SEER

RYAN BECK

This is a work of fiction. Names, characters, places, and incidents are products of the author's imagination or are used fictitiously and are not to be construed as real. Any resemblance to actual events, locales, organizations, or persons, living or dead, is entirely coincidental.

Cover art by Kayla Cunningham (CunninghamKaylaK@gmail.com)

Stay up to date with Ryan Beck at www.ryanbeckauthor.com

For Brianna and Isabelle

Prologue

Failure meant death or a lifetime in prison. Try as he might, Tiron could not keep that thought repressed. Sweat covered every inch of his body, though the hot summer night had little to do with it. Still, he continued on through the forest, each step bringing him closer to his target.

He had entered the woods an hour ago, moving quickly over a small fence with a "NO TRESPASSING" sign posted on it. After that, it had been some time before he encountered another obstacle. He had spied a few deer through his night vision display — nearly giving him a heart attack — but otherwise the woods were empty. That was how he preferred it.

A few minutes ago he had hit the second obstacle, a fifteen-foot-high fence with barbed wire looping along the top. The woods around it had been cleared for twenty feet on either side, tearing a manicured strip that stretched as far as he could see into the distance. For ordinary trespassers it would be the end of the road, but for Tiron it was the last simple obstacle he would face.

In this case, simple meant climbing a tree, shooting a line across to another tree, and zip-lining over it. Not as easy as cutting a hole in the fence, but his mission required him to leave no trace. Retracting his line was not too difficult either, thanks to the small but powerful electric motor on the reel.

After descending from the tree he had set a slower pace, moving carefully through the brush. Signs posted on the fence had warned that trespassers would be shot, and he knew they were not bluffing. Rays of light broke through the forest canopy above, only a faint green tinge in his visor reminding him that it was moonlight he was seeing, not sunlight. The enhanced image never ceased to amaze him. It could have almost passed for the middle of the day if he had not known any better. He avoided these gleaming shafts of light, sticking to the dark where the form-fitting black fabric that covered his body would be impossible to make out.

Tiron silently thanked the droning insects for concealing the occasional snap of twigs under his feet as he stole toward the next obstacle. He could see it now, the woods up ahead coming to a sudden stop. Beyond the tree line was a large open area. In the center of the clearing, a high concrete wall stretched from side to side, close to five hundred feet wide. Along the top of the wall were a series of thin wires, which he assumed to be electrified. Concrete guard towers jutted upward just inside the walls, barely peeking above the surrounding treetops. A hundred feet of mowed grass separated the compound from the forest, giving the guard towers plenty of open space to spot would-be intruders.

Tiron's heart pounded as he crept to a tree near the edge. He surveyed the towers and wall, searching for any signs of movement. There were none, and no signs of light. But that did little to comfort him.

While he scanned the area, his eyes paused on a slight shimmer over the top of one of the guard towers. He gestured to zoom in his visor, and his mouth dropped open in amazement.

Above the compound, stretching from guard tower to guard tower and out into the surrounding forest, was a fabric canopy. But it was a translucent fabric, at least from below, made from what he guessed was some kind of glass composite. From above, he knew it would be made to look like the rest of the forest. And whatever it was, it would prevent any scans from penetrating.

His team had sent several drones over the area, but had found nothing. They had wanted to send a drone on this mission instead of him, but they could not risk controlling a drone remotely for fear of the signal being intercepted. With no intel, they did not know what capabilities a drone would need and could not program one to do the mission autonomously, especially with their tight schedule. So here he was, tasked with finding out what the compound was hiding. Without that information, their plans would be useless.

He pried his eyes away from the aerial camouflage, turning his attention back to the wall. Though he could not see them, he knew there were cameras riddled throughout the compound, waiting to alert security. He had come prepared for this. His outfit was woven with strands of a material made of thousands of lights and sensors that would emit light to match whatever background he was in front of, in a wide range of wavelengths. It was not perfect, and it would be unable to blend him in with detailed or sharply changing backgrounds, but in the dark he would be virtually invisible.

He had left his suit off to conserve his backpack battery, but now he switched it on. His hands and arms instantly turned to a light shade of green in his visor, a virtual overlay visible only to him so that he could better see where his own body was.

Tiron took a deep breath to steady himself, but it did little to slow his racing heart. He stood from his crouch and moved out into the clearing. His feet moved fast but he kept his arms still, allowing his suit to portray a steadier image of the ground behind him to any infrared cameras that were pointed his direction. It took all of his concentration to keep his breathing steady, and he felt as though thousands of eyes inside the compound knew exactly where he was.

As he passed the halfway point, he reached over his shoulder to the side of his backpack and unclipped an automatic rifle with a grenade launcher attached beneath the main barrel. It was covered in the same material as his suit. He turned a dial on the side to the setting he wanted and pressed a button near his thumb. His targeting overlay appeared in his view and he raised his weapon to aim toward the top of the guard tower.

At twenty feet out from the wall, he stopped to make sure his aim was true, and fired. The fat barrel spat with a muffled thump, a gelatinous sphere launching out from it. It arced toward the tower, trailing a wire that unraveled from the side of the gun. It hit his spot with a faint slap and stuck there. Another pull of the trigger and the line went taut, the reel of wire unlocking from the gun.

He clipped the wire to his suit and placed his hand over the retraction control. If he was even a little bit off on his ascent, he would risk being dragged through the electric fence atop the wall. His timing would have to be perfect. A thumb rolled over the dial and the reel began to retract, pulling him up. He swung forward, making quick tweaks to his speed as his arc carried him toward the electric fence. His feet connected with concrete inches from the top of the wall, and in one fluid motion he absorbed the impact and sprang away, soaring up and over the wires. He swung the last ten feet to the guard tower, bending his legs to his chest to lessen the impact as he hit the side. Hanging from the side of the tower, he waited, listening and watching to see if his entrance had been noticed. But the night was still quiet.

Breathing a sigh of relief, Tiron surveyed his surroundings. He was suspended on the middle tower of the wall, about twenty-five feet above the concrete below him. To either side he could see several two-story concrete buildings in a line. They were plain, with flat roofs and parapet walls. Solar panels filled the available roof space.

With a subtle gesture, he rappelled down the tower. Another gesture at the bottom sent a current through the wire, causing the sphere at the top to unstick. The wire coiled back up as it fell, rolling into a tiny spool that he clipped back onto his weapon.

He inched his way to the corner of the tower and peeked out, gazing down the length of the compound. The ground was entirely concrete from wall to wall, with a large empty corridor running the length of the compound to a solid steel gate at the other end, close to a quarter mile away. To either side of the corridor were rows upon rows of large identical buildings, two stories tall, plain and windowless, each with a large steel garage door and a smaller steel entry door on the front. The space between each building was wide enough for two trucks to pass side by side.

Tiron crept to the side of the nearest building, stepping lightly across the pavement. The emptiness of the compound unnerved him. Every muscle in his body was tense, ready for alarms to sound at any moment. But none did. He began to walk down the main corridor, moving cautiously and sticking close to the sides of the buildings. He passed the first garage door, its heavy slab of steel stretching tall over his head. After that came the regular-sized entry door, secured with a fin-gerprint pad on the wall near the handle and an eye scanner at head level. When he reached the end of the building, he paused to look around the corner before crossing the gap to the next one.

He continued this for what seemed like an eternity, weaving in and out of the buildings, exploring as much of the area of the compound as he could. The minutes crept by, the far gate not seeming to get any nearer.

Finally, the towers guarding the entrance began to loom taller as he approached the end. At the second-to-last building on the right side, he paused near the door and pulled a small device from his backpack, holding it up to the wall. His heart went into overdrive, thudding so loud he thought it may give him away. This was the last thing he needed to do here, and then he could escape this place and its overwhelming stillness.

An image appeared in his view, captured from the device. He let out the breath he had been holding. It was a scan of the inside of the building, and it was empty.

There was a sudden flash as his night vision cut out, switching back to regular vision. A light on the wall above had turned on. His heart jumped into his throat, panic setting in. He sprinted for the corner of the building, heading for the perimeter wall. Lights were on everywhere now, and the compound was bright as day. He raised his weapon and checked that it was in the right fire mode, the flexible ammo feed line trailing back to his backpack. His feet pounded the pavement as he rounded the corner, and he could see the perimeter wall at the end of the aisle over a hundred feet away.

He flew toward the wall, passing one building and then the next. As he reached the halfway point, he turned to look over his shoulder and was relieved to see that nothing was following him. But when he turned back to the front, three shapes rounded the corner at the far end of the buildings and shot toward him.

His heart skipped a beat as he identified the drones whirring his way, quadcopters as wide as his shoulders with fierce barrels pointing out from their round bodies. In a flash, his gun was up, spitting rounds in quick succession. The targeting reticle in his visor strafed across each of the drones, but they dodged to the side and his shots whizzed harmlessly past.

Tiron skidded to a halt and looked behind him, hoping for an out, but three more drones were rounding the corner into the corridor. He was trapped. The drones in front were almost on him, forty feet away and closing fast. Gritting his teeth, he charged toward them, his weapon blasting. The drones dodged, continuing their advance, but one of his bursts hit its mark, flinging the middle drone backwards with a crunch. It landed in a twisted heap ahead of him.

They were on top of him now, spitting a barrage of small globs toward him. He leapt forward, somersaulting in midair and tucking his gun and shoulder underneath him. His shoulder hit the ground and he rolled to his feet; the globs impacted harmlessly behind him. He recognized the globs as blitz rounds, gelatinous balls charged with electricity that stuck to whatever they hit. They could be charged to different levels for warning, incapacitating, or killing targets. He had no plans to stick around and find out which level they were using.

He made for the wall, his breath coming in ragged gasps as he pushed his body to the limit. They were behind him now, but not for long. The drones were far faster than he was, and they would be on him any second.

Blitz rounds whizzed past his head and stuck to the ground around him as he ran. The wall was right in front of him, he just had to round the corner of the building and swing over it at the nearby guard tower.

Something hit the back of his ankle as he made to turn the corner. His whole body erupted in pain. He screamed, dropping to the ground as electricity coursed through him, his muscles spasming. As suddenly as the electricity started, it stopped. With his last remaining strength, Tiron pulled himself around the side of the building, out of view from the aisle.

The electricity had overloaded his suit, and now that he was completely visible there was no way the drones would miss, even if he could still move. With his suit power gone, he no longer had vision through his mask. He pulled it off, taking one last look at the night sky and a last breath of fresh air.

The whir of rotors warned him that his time was short. A final plea consumed his mind: that it had not all been for nothing. Reaching his arms across his chest, he used his ring fingers to simultaneously press a sensor on the outside of each arm. The drones sped around the corner, the first one firing a blitz round toward his heart. But he never felt it hit him.

Heat exploded from his backpack, engulfing Tiron and spreading outward, the flames swallowing the drones. The corner of the building he had been leaning against collapsed inward from the force of the blast, carving a hole halfway up the wall. The sound of the explosion echoed across the compound.

Miles away, outside of the forest, an abandoned building sat on a quiet road on the outskirts of a city. It stood two stories tall, the sheet-metal walls marking it as an outdated manufacturing building. A signal was received and a second later the corner of the building exploded, fire and debris erupting outward. Flaming chunks of steel rained down on the road. A flock of pigeons took to the night sky, startled from their normally peaceful roosts. Smoke rose from the smoldering hole as the echo of the blast faded. In the distance, a siren began.

Chapter 1

It was her last few hours of freedom. If Maria had known that, she would have spent her morning visiting friends and family, maybe walking through the park or playing video games together. Instead she spent it like most other Tuesday mornings, preparing for work after the weekend.

Her two orb drones assumed their position a few feet in front of her face when she got up, and her plain apartment turned into a work of art. The previously unadorned white walls filled with colorful murals and decorative hangings depicting live feeds of mountains, woodlands, and beaches. Virtual replicas of video game characters floated in a few corners. In others were models of animals in candid positions. The drones hovering in front of her vanished from view, leaving her alone in her augmented living space.

She pulled her unkempt black hair into a ponytail and walked into the living room. An eagle resting on a branch turned its head to look at her as she entered. The bust of a news anchor appeared on the counter of the attached kitchen and began reading the news, in sequence based on Maria's interests. It was a slow news day, the anchor starting with a brief story about Labor Day parade preparations.

The anchor's voice faded into the background as Maria's eyes were drawn to an image on the wall. The smiling faces of herself, her parents, and her little sister, Ana, stared back at her. It was the last picture of them all together, sitting at a picnic table on a sunny day. Ana could almost have passed for Maria's twin. She had the same wavy black hair and tan skin, the same smile.

Tears welled up in Maria's eyes. It had been over a year now but it never seemed to get any easier. Part of her never wanted it to. The signs had been there. Skipping family get-togethers, withdrawing from friends. Maria had noticed it but thought it was just a phase. She owed it to Ana to never forget how she had failed her.

The news anchor said something that registered in her brain, and she pulled her attention away from the picture, wiping her eyes. Something about an explosion in an abandoned manufacturing building on the edge of the city. Her brow furrowed. On a slow day like this, an explosion should have been the first story.

She brushed it off as a glitch. The story entered expanded mode, a summary of the details appearing near the anchor along with a three-dimensional view of the early morning scene. A hole gaped in the second floor of an abandoned manufacturing building, smoke billowing out and fire crews spraying water in. The authorities were saying some kids had been messing around with fireworks and caught some old equipment on fire. Thankfully, no one was injured. Maria's concerned expression faded, and she grabbed some breakfast. The anchor vanished with her loss of attention.

When she had finished her morning routine, she walked to her desk in the corner of the living room. Work modules appeared above it as she sat down on the black faux-leather chair. Her calendar opened, reminding her she had a meeting today in several hours. She and her coworker, Sandara, had to make a pitch to a client for an extension of a security contract. It was mostly a formality; the company they worked for was one of the best cybersecurity businesses around and as far as she knew, the client was extremely happy with their service. Even so, there was some work to be done to get everything prepared.

The coworker status bar popped up and she saw that Sandara was away, a timer displaying the estimated time until she would be available. It was only a few minutes, so she pulled up their presentation and began to look it over.

When the timer reached zero, a chime sounded and the head and shoulders of a smiling young woman in her early twenties appeared in front of her. She had curly black hair and her brown eyes nearly matched her complexion. "Hi Maria," came Sandara's cheerful voice, the invisible drones projecting the sound so that it almost seemed like Sandara was actually in the room with her.

Maria smiled warmly back at her, her doleful mood lifting. Sandara's positive attitude was notoriously infectious and even brief interactions with her were known to brighten everyone's day.

They talked about their weekends for a bit, Sandara describing her and her husband's trip to the capital. Maria's weekend had been less eventful, just relaxing with a few books, playing video games with friends, and jogging at the park. When they had finished catching up, Maria remembered something she had wanted to ask. "Hey, did you happen to watch your news feed this morning?"

"I watched a bit of it, but I lost interest just a couple stories in. Seemed like a slow news day," Sandara replied. "Why do you ask?"

Maria's eyebrows raised, a look of surprise on her face. "So you didn't see anything about the explosion then?"

It was Sandara's turn to look surprised, her smile fading. "What explosion?"

"There was an explosion at an abandoned manufacturing building on the edge of the city. You know all those older buildings on the east end in the dead part of town? It wasn't a huge explosion but it took out a good chunk of the building. No one was hurt or anything, but what really surprised me was how far down my news feed that story was." Maria paused. "Heck, I think they even showed some dog doing a goofy trick before they played that story," she said, laughing softly.

"Wow," replied Sandara, smiling in amusement. "That's weird. Must be some kind of issue with the feed system since it was in the wrong order for both of us."

Maria voiced her agreement. They turned their attention back to the presentation, spending the next few hours practicing their speaking parts and fine-tuning the content. Sandara

was a lead in the marketing and media department, and it
was common for the company to team cybersecurity leads
with marketing leads for proposals. It worked well; the cybersecurity lead highlighted their expertise and the marketing
lead fostered relationships with the client and made sure the
proposal was eye-catching.

They performed a final practice run of their presentation
and finished shortly before noon. Maria leaned her chair back
and stretched, feeling confident that the presentation was in
good shape and that the contract would be renewed.

They agreed to meet a half hour before they were due to
present, and then signed off. Sandara's face vanished, and
the rest of the work modules did too. Maria walked to the
kitchen for something to eat. As she approached, an opening
on the side of the fridge dispensed two slices of bread, cultured
chicken, a slice of cheese, and some lettuce onto a tray on the
counter.

She assembled her sandwich and took a bite as she walked
to her room. Four scale-models of herself appeared in the air
when she stepped inside, each wearing a different outfit. As
soon as she knew which one she wanted, a panel in the wall
slid open, her selected attire extending out from it on a rod.
She scarfed down the rest of her sandwich and grabbed the
black dress pants and matching black blazer with a light green
button-up underneath.

When she had finished getting ready, she grabbed a small
handbag and stepped out her apartment door. A short walk
down the hall and two flights of stairs and she was outside,
squinting as her eyes adjusted in the bright sun. The sidewalk

extended ahead of her, cutting through a grassy area with a few trees and picnic tables.

A pod pulled up as Maria approached the small parking area at the end of the sidewalk. It was small and white, with a single seat inside. The front and back of the pod were sloped aerodynamically, making the same shape so that the front of a pod would fit perfectly against the back of another pod. The sides were flat and completely vertical, painted metal on the bottom half and glass windows and roof on the top half. The door opened as she approached and she ducked inside, setting her bag down on the sloped, desk-like surface in front of her.

The door closed behind her and the pod took off, the electric motor silently turning the three wheels, two in the front and one in the back. Her two drones had moved with her into the pod and were resting on charge ports near the top of the desk, still cloaked from her view. The destination and arrival time floated near the front window, the drones feeding the information into her vision. They projected light right onto her eyes, which meant her vision could be augmented in any way imaginable. It enabled holograms and virtual displays, and it meant her surroundings could be decorated however she liked. Either with downloaded content such as the video game replicas and nature scenes in her apartment, or with her own creations like some of the murals on her walls.

Her arrival time was right on schedule, which helped settle her mounting nerves. She leaned back in the seat and closed her eyes, relaxing and collecting her thoughts before the meeting.

A gentle jolt startled her from her meditation. Her eyes flicked open, seeing that her pod was now on the highway and had joined with a group of pods, locking in to gain efficiency from the improved aerodynamics. The front of her pod nestled into the back of the pod in front of her, and the vertical sides allowed pods to attach to her right and left. All four windows were able to roll down, including the front and rear, so that families or groups could still be part of the same vehicle when traveling, and so that people who wanted to be sociable with strangers, could be. Maria, however, wanted to continue meditating before her meeting. The windows darkened, blocking out the view of the other passengers, and she closed her eyes.

Several minutes later she felt the pod detach from the group and decelerate. She blinked her eyes open to look out the now-translucent windows, revealing that she was moving down the exit, approaching a cross street. But something was wrong. This was not where she was supposed to be. She checked the destination on the dash, worry washing over her. It was no longer there; the graphics were completely gone. "What the hell?" she groaned, feeling sick. "SEER, where am I?" she asked, speaking to the computer system that managed nearly all human interaction with technology. The acronym stood for Statistical Engine for Early Response. Or as the popular joke went, someone just really wanted it to spell SEER.

There was no response from SEER. Something was seriously wrong. SEER could normally anticipate human behavior and handle most interactions with technology without people having to lift a finger. It was how her refrigerator knew what sandwich components to dispense, how the computer knew when to initiate a video call, and how the pod knew when to pick her up and what destination to take her to. It sometimes made mistakes, though it was fairly unusual. But it was extremely unusual and somewhat frightening for SEER to not respond when addressed.

Panic began to set in as the pod continued driving, taking her toward the edge of the city. She had to stop it. She had never had to do this before, but there was an emergency lever equipped on every pod that would pull out a contact between the battery and motor, leaving the braking and steering systems powered up so that the pod could still be guided to safety.

She reached under the dash, above her legs, feeling around for the lever. "Come on, come on," she muttered, not feeling anything. She slouched down a bit in order to see. It should be clearly marked and noticeable, but there was nothing there. Realization dawned on her and her breath caught in her throat, her stomach twisting. Someone had tampered with this pod and sent it specifically to kidnap her. Questions streamed through her head. Why her? How had they done this without SEER noticing? She pushed her questions aside, focusing on the more important task at hand. She had to escape.

A few deep breaths helped her focus. She needed to think clearly, but could not waste any more time. Every passing second took her farther from the city and closer to her kidnapper. It was clear that something was blocking the signal into this pod, since her drones had not conveyed her question to SEER.

In fact, they seemed to have stopped working completely. The two black, grapefruit-sized orbs were plainly visible on their charging docks, no longer cloaked from view. That meant she could not call for help. She was completely on her own.

Leaning back in the seat, she lifted her feet over the dash and lashed out at the windshield. The glass did not budge. She tried several more times, but still nothing. She gave up, not wanting to waste any more of her precious time. Pods had strong glass for safety reasons, and it was likely that her kidnapper had sealed the pod up to prevent an easy escape.

Sweat rolled down her forehead as her panic mounted. The sparse houses and buildings around her were becoming even less frequent the farther she traveled from the city. The road began to wind through a wooded area, the afternoon sun strobing across her face as it streamed through the trees. Her mind raced, trying desperately to come up with a plan, but she was drawing a blank. Suddenly, her eyes widened, an idea forming in her head. It was risky, but she was out of options.

She grabbed one of the orbs from its dock. Raising it over her head, she smashed it down on the desk surface repeatedly until the tough plastic case began to break. Shoving her fingers into a broken part of the case, she pried it the rest of the way off, exposing the built-in battery pack and the internal circuits. The sharp plastic cut her fingers, but the pain hardly registered. She grabbed her bag from the desk, taking hold of the clasp on the strap, wielding the metal prong like a dagger in her quivering hand. She stabbed downward, driving the prong into the exposed battery. Nothing happened, so she continued lifting up the clasp and stabbing it back down, trying to drive it into the same spot.

After continuing this frantically for nearly a minute, the pack finally punctured. She drove the metal prong into the opening and pushed it inward, twisting it around. The pack began to smoke, a small flame growing inside as the chemicals combined. She dropped her bag and lifted her elbow to her face, breathing through the fabric of her blazer in an effort to filter out the acrid fumes of the smoking battery.

Maria closed her eyes against the stinging smoke, silently praying that whoever had sent this pod had not disabled the emergency fire shutoff. If they had, she might have only succeeded in suffocating herself.

The pod was filling up with smoke and still carrying her away from the city. It was becoming difficult to breathe, even through her sleeve. She began to lose hope, realizing she may have just guaranteed her death. Then a brief klaxon sounded and the pod decelerated. A voice sounded from the speakers, "Fire detected, please exit the vehicle once stopped."

The voice played on repeat as the pod came to a stop, the door popping open. She crawled out, collapsing to her knees. Her body racked with uncontrollable coughing, clearing the smoke from her lungs until they were filled with fresh air. Her face lifted into an exhausted smile, relieved to breathe again and to be out of the pod. But her smile faded as she remembered that she still was not safe. She was several miles outside of the city and her would-be kidnapper could be nearby.

She climbed unsteadily to her feet. Taking a deep breath, she plunged her arm back into the pod, fumbling in the thick smoke for the other drone. Her hand closed around it and she pulled it out, breathing again as she moved away from the smoke and headed into the cover of the woods alongside the road.

Once past the first few trees, she turned the drone over in her hands, hoping it would work now that it was out of the pod. No such luck. It was dead, its battery drained by the sabotaged charging dock.

She needed to move away from the smoke in case the kidnapper came looking, and decided it would be best to follow the road, but stay in the safety of the woods. There had been no pods on the road since she had taken the exit, but she hoped that someone would find hers and report it, summoning the police. She began to run through the woods, following the road back toward the city. Normally she was a good runner, and her brain was screaming at her to sprint, but the smoke and stress had taken a lot out of her. Instead she kept a steady pace, holding onto the drone in case she came across somewhere she could charge it.

After several minutes of running, she saw a pod coming toward her down the road. She stopped and hid behind a large tree trunk, since there was no way of knowing if the person in the pod was her kidnapper or someone who could help her. It took everything she had not to run out on the road and get this person to help her. But her good sense prevailed, knowing she could not risk it. The pod passed by almost without a sound, at an agonizingly slow pace. She could not be sure if it was because they were scanning the woods for her, or if it was going at normal speed and it just felt like forever. Finally, it passed out of view and she continued on. If that pod was really just a random citizen, they should see the smoke soon and the police would be on the way.

She continued jogging through the woods, ducking tree branches and maneuvering around bushes. It seemed like an eternity passed before she heard the sound of sirens in the distance, growing louder as they approached. She could have cried out with joy when she heard them. Now it sounded like they were on the road she was on, still a way off but approaching fast. She ran out on the road, not wanting them to miss her. The road stretched ahead of her for maybe a mile before curving out of view, disappearing into the distant woods. The rescue vehicles were not visible ahead of her yet, but it sounded like they would be rounding the bend any moment now.

She glanced behind her as she jogged ahead, and her heart nearly stopped. A half mile back, she could see smoke rising from her pod, stopped in the middle of the road. Just beyond that there were three figures speeding toward her. Buried underneath the sudden terror, she felt a hint of surprise. She had only seen pictures of what these people were riding, never one in person. They were motorcycles, and she could tell that they were extremely fast, moving faster than a pod ever could.

She turned around and began to sprint, adrenaline coursing through her and pushing her faster than she had ever run before. The police just had to reach her before the motorcycles did and she would be rescued. She glanced back, seeing that two of the motorcycles were still speeding toward her, halfway between her and the dead pod. The other one had stopped at the pod. The sirens sounded close, and she turned back toward them, now able to see one of the police vehicles through the trees in the distance, black and white and larger than a pod, able to hold two officers with room for two passengers — or troublemakers — in the back.

She frantically waved her arms, calling out for help. But as it came fully into view she heard the squealing of tires and one of the motorcycles skidded around her, coming to a stop right in her path. It startled her momentarily, but she did not slow down. She leapt forward into the air, sticking her forearms out in front of her, crossed over her face. The rider was caught off guard, only just beginning to raise their arms as they realized what she was doing. She connected with the rider just below the helmet, knocking them off the bike and tumbling to the ground on top of them. Scrambling to her feet, she stumbled ahead toward the distant rescue vehicles. The impact had jarred the dead drone out of her hand, but it no longer mattered.

A hand grasped her ankle, the fallen rider grabbing her from where they lay on the ground. She kicked her leg backward, feeling her foot connect with the rider's helmet. The grip on her ankle loosened and she pulled free, running and waving her arms, screaming for help.

Something hit her hard, tackling her to the ground. It was the second rider. Pain shot through her elbow where it had smashed into the ground. She struggled to breathe, the wind knocked out of her and a sick feeling in her stomach. Still, she writhed and flailed, trying to break free of the grasp of the rider. Her elbows connected with the assailant, but the pressure of the elbow pinning her to the ground did not loosen. If she could just fight them off for another minute, she would be rescued! Elbows, head, legs, anything that could move she moved, trying to make contact with the rider.

A hand grabbed her head to hold her still and she felt the sharp sting of a needle driving into her neck. A cold feeling spread through the nearby veins. She knew what had just happened but could only feel indifference as the drug did its work, her vision fading. The last thing to go was her hearing, the scream of the sirens echoing in her ears and fading to nothing as she lost consciousness.

Chapter 2

"She's coming to. Get Vincent." A woman's voice broke through the black fog of Maria's senses, sounding distant. She heard footsteps and then a door closing. Her eyelids felt heavy as she struggled to open her eyes, and when she managed to open them, her vision was blurry. She tried to lift her arms to rub the blur away, but they would not move. It took her several seconds to realize it was because they were restrained. Instantly she remembered everything that had happened and her eyes went wide, her heart skipping a beat. Where was she?

A glance down confirmed that she was sitting in a metal chair, her wrists tied to the armrests. She was in a small, dimly lit room, which slowly came into focus as her eyes adjusted. There was a desk in one corner and some shelves with medical supplies on the walls. A hospital bed was pushed up against the wall in another corner with an empty IV stand next to it.

Maria heard footsteps in the hall and the door slid open. An older man, maybe in his fifties, walked in. He was just under six feet tall, skinny with tanned skin and dark brown hair that was turning gray. Behind him a woman entered, slightly shorter than him with long blonde hair and wearing a lab coat a shade of white that nearly matched her skin. As the man walked in, he flipped a light switch, the sudden brightness blinding Maria, who winced and lowered her head to avoid the glaring overhead lights.

"Where am I? Who are you people and what do you want with me?" Maria demanded, trying to pull her arms out of the restraints, afraid of what they might do to her. She tried to stand with the chair attached but it was bolted to the floor.

"Everything will be explained shortly," he said, his voice smooth and relaxed, "just remain calm and please allow Doctor Jeffreys to do a quick checkup." The woman came over and pulled a medical scanner out of a nearby drawer. Maria shrank back in her chair as she came towards her, but she only used it to shine a light in Maria's eyes and to get a blood scan from her wrist. Maria settled down and allowed her to work, realizing that struggling was not going to get her anywhere.

"She's doing fine, Vincent," said Doctor Jeffreys, who sounded British. Addressing Maria, she said, "You'll be okay. The sedative has worn off and you'll feel groggy for a bit, but you should feel completely normal after a few hours."

"Thank you, Lily," said the man. Doctor Jeffreys walked over to the desk and sat down at the chair, making a couple of notes on a display Maria could not see.

"I know you're confused, and we're terribly sorry that you had to be introduced to us in this manner, but I'm afraid there were no other options," the man said. "My name is Vincent Daniels, and we're already familiar with you, Maria Rosado."

Maria frowned, unnerved by him providing his name. If it was his real name, it meant he was confident that she could never give him up to the police. Did that mean he planned to kill her? Her stomach churned. "Is that your real name?" she snapped at him, trying to disguise her fear with bravado. "If it is, I'll make sure the police know who you are as soon as I get out of here."

Vincent just smiled and shook his head. "It is my real name. And I can tell you my real name because you're not going to be able to get to the police. And even if you could, I don't think you'd want to after you hear what we have to say."

Maria scowled, waiting for him to speak so she could figure out what he wanted from her.

"In order for this to make sense, let me start by asking you a question or two to see what you know," Vincent said. "What do you know about SEER?"

Maria raised an eyebrow. "I suppose what everyone else knows," she said, deciding to cooperate for the time being until she could figure out what they wanted. She tried to sound confident but could not keep her voice from wavering. "It's a system that makes our interaction with technology simpler. It uses statistics and behavioral patterns to predict what someone is going to do next, and it uses its prediction to try and make life easier, either by providing information or bringing a pod, or a bunch of other stuff. What does that have to do with you kidnapping me?" She spoke the last sentence sharply, impatience and anger in her voice.

"That's what I expected," he replied. He paused, seeming to think over how to word his next sentence. "I'm sorry, I've done this several times but it's always difficult to figure out the best way to convince people."

"Are you saying you've kidnapped more people than just me?" Maria felt sick. None of this made any sense. He talked as if he was part of some noble cause. But noble causes did not kidnap people. Was this some kind of human trafficking operation? She dismissed the thought. There would be no point in lying to her if she was just going to be sold or killed. No, this guy wanted something from her.

"Yes, a little over half of our group here consists of people who have been... conscripted. But they all came to support the cause after they were brought up to speed." Vincent paused for a moment, lost in thought. "Actually," he said, "let me bring you out to meet the other members of our group, I think that may be the best way to introduce you to all this. Lily, the straps please."

Doctor Jeffreys, or Lily, stood up from the desk, where she had been observing after finishing her notes. She moved over to Maria and reached for the straps. She paused to look at Vincent before undoing them, as if to make sure he knew what he was doing.

"Maria, before you're released from the chair, please know that we have no intention of harming you, but we must keep you here," he said. "We're in a remote location and have great security. Please don't try anything." With that, he nodded to Lily. She released the straps.

Maria massaged her wrists where the straps had been digging into her skin, happy to be free of the restraints. Lily stepped back from the chair but remained near Maria.

"Please follow me," Vincent said, walking to the door. Maria stood slowly and took a step, shaky on her feet. Lily reached for Maria's elbow to steady her, but Maria pulled back, reflexively avoiding her. Cooperating seemed to be her best option at the moment, but that did not mean she had to be anything but cold to them.

Maria walked to the door and stepped through into the hallway. It was bare, with several closed doors on each wall. It looked like a hallway in a hospital. Lily stepped through the doorway behind her.

Vincent turned to the left and walked down the hall. "This way please," he said. Maria followed, resisting the strong urge to kick him, tackle Lily, and try to escape. Even though she had not seen anyone else, she remembered the three motor-cycle riders and believed what Vincent said about the security.

The hallway turned to the right at its end and they followed it around the corner into another long hallway. A door at the end of it was open, raised voices spilling out. As they neared she could see a man pacing angrily and chastising a woman seated at a desk.

"... jeopardized the entire operation!" he shouted, Maria now able to hear his fiery speech as she approached the room, making out a hint of a Central American accent. "How could you have overlooked the fire shutoff? We were less than a few seconds from being seen by the authorities, and with all the commotion it's still possible someone saw us!"

"That system was left in place on purpose!" the seated woman snapped back at him, her dark brown curls bouncing and a red flush on her tawny cheeks. "If it had been disabled, she would have suffocated or burned to death, and of course there would have been a huge investigation into why the fire shutoff on the pod failed, and where do you think that might have led?"

The pacing man opened his mouth to retort, but was interrupted by a woman who stepped into view. "Cut it out," she said, her mild accent indicating Russian heritage. "It's not her fault, Antonio, and you should just be happy that we managed to complete the mission."

Vincent reached the doorway ahead of her and paused, turning back to her. "It seems your little stunt has upset the team," he said, a slight smile curving on the corners of his mouth. "Lily, we can take it from here, you can go."

Lily nodded and turned back the way they had come. Vincent ushered Maria into the room. The three occupants glanced up as they entered, with what Maria assumed were expressions of surprise on their faces, probably because she was unrestrained. The room itself was a sparse office, fairly large, with two desks on opposite walls. Both desks were empty, aside from the woman seated at the one opposite the door.

"Did you convince her to join already?" the Russian-sounding woman asked, strands of sandy-brown, bob-cut hair falling across her pale cheek as she cocked her head to the side. "That's gotta be some kind of record, I know I was pretty stubborn at first."

"No, I actually thought it might be best if you three participated in our discussion," he replied. "I think it might be beneficial for people who have been in her situation before to offer their perspective if needed. Let's start with some brief introductions." Vincent turned to look at Maria. He gestured toward the woman at the desk. "This is Doctor Karen Hansen, one of our programmers." Turning toward the man he said, "This is Antonio Thomas, a member of our field team. And here is another member of our field team, Irina Barkova." He turned toward the standing woman as he said her name, and then gestured back at Maria. "Everyone, as you know this is Maria Rosado."

The three in the room murmured greetings to her, each of them giving her a slight smile. Antonio's smile seemed forced, probably still upset at the turn the kidnapping had taken.

"Please, have a seat," Vincent said, gesturing to the empty chair at the other desk. Maria complied. Vincent grabbed a stool from the corner of the room and sat down near the middle of the group. Maria crinkled her nose at the strangeness of the situation, like a meeting in a professor's office instead of a kidnapping. The mostly friendly demeanor of her captors had begun to dull her fear and anger a little. She resisted the feeling. Her only hope was to be alert and suspicious, ready for their attitude to change, ready to fight back if necessary.

"Okay, Maria, so you had just been saying that you know what everyone else knows about SEER," Vincent said. "Basically that it's a system that anticipates human behavior in order to facilitate efficient interactions with technology. Well, this group exists because it's actually more than that. Much more. SEER doesn't just use statistical modeling and previous behavior to anticipate future behavior, it records nearly every sensory input into a person's brain, coupled with genetic information, and accurately predicts how that person will respond to those inputs."

Maria's eyes narrowed, a skeptical look on her face. "Even if this were true, why do you care if SEER collects more data than people think it does? How does it get and use our DNA? And what does any of this have to do with me?"

"We'll get to what this has to do with you later, it will make more sense after we explain the rest of it," Vincent said. "As for your other questions, you're aware that our DNA is collected and analyzed at a young age, and that information is put into our medical file to help us track and monitor potential heritable diseases that we may be at risk for. Our biological information is also put into an FBI database, which is used when DNA evidence is collected to find potential matches. Well, what people are not aware of is that our biological data is also provided to SEER, and it's used as the foundation of SEER's behavior prediction. SEER uses our genetic data to determine what our impulses and instincts are. At birth our behavior is mostly instinct, as we haven't absorbed much information yet. Genetic information and conditions in the womb form our brains, which only contain the information our genes placed there or that we learn during gestation. Upon birth, our brains are what determine how we absorb the inputs we receive. You throw information at the canvas and see what sticks. After information starts to stick, it creates a new basis for how future information is absorbed. Every input you receive becomes a part of who you are, and it determines how you absorb or react to future information. Over time the initial genetic information becomes less important as you become more heavily influenced by the information you're absorbing, but the foundation of all of it is our genetic information. can build a pretty good model of who you are as a person just based on inputs and observed behavior, but in order to truly capture the full picture and build an accurate model from a young age, it needs your genetic information."

Vincent paused, looking for feedback from Maria. She played along, interested in what he was saying, but impatience still evident in her voice. "Okay, so they're using our DNA for prediction purposes. But if it makes the system function better, I think a lot of people would consider that worth it. I'm sure the public would be concerned about the lack of transparency and the unauthorized use of DNA, but this hardly seems to warrant kidnapping people for whatever it is your little group is trying to do."

Vincent gave her an amused smile. "Yes, but it's not the data collection that we're concerned about, it's what's done with that data. The public has basically already decided that it's okay with data collection if it's being used for their benefit, and if that data is used only by computers and not people." Vincent paused to think for a moment, and then continued. "How accurate do you think SEER is?"

Maria considered for a second before answering. "Pretty accurate, but it definitely makes mistakes. Just this morning it put a news feed story I was interested in way at the bottom."

Vincent glanced over at the other members of his team, all of their faces suddenly grim. "Yes, well..." he trailed off, and then continued after a few seconds. "SEER did make an error there, but not in the way you're thinking. I'm assuming it was a story about an explosion, is that right?"

Maria nodded, eyes widening as she began to suspect what he was going to say next.

"That explosion was related to our group's activities, and we'll tell you what that was all about later," Vincent said. "But the fact that the story was so far down your news feed was no accident, and you seeing that story at all was probably the mistake that SEER made. You see, SEER is not just passively using your genetic, behavioral, and environmental information to ease your interaction with technology. Instead, SEER is being used by those who control it to influence every aspect of people's lives. As you said, SEER makes mistakes sometimes. But this is normally by design. SEER intentionally makes small mistakes to keep the public from growing suspicious of what it can really do. In reality, SEER knows nearly everything you'll do. It knows what you'll do before the thought crosses your mind. It even knows what you'll be thinking before you think it. Each individual has thousands upon thousands of thoughts and actions in a day, and SEER will maybe make only a couple real mistakes out of all of those predictions."

Maria swallowed, unnerved by the thought, but not trusting what she was hearing. "If that were true it would be... alarming," she said. "So, if we pretend you're telling the truth, how is SEER manipulating people? Just through the news?"

"Oh no," Vincent replied, "it's much more than that. SEER has so much data that it knows what kind of information would sway your opinion on a subject. That includes talking to certain friends, or sometimes even just seeing some random object that makes you have a change of heart. Like a eureka moment, if you will. SEER controls the technology that runs our life, so if it thinks a person is on their way to talk to a friend and that conversation will likely result in that person wanting to protest a cause SEER is programmed to subdue, then it may interfere. For example, by causing your pod to run late or making you come across a piece of information that reduces your conviction. And if that doesn't work, SEER can subtly influence you into unhealthy behaviors and addictions that crush your spirit. If all else fails, it can put a stop to you in much more sinister ways. However, that's less common because the subtler methods are extremely effective."

Maria frowned, trying to figure out if this man was some lunatic conspiracy theorist or just lying to get her on his side. But despite herself, she was beginning to feel frightened at the possibility that he was telling the truth. She laced her reply with a heavy dose of skepticism. "I'm going to need to see some proof of these claims you're making. On the unlikely chance that what you're saying is true and SEER is manipulating the public and even killing, how is that level of prediction and manipulation possible? I can accept that SEER can predict everyday behavior and tendencies, we've all seen that that's true. But you're telling me that SEER actually hardly ever makes a mistake, and that it can predict thoughts, feelings, and opinions? And to such a level that it knows in advance how new information will affect us? What about free will? You're implying that we have no freedom to choose our actions, and that instead our actions are determined only by genes and what we've experienced before."

He smiled grimly, seeming to enjoy Maria's bewilderment and the discussion they were having. She scanned the faces of the rest of the group, who were listening to the conversation with slightly bored expressions on their faces. Maria sensed that they had seen this discussion play out several times before. They had probably all participated in the discussion before too, if Vincent was telling the truth. She could tell Vincent liked to talk, and if she could keep him talking she would have more time to figure out how to get out of here.

Vincent got up from his seat and began to slowly pace as he responded to Maria. He seemed to feel comfortable lecturing, giving off the same vibe as a professor in front of a college class. "That's close to what I'm saying," he said. "I am indeed saying that our thoughts, ideas, and actions are entirely based on our genetic information and the information we receive through our sensory interactions with the world. We have genes and we have what we learn. What else is there? We all operate under the assumption that we have free will, but free will is just a term we use to describe our ability to make decisions. What decisions we actually make depend entirely on our genetic disposition and the information we've absorbed during our lives."

Vincent paused his speech and his pacing, looking at her to see if she had anything to say. She did not have a response, unsure if she bought the idea that her choices were inevitable. She waited for him to go on. He noticed this and continued speaking, resuming his slow pacing as well. "Now, what I'm saying does not necessarily preclude free will, depending on your definition of free will. Humans can't store unlimited information, and they're not acutely aware of every bit of information stored in their brains. The information we have stored in our brain is used when we make decisions, but we don't know exactly what information is influencing us. I could've read a book ten years ago and the message of that book could be influencing me, even if I'm not actively thinking about that book as I make a certain decision. From my perspective I'm freely choosing what I'm doing. In my eyes I could have done any number of things. But SEER has data on everything I've ever done at the ready. It looks at the data and knows exactly what that book contained and what parts of it influenced me. It analyzes my decision before I make it and knows, based on all its data about me, exactly what decision I will make. From SEER's perspective, I was only ever going to make that one decision. It may know what other options I considered, but based on who I am and what I've experienced, SEER knows exactly what I will do. So from SEER's perspective, I do not have free will. My decisions are a result of my genetics and my life experiences. I am completely predictable and an inevitable result of those influencing factors. Although, there are still some influencing factors that are outside SEER's ability to measure, like the movements of stray microscopic particles and things like that, which is likely part of why SEER does make a few mistakes. But for the vast majority of the decisions made, SEER can find the data that led you to your choice and it can know what you'll choose before you yourself know."

Vincent stopped pacing and sat down on the stool again. His speech had been steadily increasing in excitement as he lost himself in the topic, his energy similar to that of a youth explaining something amazing they learned in school. Maria had been taking advantage of his rapt speaking to survey the room, but she returned her gaze to him as he faced her. "Think of a kid raised in a group of violent people," he continued, "who's never taught to be nice, and is only taught hate and violence, and is surrounded by hate and violence his entire life. Let's assume there are no 'nice genes' in him either. Could he really have chosen to be nice instead of hateful? In his mind there's no such thing as being nice, it's not something that he knows exists. Does he truly have free will if being nice was never a possibility? And if he doesn't, how can anyone else be considered truly free if their choices are limited to the information they've been conditioned with during their life?"

"But that's an overly simplistic scenario," Maria said. "In the real world, we're exposed to thousands of new ideas and philosophies over the course of our lives. Almost no one is that isolated from new ideas."

"Sure, it's an extreme example," he replied, "but even if the hypothetical kid I'm talking about were exposed to niceness a few times in his life, do you think he would really jump off the hate train and start being nice? I don't think so. For people to change their opinions or their lifestyle, they have to be exposed to a new idea enough that the idea makes sense and for them to feel comfortable with it. A new idea could catch on pretty quickly with people who have been raised or genetically predisposed to be more open-minded. But for someone who is pretty set in their ways, it's going to take a lot of exposure for them to change their mind. If we consider my hypothetical, a kid who has been raised in a hate-only society is going to need a lot of convincing before he decides to start being nice. I think if you look around at the world we live in, it's pretty easy to see that people are raised with certain perspectives and they don't get a whole lot of exposure to new perspectives. People do change, but only if they're exposed to ideas or events that make them change."

Maria tilted her head thoughtfully. "I suppose it's like brainwashing," she replied. "We accept that people who are brainwashed have a diminished level of free will. But what you're saying is we're all brainwashed in a sense, since we're only made up of the ideas, attitudes, and experiences we've been exposed to."

"Exactly," Vincent replied. "Even our criminal justice system has made good strides in embracing this understanding of behavior. Now it prioritizes reform instead of retribution, moving toward the idea that introducing positive influences to people who have committed crimes can do a great deal of good. And SEER uses this concept to discourage crimes before they're committed by exposing people to positive influences. But even though this is a noble goal, it raises ethical questions. People trying to influence other people is generally seen as okay, since most people aren't good enough at manipulation to really control anyone. But when you have a computer that has an understanding of a person far beyond what any other human could comprehend, it becomes a simple task to change someone's opinion, or even their beliefs. And SEER is now being used to go far beyond trying to put potential criminals on the right path. Those who are in control of SEER are using its manipulative abilities to control outcomes of elections, to influence politicians, and to change public opinion and behavior to better match their ideal vision of society."

Maria was starting to worry that he might not be just a raving lunatic, that he might actually be telling her the truth. She had already guessed the answer to her next question, but asked it anyway. "That would be terrible," she said, "but how can SEER manipulate people so easily when it's so easy to create an echo chamber with your chosen media sources?"

"SEER is in control of what media sources reach you," Vincent replied. "Even if you say you only want to see media from certain sources, SEER can manipulate what information you see from those sources so that your biases slowly shift. You may not even notice at first, but over time your media preferences will change. The echo chamber you prefer to live in will slowly shift its bias until it's right where SEER was told it needed to be. From your viewpoint, it was your tastes changing that made your opinions shift, when in reality SEER was manipulating you the entire time."

"You've mentioned that people in control of SEER are telling it to manipulate people," Maria responded, "but if you're telling the truth, how can you be sure that SEER isn't just malfunctioning, or that it somehow gained sentience and is acting on its own?"

Vincent gave her an amused smile. "I doubt anything like that would be possible. I'm sure you know that achieving human-level general intelligence has been more challenging than it was originally thought to be. I don't think we'll be stumbling on the answer to that problem by accident. No, SEER is just an advanced computer program, extremely good at collecting data and using that data to predict human needs and to achieve commands entered by those who control it. Besides, I've seen the documents with these commands listed on them. We can show you proof soon, once you understand what this is all about."

Maria narrowed her eyes. "So what makes you so special that you figured out this was happening when no one else could? How do you fit into all this?"

"I was one of SEER's mistakes. I was hired by the agency in control of SEER to put my doctorate in human development to good use by improving SEER's behavioral model. At the time I was hired, SEER was fully functioning, but they're always trying to improve the model, to reduce the amount of statistical analysis used and to make it solely rely on an individual's data. There will always be outliers to statistics, so if you can create a logical pathway from data to decision, your model will be far more reliable. Anyway, SEER was used to vet all potential applicants to make sure they'd be supportive of the program. It also constantly monitored all employees to make sure no one had a change of heart. There were several instances while I worked there of employees disappearing..." He trailed off, a distant look in his eyes as his train of thought seemed to be swallowed by his memories. "Anyway," he said, snapping back to the present, "to make a long story short, SEER must have assumed I would be totally on board with the program. I think at first I was, but that was before I knew the full scope of what SEER was capable of and how it was being used. After close to six months, a co-worker who I had begun to befriend disappeared. That raised my suspicions, and I did some digging. I discovered everything I just told you about and I left immediately, going into hiding. SEER's mistake was in not catching my change of heart. After I left, I began slowly building this group up and we've been working to stop SEER ever since."

Maria still had a million questions, but she held them back for now. She asked the only question that was important. "So what does this have to do with me?"

"I think you may already suspect the answer to your question," Vincent replied. "We are aware of the cybersecurity work you do. It seems you're quite talented and are one of the top cybersecurity programmers in your company, and maybe even in your field. We also know that one of your ongoing contracts is with DARPA. It's common knowledge that DARPA is the public face of SEER, handling its research, upgrades, and maintenance. While DARPA is not the agency solely in control of SEER, it's responsible for providing top-of-the-line cybersecurity to prevent unauthorized access to SEER. It's likely that DARPA hasn't told you exactly what it is you're building security for, right?"

Maria nodded, mouth slightly open in awe. The Defense Advanced Research Projects Agency, or DARPA, was the main research agency of the Department of Defense. Its mission was to be on the forefront of any research and technology deemed important or useful to national security. She had known her work had been for something important, and the level of security had been extremely high. But she never would have dreamed that she had been working on cybersecurity for the program that literally kept the United States running.

"I thought so," Vincent continued. "Keeping contractors in the dark about that is the best way to keep it secure, aside from SEER already watching your every move. So the fact that you've worked on cyber defense likely used for SEER makes you a valuable asset. But that's not the only reason we chose you. Another reason is your Mexican heritage."

Maria wrinkled her nose in confusion. "My Mexican heritage, what does that have to do..." she trailed off, realization striking.

"Right, you get it," said Vincent. "You were born in Mexico, you lived there until you were nine years old. You were outside the reach of SEER's main surveillance during that time, and any time you came back to Mexico to visit after that. SEER isn't completely blind over there, it still analyzes anything foreign citizens post on the internet or any data or video transferred or stored online. But that's much less information than it has about people in the States. To SEER, your childhood is mostly a mystery. A lot of things influenced you during that time, things that SEER has little knowledge of. Now, that doesn't mean you're still a mystery to SEER. All immigrants have their blood sampled and SEER uses that data, and you've lived in the United States long enough for SEER to be able to anticipate you extremely well. But not quite as well as it can anticipate a lifelong citizen. Most members of our group are immigrants or have lived outside the US for some time, and that makes us just a little more unpredictable than we otherwise would be."

Vincent turned and gestured toward Dr. Hansen, who was still seated at her desk, listening to the conversation. "Karen is from Canada. She was actually born in the US, but emigrated to Canada after college. She's an excellent programmer, and one of the earliest members to join our team. I was able to travel to Canada to recruit her. SEER has limited surveillance presence there, so I didn't have to resort to abducting her."

Vincent then turned to Antonio, who was leaning on the edge of Karen's desk. "Antonio immigrated here from Honduras as a teenager. He was one of the first members of the team that was recruited through abduction. He made it extremely difficult for us."

"Yeah, you bet I did," Antonio replied, dimples forming in his light brown cheeks as he recalled the event. "I was just minding my own business in my apartment when the power went out. Next thing I know, there's a knock at the door. I was working a security gig at the time and I'm a pretty suspicious guy, so I go answer the door with a baseball bat in hand. I crack the door and three people come out of nowhere, barging in and trying to grab me. Lucky for them they were on me before I could get a full swing in, but even so I had knocked Vincent unconscious before the other two could pin me down and jab a needle in my neck."

"I think my head still hurts at times from that knock you gave me," Vincent said, laughing softly. "And I'm sure Henry and Tiron didn't appreciate having to carry two unconscious people down to the pods."

"I'm just glad I didn't end up seriously hurting one of you, it was a pretty sloppy operation," Antonio said with a chuckle.

"That's why we chose him," Vincent said, turning back to Maria. "Antonio has been in charge of planning our recruitment missions. Since joining, most of them have gone quite a bit more smoothly than they had previously. Until today at least. You managed to turn what we thought would be our easiest recruitment mission into a near disaster." He spoke the last sentence with a wry smile on his face.

"Yeah nice work with that battery," Antonio said. "Caught us completely by surprise."

Vincent turned toward Irina, who was leaning against the wall near Karen's desk. "Irina was born in the US to Russian parents, but spent most of her teenage years in Russia after they moved back. She returned to the US for college, studied engineering, and then joined the military. She had spent several years in the military when we abducted her. This was after Antonio had joined, and he had come up with our pod capture technique, made possible with Karen's skills. It went off without a hitch, although Irina somehow managed to put a nice crack in the pod windshield."

Irina grinned. "If we had been a mile farther away from your pickup point, I probably would have broken all the way through."

"Since then she's been invaluable to us in obtaining the weaponry and equipment we need," Vincent said. He turned back to Maria. "We really do try not to abduct people unless absolutely necessary. If we can, we take them when they're traveling outside the country. But we're trying to work fast here and a lot of the time our schedule can't wait for someone to take a vacation or a work trip."

"Yeah, I'm sure you've found a way to make yourself believe it was totally fine to kidnap people." Maria crossed her arms, sneering at him. "What I don't understand is how you can abduct these people and know that they'll wholeheartedly join your cause." Turning her attention to Antonio and Irina, she continued, "How can you just go along with being pulled out of your lives?"

"It's hard at first," Irina responded, "but the cause is important. Vincent picked us not only because we've spent time outside the country, but because we've spent time inside the country too. We love the United States, and we don't want to see the land of the free turned into the land of the brainwashed slaves."

"What she said," Antonio replied. "And another common factor among everyone that Vincent took and that we take now is that none of us have spouses or children. We have family that we miss, but if we were taken from husbands, wives, or children, there's no way we could just go along with it. Everyone who's a part of this was chosen with these factors in mind."

"Okay," Maria said slowly, "but the way you talk it sounds like I have a choice in whether I go along with this or not. Even though I'm not married, I still have family and friends. So if I wanted to, I could still leave and go back to them?"

"I'm afraid not," Vincent replied. "You can't go back, you died today."

Chapter 3

Maria was stunned, her fists clenching tightly as fury blazed over her. It would explain her awful day if Vincent meant she had literally died and this was some kind of freakish afterlife, but she knew that was not what he was saying. "How could you do that to my parents?" she moaned, her fists shaking. "I'm the only kid they have left, they've already lost one daughter. They'll be devastated!"

Vincent looked at her with sad eyes and a pained expression on his face. The other three averted their gaze, looking uncomfortable. "I'm sorry," Vincent said, his voice soft. "It was the only way. You couldn't just disappear, they look for people that suddenly vanish. With SEER and the constant surveillance, they would have looked everywhere, never giving up. So we had to fake your death. We gave them a body to keep them from looking. In your case we made it look like you died in the fire in your pod. That wasn't the original plan, and we had a better plan prepared, but we had to improvise after your little stunt. While Irina and Antonio were chasing after you, another member of the team stopped at the pod to plant a body and to destroy the evidence of our tampering with the pod. We had already planted your DNA on the body in the usual places that they test for identification, and also replaced the teeth with copies we created to match your dental records. When we planted the body, we fueled the fire to disfigure it beyond recognition. It was a sloppy operation but we're hoping it was enough to slow them down, to make them think you aren't still out there somewhere. I'm afraid it was already way too suspicious, and there will be an investigation about why the pod caught fire."

"There had to be another way," responded Maria, her voice quiet. She pictured her parents, inconsolable, both daughters gone in just over a year. If she had just been missing, at least they would have had hope. Now they had none. She put her head in her hands.

"I'm so sorry," Vincent said, "but this was the only way. SEER has too many resources, and we have to do our best to keep them off our trail."

"Where did you get the body you used to fake my death?" Her voice was hoarse and quaking, sounding almost feral.

"If you're concerned that we killed someone, we didn't," Vincent replied hurriedly. "We monitor recent deaths for people who look similar to those we want to recruit, and if we find one, we steal the body. We use DNA we pick up from our potential targets, create more DNA, and then use that to replace as much of the DNA in the body as we can. We replace the teeth with ones we created, and at times fingerprints as well. It's an unfortunate and unpleasant part of what we have to do, but it's necessary. Lily, who you've already met, is in charge of finding and preparing bodies."

"So you're a group that kidnaps people, steals dead bodies from grieving families, and fights against a computer system that has improved the lives of everyone in the United States. And you're trying to tell me you're the good guys here?" She was nearly snarling as she spoke. It was too much, she had heard enough.

Before they could respond she leapt up from her seat, lashing out with all her strength at Vincent's stool, tipping it over backwards and spilling him to the floor at the feet of the other three. The confusion brought her a few precious seconds. She dashed for the door, swinging it closed behind her. Maria allowed herself a brief moment of satisfaction when the door thumped shut on a reaching arm, a cry of pain ringing through the air.

She sprinted down the hallway to her left, looking for a way out. The few windows she had seen had all been boarded up, so she had no idea what floor she was on. She spied a sign with a stair symbol on it up ahead, the number on the door informing her it was the second floor.

A shout rang out close behind her. Too close. She ran faster, pushing through the door and rushing down the steps. Her head swam and her legs shook, the activity too much after being sedated. She fought through it, focusing intently on the steps so as not to fall.

As she rounded the landing, the door above her slammed open. Footsteps pounded down the stairs after her. Maria did not look back, focusing only on moving as fast as she could, doing her best to ignore the thudding of her heart.

Pushing through the door to the first floor, she entered a hallway like the one above it but in a state of total neglect. The tile floor was covered in dirt and debris, the walls stained and coated with mildew. The musty air made it even harder to satisfy her burning lungs. She barely registered any of that, her attention focused on the doors up ahead to her left. The exit.

The first set of doors were covered with plywood from top to bottom, hiding the glass. The left door swung open with a squeal of rusty hinges as she pushed through it into the vestibule. The next door made a similar sound, and then she was outside.

Her eyes blinked in the bright sun and goosebumps rose on her arms from the chilly breeze. A street ran side to side in front of her, with a few smaller restaurants and offices situated along it. But there were boards over the windows and the paint was stained and faded. Overgrowth had crept back in where the woods had once been cleared to make room for the buildings. The asphalt road was rutted and broken, plants growing up through the many cracks.

She cursed, taking off to her right down the street. Her hope of finding civilization shrank with every passing second. Behind her, the rusty hinges squealed again.

"Maria!" a woman's voice shouted, sounding close. Maria ignored it, running as fast as she could despite the pain in her side and the spots in her vision.

"Maria, we have proof! Your sister! SEER made her do it!"

Maria stumbled. SEER made her do it? What did she mean?

Her brief moment of hesitation was enough. A hand clamped down on her wrist. Maria pulled away, but she was tired, unsure. The hand never loosened.

Maria turned around as Irina wrapped her arm around Maria's waist to hold her still. Antonio was just catching up, and he took her by her other arm. Maria looked at Irina blankly. "What do you mean SEER made her do it?"

Irina glanced nervously up at the sky. "Everything will be explained when we get back inside. Quickly now."

They walked at a brisk pace back to the building, one of them supporting her on each side. The walk went by in a daze. Whatever drug they had used to put her under was still having an effect, and the fear and exertion had been too much. She was too tired to resist, and unsure if she would resist even if she had the strength. If there was some connection between SEER and her sister's death, she had to know.

By the time they were back to the second floor, she had caught her breath and her head had cleared a bit. Vincent stood waiting for them by a different room. Karen was not with him.

"I know we don't seem like the good guys right now," Vincent said as she approached, "but please be patient and we'll prove to you the awful things SEER is doing."

Vincent pulled a keycard out of his pocket and held it up to a sensor near the door. It slid open and they walked through into a large room, stuffed with blinking computer servers and a few desks to the point that it felt almost cramped. Seated at one of the desks was a skinny man with deep brown skin and short black hair. He turned to look at them as they entered, a smile forming on his face as he saw who it was.

"Ah!" he exclaimed. "This must be Maria." His accent suggested African origins. He stood up and walked over to Maria, shaking her hand, stooping slightly so that his tall frame did not tower over Maria's shorter figure.

"This is Zuberi Kamala, he's our IT specialist here. He's responsible for the servers and local network our group operates on, as well as some of the technology we use," Vincent said.

"Please, call me Zu," he said, smiling warmly. "That's what my friends call me."

Maria hardly registered him, although the part that did felt a twinge of guilt about ignoring this man that seemed so happy to meet her. "My sister," was all she could say.

Zu nodded and gestured to the chairs near his desk. Irina guided Maria to a seat and sat next to her. Antonio motioned for Vincent to take the last chair, opting to lean against a server rack.

"This won't be easy to hear," Vincent said, "but your sister was manipulated into killing herself."

Maria's mouth set into a grim line. "What do you mean manipulated? She wasn't weak. She wasn't dumb. She couldn't just be tricked into killing herself." She turned to Irina. "I thought you meant she was threatened or forced to do it."

"She was, in a way," Irina replied.

"Remember what I said earlier?" Vincent said. "Seer knows everything there is to know about a person. For Seer to find ways to get your thoughts and feelings to change is simple. It knows what would crush your spirit, what would make you dread getting out of bed every morning."

"But why though?" Maria was exasperated now. "Why would Seer want to—" But as the words left her mouth, she understood. Ana's vlog.

Ever since she was little, Ana had been fascinated and scared by the fact that cameras recorded everything they ever did. That stuck with her as she grew older. She thought it was wrong that a person could not opt out, not with the cameras everywhere and the surveillance drones in the sky. It had been Ana's passion. So much so that she had been working on a double major in history and computer networks to learn more about how the public opinion shifted to accept constant surveillance and how these surveillance networks worked. Early on in her college career she had even started a vlog advocating for the ability to opt out of surveillance.

"Her vlog was growing fast," Vincent said, "so fast that whoever is controlling Seer must have thought it was a risk. Seer needs constant surveillance on everyone in order to provide the most accurate predictions. The people in control need accurate predictions so they know who's a threat. Being able to opt out of being monitored would not fit with their goals."

"But you claimed before that Seer can manipulate beliefs and opinions. If they wanted to stop her, why not just manipulate her to believe surveillance is fine?"

Vincent gave a slight, sad shake of his head. "We can't say for sure, but I would bet at the rate her vlog was gaining popularity they thought if they didn't shut her down fast it might get too big, might convince too many people. Sadly, it takes a lot longer to change a belief someone has spent years devoted to than it does to ruin their life."

Maria had never been as concerned about surveillance as Ana, mostly seeing it as providing a lot of benefits with few downsides. It had always been surprising to her that so many people had shared Ana's belief. Maria had watched every video Ana had posted multiple times since her death, just to hear her voice and see her face again. She had noticed how each video had more commenters thanking Ana and agreeing with her than the last. Although if what Vincent was saying was true, Ana's vlog had been even more popular than Maria had guessed.

It all seemed to fit so well, and it would explain so much. Maria's stomach churned, emotions twisting inside her. Ana had lived with so much passion, and she had always seemed so happy. They had played video games online together at least once a week, chatting and laughing as they played. Ana had always taken the time once a month to come visit Maria and their parents, despite Ana's heavy school load. But then it had all gone downhill so fast. Ana stopped visiting, stopped responding to calls and messages. And then she was gone.

"You told me you had evidence," Maria said. "This... would explain a lot, but depression can really mess people up too."

Vincent nodded. "Did you know your sister made a final goodbye video?"

Maria's eyes went wide. "No, she stopped publishing videos a month before she died."

"Yes, she did stop, but she created one last video, saying goodbye to her friends, family, and fans. Ana uploaded it, but SEER made sure it was never seen." Vincent turned to Zu. "Pull up the video please."

Zu made a few quick gestures and a 3D video of Ana's upper body appeared in front of them. One look and Maria's hands went to her mouth. Ana had looked increasingly disheveled and unenthusiastic in the last few vlogs she had posted, but this was something else entirely. She looked gaunt and skeletal, her eyes red with heavy bags, her hair unkempt.

When Ana began speaking, Maria felt a familiar ache in her heart, and tears formed in her eyes. "This is goodbye," Ana said, her cheeks wet, her voice on the verge of breaking into sobs. "I've just stopped enjoying life. I don't know why. And it's no one's fault. I can't sleep, but I don't want to get out of bed. My appetite is small, but when I do get hungry, I don't want to eat. I know there's good out there in the world, but all I can see or think about is the bad. I know I have loving family, friends, and fans, but all I can think about is the many who hate me. It's been so hard for me to care about the things I used to love."

Tears streamed freely down Maria's face, rolling over her quivering lips. Watching Ana's other videos had been hard but this... this was on another level. Ana's despair seemed to radiate out from her body.

"Mom, Dad, Maria, please don't think any of this is because of you. You've always been there for me. I know this will be hard for you, but I'm doing what I need to do. I love you."

Ana paused, fighting off a sob, before continuing. "And for the few actual supporters of this vlog out there, the conversations we've had and the comments you've left have meant the world to me. Thank you so much. Goodbye for the last time."

The video ended, leaving the room silent except for Maria's restrained sobs. Antonio handed her a tissue, wiping his own eyes with another one. Everyone remained quiet, giving her a moment to recover and process what she had just seen. It made little sense, and Maria voiced her concern. "I don't understand," she said, wiping her eyes, her voice wavering. "Ana had so many fans, and as far as I know hardly any detractors. You really think SEER stopped this video from going up? Where did you get it? How could SEER make her miserable like this?"

Vincent looked at her, his face soft and sad. "I don't just *think* SEER stopped this video and compelled your sister to kill herself, I *know* it did. I copied this video from SEER's files before I left, as well as commands relating to your sister's death. As for how, it's hard to say exactly, the commands aren't specific enough. But I think it's likely that SEER only showed Ana the worst things about the world. Every day she would wake up to the evils of the world and only hear bad things in the news. Every time she looked for reactions to her vlogs, SEER would only show her the comments that hated her and her work. SEER knew her fears and insecurities, and it exploited them to ruin her life. I think SEER even messed with her sleep, playing subtle noises through her orb drones that would wake her up but that she would be unable to actually register. She would think her inability to sleep was just because there was something wrong with her. I think SEER spent the last few months of Ana's life torturing her until she could no longer take it."

Maria had to push that thought out of her head. If she allowed herself to think about the agony of Ana's final days, there would be no recovering. In a strained voice she asked, "Do you have the commands you copied?"

Zu nodded, and a moment later an array of documents appeared in the air in front of her. They were sorted by subject, and she quickly flipped through until she found the documents relating to her sister. They were labeled "Ana Rosado, compelled to suicide." Her final vlog post was in the file, as well as background information. The documents Maria wanted to see were called out as "SEER commands."

She opened the first document. It looked like an official form, the header and seal of the National Security Agency, or NSA, at the top. Below that were several lines indicating the officials approving the commands and the date. The names were blacked out, leaving only the timestamp of February 5th, 2123. A year and a half ago.

Filling the rest of the page was a smaller subject box followed by two large boxes labeled "INPUT" and "RETURN", respectively. The subject line read, "Increase public support for surveillance, identify influential leaders of surveillance opposition movements."

She read down to the input section. SEER's programming language appeared modern, the commands and styles very close to regular English, like most other programming languages. There were only two lines in the input section, which read:

```
SEER action: Increase PUBLIC support for
GOVSURVEIL. Authorize modes: MEDIA; IN-
TERACTION.

SEER return: ID of GOVSURVEIL(OPPOSITION)
PUBLIC(INFLUENCERS).
```

The only thing listed in the return box was:

```
Reference: GOVSURVEIL(OPPOSITION)_PUB-
LIC(INFLUENCERS)_LIST.
```

"So it looks like they feed commands into SEER and have some groups and code words pre-defined to simplify the commands, like PUBLIC and GOVSURVEIL," Maria said. "And they also input the acceptable means of accomplishing the tasks. This return looks like it's referencing some kind of list or spreadsheet right?"

"That's correct," Zu replied. "They define groups, programs, and ideas to make it easy for commands to be issued. And with each input they authorize the accepted means to achieve the goal. And yes, you're right, the return is larger than the room they have on the form, so SEER provides the details in a separate list document. It should be in the files."

Maria found the file and opened it to reveal a list of names, identifying numbers, and addresses of the people

SEER deemed significant influencers opposing surveillance. Second from the top was her sister's name.

The next file she opened was another SEER command. The date was a little over a month after the previous input. The subject read, "Terminate specific uncoerced surveillance opposition leaders."

Maria's heart felt heavy. Her eyes moved down to the input section. It read:

```
SEER action: Terminate GOVSURVEIL(OPPO-
SITION)_PUBLIC(INFLUENCERS)_LIST{AR325,
HD293,OS114}. Authorize modes: ACCIDENT,
PSYCH.
```

There it was. The order that killed her sister. Ana's ID code on the list of public influencers had been AR325, and this command called out ID AR325 for termination. For a moment she questioned whether these commands could have been faked by Vincent's team to convince her, but she brushed that thought away. It would be easy to fake the documents, but not a missing vlog post. Ana's sudden downward spiral made so much more sense this way. These documents were legitimate; there was no doubt in her mind.

"How did the others die?" Maria asked, her voice regaining some strength.

Zu looked grim. "One was a journalist, he got drunk and fell off a bridge. The other was a New York City Council Member advocating for privacy, and she was murdered in a robbery."

Maria's fury toward Vincent had faded, but it was flaring up again at a new target. She began making small hand gestures, rifling through the files, reading quickly. There were hundreds of files, each documenting coercion of politicians and media personalities, commands to increase or decrease public support for different policies, and several more terminations. One made her pause, her eyes widening. "Termination of American citizens by drone?" she asked.

"Yes," Irina replied, "not our high-altitude drones we've used against foreign threats, but the small drones, similar to the commercial and private drones that are available. Like the weaponized rapid response police drones, but more advanced. They use electrified weapons that can make it look like a person had a heart attack. Usually they reserve the drones for cases where they need someone gone fast and don't have time to wait for SEER to convince them to kill themself or cause their death some other way."

Zu gestured several times and pulled up a video file, expanding it to a large size. "Vincent was able to steal this video file when he left. It shows one of the drone assassinations. In this case, it was someone inside the SEER program who was going to try to go public with inside information."

He gestured again and the video began, showing a street at night, street lights illuminating the road. The video seemed to be taken from a camera mounted on a building, showing the road and the sidewalk on the opposite side of the street. Several pods passed by, and then a few moments later a woman stepped into view, walking along the sidewalk. She looked agitated, moving fast and stealing glances over her shoulder. Even from this distance, paranoia was evident in her behavior. She passed in front of an alley, but then stopped, her head snapping to the side as something down the alley drew her attention.

Zu whispered as the video continued. "You can't hear it on this video without amplification, but she heard someone say her name down the alley," he explained. The woman stepped cautiously into the dark alley. The camera angle changed, switching to a camera at the end of the alley looking out toward the street, the camera up on a building.

"H-hello?" the woman called out, fear in her voice. She took another step and then paused, perhaps realizing that she should not have entered at all. She pivoted, moving as if she were about to break into a run. But before she could, an object rose from where it had been hidden on the ground and darted toward her. Something shot out from it, a small glob that struck the woman's neck and stuck there. Instantly the woman convulsed, dropping to the ground and writhing, mouth open but no noise coming out. As suddenly as she began convulsing she stopped, her body limp. The drone flew toward her and a mechanical arm reached out, its claw closing around the glob on the woman's neck. It pulled it off of her and then flew upwards and out of view.

Maria's mouth set in a grim line. She recognized the projectile as a blitz round, a small gel ball that would stick to targets, commonly used by police drones. She remembered learning somewhere that the blitz rounds were originally invented in Germany with the brand name of Krugelblitz, the German word for ball lightning. They were charged with electricity, the amount of charge depending on what the intended purpose was. Police drones commonly used lower charges to slow or stun dangerous suspects. This one had been intended to kill, the blitz round removed from her body to leave no trace.

The room was silent. Zu said nothing, but gestured subtly a few more times and pulled up a news article. There was a picture of the woman, and the title read, "Body Found in Alley". The article said the cause of death was ruled as a heart attack. No foul play was suspected.

"They have to be stopped," Maria said, her hands gripping the arms of the chair to stop them from trembling with rage. "The people in charge of SEER have to be exposed and punished for this."

"That's what we intend," Vincent replied. "We want to expose the abuse of power to the public and show everyone the terrible things SEER has been used for. We want to transfer control of SEER to the people and make the operation of SEER as transparent as possible."

Maria frowned, unsure if that was the right move. "After everything you've said about what SEER is capable of and what it's being used for, how can you let it continue to exist? It killed my sister and countless other people. The people in charge need to answer for these deaths, but SEER makes them like gods. It's too dangerous."

Vincent nodded. "A lot of things are dangerous in the wrong hands. I definitely understand your point, but the entire country relies on SEER. Our transportation, communications, manufacturing, farming, healthcare, emergency services, crime prevention, basically everything. It all depends on SEER, and is so much more efficient than it otherwise would be because of SEER. If SEER were to shut down, the country would grind to a halt and erupt into chaos. It would take a long time to get everything running again without SEER. Tens of thousands could die without all of those necessities I mentioned. And even after we transitioned from SEER, we would never achieve the same level of care in our hospitals or the same efficiency in our lives as we have with the data SEER collects and uses. Quality of life would decline, and many people would die from the lower-quality healthcare. SEER is dangerous, yes. But quality of life without SEER is worse for everyone in the US."

Maria pursed her lips, thinking over what he said. Then she nodded. "I'm with you. I don't blame SEER for Ana's death. I blame the miserable assholes feeding it commands, who think lives are play-things they can mess with to achieve their goals." She paused a moment to relax her hands, which had been clutching at the arms of her chair as if they were the necks of the people responsible for Ana's death. "So, what's your plan? How do we stop SEER?"

"We recently found the location of one of SEER's data servers, in a base not far from DC. Until today, we'd only suspected it was the server location. We had tried to send drones into the area but interference kept us from getting close enough to see anything. So we sent one of our team members in to verify that it was the server location and to gather data. His name was Tiron, and unfortunately the mission cost him his life."

Vincent paused, looking down, a slight tremble passing through his chin. The faces of the others were a mixture of pain and sadness. Vincent gathered himself and continued.

"Tiron managed to break into the compound and gather intel. Specialized scanning equipment in his backpack imaged below the base as he walked around, and from that we were able to verify that there's a large area below the base that likely contains the servers. Unfortunately, Tiron was discovered and became incapacitated. In order to prevent the NSA from discovering anything about the mission, Tiron blew himself up, destroying all the evidence. He also sent a signal out, detonating another bomb at a decoy hideout we had set up on the outskirts of the city. This was the explosion you saw in your news feed yesterday. There was nothing at this decoy hideout, but by sending a signal we were able to send the data he captured as well, disguising it as a signal to detonate the decoy bomb. If we hadn't disguised the signal it's likely that SEER would have intercepted and analyzed it, finding out that Tiron was working with a team and that the team had received all his data. We wanted to prevent SEER from finding out just how much information he was able to discover. Because of Tiron's sacrifice, we now have a video of the compound and confirmation of the likely server location."

Maria nodded, but a puzzled expression crossed her face. "So what do we do with that information? There won't be access through the data servers to the SEER command terminal, so there's no way to take control of SEER from there."

"That's correct," he replied. "Now that we've confirmed the location of one of the server groups, our plan is to hack into these servers and modify the user files so that there are fake records for all of us. Doing this will allow us to be out in public without triggering alarms in SEER's system, and it will make our approach to the SEER input terminal at the DARPA headquarters much easier. Once we're in the system, we'll break into DARPA and access the SEER terminal. We'll immediately order the shutdown of all of the programs we're concerned about and alert the public about these programs. Then we'll transfer control of SEER to ourselves until the public has decided what should be done with SEER."

Maria gave Vincent a look of dismay. "Whoa, hold on. Two things. First, why not just hack some pods like you did to kidnap me to get us close. Or hack a couple of the surveillance drones to hide our approach? You had to have done that when you rode in on your motorcycles to get me, otherwise you would've been caught."

How they had managed to fool the surveillance drones was something she had been wanting to know. Surveillance quadcopters hovered in the sky, forming a grid over the whole country, recording and feeding data back to SEER. It made for a nearly impenetrable network of cameras, even in rural areas, that allowed SEER to better predict behavior and to have emergency drones to most locations within minutes. Replacement drones were always at the ready in case of low battery, lightning strike, or mechanical failure.

Antonio spoke up to answer her question. "It takes too long and there's a lot of risk. It took months to find a pod and modify it so it would send fake data to SEER without looking suspicious. But then you torched it so now we don't have any." His lips stretched into a teasing smirk. "Besides, we'd need to get a cargo trailer to carry all of us. And the contents of those face pretty heavy scrutiny. The drones aren't easy either. We had one location prepared where we replaced a surveillance drone with one of our own. It fed pre-recorded data to SEER so that we'd be invisible on it. But that only lasts as long as the battery does. To try to replace all the drones on the way to the SEER terminal would take a lot of drones, perfect timing, and a lot of risk of being discovered. Not to mention there are a lot more cameras than just the aerial surveillance drones when you get closer to the city."

"And we already have the gear we'll need to infiltrate the data center," Irina added. "Most of it we already needed for our other missions, stuff that we've stolen from the military or bought from black market contacts. Thanks to Tiron, we think we have a way in, and if it works we'll practically be able to walk right up to the DARPA headquarters without any trouble."

Maria gave a small shrug. "Okay, makes sense. But my second issue is the most important one. You said we have to hold the SEER terminal until the public figures out what to do with SEER. That's a lot of power for a small group of people. How do I know you won't just hold onto the power forever?"

Vincent looked hurt. "You aren't the only one who's lost people you cared about because of SEER. I watched as my coworkers disappeared when I worked there. Antonio lost a brother. Irina has lost friends during her time in the military. We know it's hard to trust people who have kidnapped you, so we've made sure that the people we've had to abduct have strong motivation to change SEER. And aside from personal relationships destroyed by SEER, everyone on this team has lived in the US for quite a while. We all love the United States, and everyone has been horrified when we've told them what SEER is doing to the people it's supposed to be helping. We will not become like the people who hold it now. We want everyone to know what's been happening and that things need to change."

Maria rubbed her chin, not fully convinced. Vincent noticed her reservation. "Trust me," he said, "I'm concerned about so much power being in so few hands as well, but there's no other way. We can't trust the government to take control of SEER without a democratic process to determine what to do with it. And until they make a decision, it needs to be safeguarded. We're the only ones that can be trusted to safeguard it. And every order that gets entered into SEER while we're guarding it has to go through you, Maria, because you'll be the one writing the inputs."

She considered for a moment, and then nodded. "Okay. So I'm guessing you want me to create a program that can hack into the data servers that you can use when you break in? And one that will hack into the input terminal for the next stage too?"

Vincent tilted his head to the side. "Yes, but you wouldn't just be handing us a program. We need you to come with us on these missions too."

Her stomach twisted into knots. Go on the missions? It was dangerous enough even working with these people, but infiltrating bases and government headquarters was an entirely different level of danger.

"Why would you want me to go? Wouldn't I just be a liability?"

"We need you in case something goes wrong, or in case there's something else that needs to be hacked in order to access the servers. Same with the SEER terminal. We can't risk any communications because SEER could easily intercept them. So you can't monitor the missions remotely. You have to be there. Don't worry, though. Our field team will get you in and out. All you have to do is follow their instructions."

Maria bit her lip. "And if I were to say no?"

Vincent frowned. "You would be allowed to live here semi-independently. But we couldn't let you go back to your home. As far as SEER knows, you're dead. Showing up again would alert SEER and ruin our whole operation. And without your help, it will be even longer until we can stop the brainwashing and killing that SEER is being used for. If we even can at all. We need your help, Maria."

It was so much pressure, so much responsibility. And the alternative was to wait here, unable to return to her life, to her parents and her friends. It had to be that way, she knew that, but it was so unfair. Why did it have to be her?

Disgust filled her as soon as that thought crossed her mind. Ana had never asked for this either. Ana had never known why her life had become a living hell. And how many more were suffering because a few powerful people thought the country needed to be molded to better fit their vision? Even those not suffering were living a lie, their beliefs changed to better suit the goals of whoever was feeding the commands to SEER.

"I'll do it," Maria said, meeting Vincent's eyes with a hard stare. "But I don't have access to my company's program, which we use as a basis for all our work. It's kept under tight security and we aren't allowed to take the program off the premises or even work on it from home. I can recreate it, but it would take a long time."

Vincent smiled reassuringly. "Not to worry," he said, "we've already taken care of that. The night before you were captured, Irina broke into your office and retrieved the program."

Maria looked at Irina incredulously. "But how?"

"We used your DNA and fingerprints to fool the biometric scanners and to access the building and your station," Irina replied. "I disguised myself to look similar to you so the surveillance cameras didn't raise suspicions either. Once I accessed your station, I loaded a program onto it that Karen wrote. It converted your file into sound and I played it over your station's speakers, bypassing your copy and transfer protection. When I got back to our base, all Karen had to do was run the audio through the program again and then we had a copy of your file."

"Wow, nice," Maria said, giving an impressed smile. "Clearly I have some security improvements to make when things get back to normal." Her smile faded. Would things ever be normal again? Certainly not if they failed. And if they were successful, how would the country react?

She shook that thought from her head. There would be time for it later. Another question had been bugging her. Her escape attempt and the image of abandoned and water-damaged buildings came back to her. "Where are we anyway?"

"We're in southern Nova Scotia," Vincent replied, "in an area that's been abandoned due to rising sea levels and the associated flood hazard. It's the perfect location, unpopulated and remote but within a decent distance of DC, where most of our activity will be."

"Yeah, the perfect location," said Zu, giving Maria a sarcastic smile, "unless you're the one who has to keep the lights on in the building or set up the servers."

Maria's look of surprise gave way to a small smile. "Wow, I didn't know it was so far away, how long have I been under?"

"About twenty hours," Vincent replied.

Maria gaped at him. No wonder she felt like crap. "Why so long?"

"I wasn't on the boat so we thought it best to keep you under until you were back here to talk to me. It's a long trip by boat, a trip we'll have to make again when we go on our mission. We're on a fairly tight schedule, once you've had a chance to dig in a bit I'd like to talk about how long you think it will take to finish your part. But for now, do you feel you have enough information to begin?"

Her mind was a whirlwind, her thoughts swirling around in no particular order, her head beginning to throb. She could hardly make sense of her emotions, having exercised every one to the point of exhaustion. And her body felt like she had slept on a bed of boulders. But at the forefront of all of that was Ana's smiling face, urging her to make sure no one else would suffer the way she did. Maria met Vincent's eyes and nodded. "Let's get started."

Chapter 4

Maria spent the next few days working on her program, modifying it so that it no longer just identified vulnerabilities, but exploited them. She was given the empty desk across from Karen's, in the room where she first met Karen, Antonio, and Irina. Her progress in the first few hours was agonizing, as she had to relearn how to manually do the things that SEER had always done for her.

The first time she sat down at her desk, she had waited for close to fifteen seconds for her station to turn on, slight frustration setting in before she realized her mistake and her frustration was replaced with embarrassment. She had never had to access a station manually before, and it took her a little while to figure out how to do it. Even after working at her desk for several days, she sometimes still caught herself waiting for her station to start automatically before she remembered to do it manually.

However, she found the biggest inconvenience and inefficiency to be text input. She had never written at a station before without SEER's predictive text assistance. And it was much more than assistance. SEER's predictive capabilities had meant that it could type as fast as you could think, hardly ever making a mistake. With SEER it felt smooth and natural, the words appearing on the screen immediately after you had thought of what you wanted them to say. When SEER did make an occasional mistake, the fix was as simple as selecting the incorrect word and choosing from a short list of alternatives, the desired word always appearing in the list.

Coding without SEER was an entirely different story. Her station did have a text prediction program loaded on it, but it was old and inaccurate. No one had bothered to make an improved program in the last twenty years, SEER having completely eliminated the need for one. So she was stuck with this ancient program, which made her writing feel about as quick as etching words into stone. After the first few hours, she began to figure out the program's quirks and shortcomings, and her speed with it picked up. But even with her increased competence, she was still operating at half the speed she was used to.

In retrospect, it was almost surprising that SEER's predictive text capabilities had not caused more people to fear SEER or call for its destruction. That ability was proof enough that it could predict people's thoughts with high accuracy. Somehow she had never considered that a cause for concern before. SEER had always just seemed like a natural part of life, a ubiquitous but benevolent tool that she had no reason to fear. Sure, there had been the occasional article from tech reporters wondering if all this data that was being collected could be used for malicious purposes. But the public mostly treated these concerns with indifference or as if they were only vague hypotheticals. Looking back on it now, she realized that SEER most likely influenced everyone to care less about these concerns, or to ignore them entirely. And it had worked on her as well. How much of who she was had been put there by SEER? What would she be like if SEER had never manipulated her? Thinking about it too much led her down an even deeper rabbit hole. How much of who she was had been put there by her parents, her friends, or her genes? The answer seemed to be that everything about who she was had originated from outside herself. All of it was outside her control. Just like SEER's influence.

Too much of that kind of thinking would only lead her to an existential crisis. Instead, she focused on her work. The lack of SEER slowed her down in other ways too. Programs and answers to questions did not just pop up when she wanted them, she had to load the programs and search for questions manually. Another issue was the lack of internet access. They could not risk sending or receiving any signals from the outside world for fear of detection, so instead of full access to the internet, they only had access to pieces of it. Zu had loaded their servers with portions of the internet that he hoped contained the most relevant and useful web pages and data. He had gathered these chunks of data as they were needed, taking trips to countries where SEER had a weak surveillance presence but where internet was available.

Zu had done a pretty good job, gathering relevant portions of the internet containing manuals and discussion threads for the computer language her program used as well as theory and educational material on cybersecurity to help refresh her memory when needed. Even so, there were gaps in the information, and she often found her questions and searches yielding useless results. Every unanswered question brought a curse to her lips and forced her to recreate certain code sections by reasoning through obscure cybersecurity logic.

Still, she made progress. Her program began to take shape, and she coordinated with Karen to figure out what Karen would need access to. This involved a lot of guesswork, since they had no concrete information about what format the user data files were in. It meant Karen had to write several different routines to modify the SEER data. Once Maria had accessed the servers, Karen would have to manually pull up several data files, identify which of her routines looked like it fit the best, and then run that routine. From there, the routine would identify how the data file was organized, rearrange the fake data they had created in a format that matched, and then input that fake data as new user data files into SEER.

Occasionally, Karen asked Maria for her opinion on the actual user data files she was creating for the team members. Karen had to populate the files with enough information to make them appear as if they had existed in SEER's servers all along. This meant they could not just be empty files with generic information such as height, weight, and appearance. Instead they had to have a brief history, with snippets of information that SEER would be reasonably expected to have. To make this realistic, all of the team members were designated as residents of foreign countries who previously had limited access to internet and technology. Their files only contained brief bits of information, such as times they may have passed through a surveilled area or fake phone conversations they may have had with someone who would be in a surveilled area.

The beauty of this was that once this fake data was input into the system, the team would be able to take public flights into the country, appearing to SEER to be tourists coming to the United States who had little available background information. If they were to suddenly appear in America, it would raise alarms since there was nowhere within the country where a person could have disappeared in the first place. But taking flights in from other countries would not raise any red flags in the system, and they would only be subjected to the increased surveillance typical to tourists who had limited background information for SEER to use.

After only a short time working together, Maria had developed a great respect for Karen. She could tell immediately that she was brilliant and meticulous, catching on quickly to Maria's work even with little previous exposure to the defense side of cybersecurity. Karen was typically serious and focused, unlikely to begin a conversation unless she was engaged by someone else or if she needed to discuss an aspect of their work. But she was not cold, and when spurred into conversation she was friendly.

Maria enjoyed working with her, and Karen's usual restrained demeanor made her unexpected jokes or outbursts of laughter all the more endearing, as if Maria had achieved a rare victory by getting her to open up. Such as at one point during the second day when Karen had caught Maria hiding a grin.

"What's so funny?" Karen had asked.

"Oh nothing," Maria had responded, letting a small giggle escape.

"What is it?" Karen demanded. "Is there something on my face?" Then her eyes had widened as she realized what she was missing. "Share your reality right now!"

Maria complied, sharing her augmented-reality provided by the light stations situated around the room which projected light onto their eyes, allowing them to see their virtual workstations and any other virtual decorations they added. They were basically a stationary version of the orb drones she had back home.

"You're such a child," Karen snapped, as she looked at a virtual reflection of herself to see that in Maria's augmented reality world, Karen had been dressed in a full body gorilla suit.

Maria shook with laughter. "Pound your chest!"

Karen just crossed her arms, but a moment later a chuckle escaped the gorilla suit and then Karen was roaring and pounding her chest. Since then they had kept a running competition to see who could come up with the goofiest virtual outfit for the other person.

When they weren't playing augmented-reality jokes on each other, Maria's work style differed significantly from Karen's. Where Karen was quiet and focused, Maria fidgeted and muttered under her breath. She had periods of calm, punctuated by muttering and curses. Sometimes the cursing was caused by problems in her code, but much of the time it was directed at the quirks and difficulties caused by working without SEER.

Vincent occasionally stopped by to get updates on progress and to let them know about various things. He never stayed long, usually just long enough to get an update or to ask and answer questions, and then to let them know when lunch or dinner would be. Each day the team held lunch and dinner upstairs on the third floor in a room they called the lounge. At first it struck Maria as a little odd, but, as Karen explained, most of their tasks were isolated, and it would be easy to spend the majority of the day with little human interaction. Holding lunches, dinners, and other events kept everyone sane and sociable and helped the team mesh. It made sense to Maria, especially considering that everyone else here had been living in this abandoned building together for months.

Vincent had shown Maria around shortly after her arrival, introducing her to the rest of the team. He had taken her around to each of their offices on the second floor, the first stop being the team's surveillance expert, Liu Min. She was a young woman from China, who went by the name Min. Her job was to make sure the team was not detected by surveillance and to keep their activities hidden.

Next, Maria had been introduced to Clarissa Harris, originally from New Zealand, who was the head of security and a member of the field team. Clarissa worked frequently with Min to keep their activities hidden and was in charge of protecting and securing the operation in case of discovery.

After Clarissa, she had met Henrik Martinsson, a man from Sweden, who went by Henry. Henry was a member of the field team, and was in charge of procuring secure means of travel for the team.

Finally, Maria had been introduced to Vasu Jatav, a man from India. He was the team's engineer, in charge of equipment and technology, especially maintenance and improvements.

Maria had been surprised when Vincent had told her she had met all of the team members. There were only ten of them, eleven if she counted herself. It seemed to her that there should have been more, especially considering how well-equipped their base was. She had felt anxiety creep in at that point. The chances of eleven people succeeding against the government and a seemingly omniscient computer system felt slim.

Since that point, the fear had not faded, but had instead been pushed into the background as she focused on her work. She adjusted quickly to the long hours they worked, usually even continuing several hours after dinner. But they did not work around the clock for fear of burnout and mistakes, as Vincent told her. Late in the evenings, everyone took some time to relax, moving up to the third floor where they had set up some community rooms. There was the lounge, with an attached kitchen and walk-in freezer, meeting rooms, a library, and a game room. The game room was well stocked with video games, and even had a makeshift ping-pong table and dart board too. Each night they would take the time to unwind, some watching movies or shows, others reading or playing games.

When sleep called, they would head upstairs to the fourth floor, where they each had their own room. Each room only had a cot and a dresser, and they all shared the public bathrooms, which had been modified to include showers and a washing machine. The clothes they wore had been gathered by Henry and were collected in one of the rooms on the fourth floor. They could each pick clothes to keep for themselves from the collection, although the selections and styles left a lot to be desired.

Every Wednesday they had movie night, another opportunity to socialize, and also an opportunity to watch pirated copies of new movies that had recently hit theaters. Overall, the atmosphere felt like that of a company trying to build a strong culture instead of a secretive team fighting against government control. They were warm, friendly, and seemed to honestly care about one another.

That had been especially evident on the day of her arrival. At lunch, Vincent had announced to the group that there would be a ceremony to honor Tiron at two PM. When that time came, they had all gathered in one of the meeting rooms on the third floor. A large picture of Tiron had been placed on a stand at the front of the room, his smiling face flanked on either side by glowing candles. The whole group had been there, and she had sat on the edge of a row of chairs next to Karen.

Vincent had started the ceremony with a few words about Tiron, beginning with Tiron's background before moving on to the impact he made on their lives. Maria gathered that his role had been as a field team member in charge of purchasing equipment from the black market using money Karen had hacked from various banks.

Maria had looked around the room while she listened, observing the varying expressions of grief on each person's face.

Some had been weeping openly. Others had tried to restrain their emotions, quivering lips and moist eyes betraying their feelings. Maria could feel their sadness, and her eyes had teared up as she remembered the pain she had felt at Ana's funeral.

After Vincent had finished his short eulogy, he invited the others to say a few words if they wished. Zu had spoken briefly, with tears on his cheeks, of the friendship they had. He recounted a story of the time Tiron had returned from a trip dressed as the Easter Bunny and handing out candy, earning a tearful chuckle from the crowd. Vasu went next, speaking fondly of Tiron and then ending with a word of prayer, spoken in Hindi.

What moved Maria the most was when Karen had gotten up to say a few words after Vasu. She spoke briefly about the sacrifice he had made for them, and as she finished speaking, her normally reserved demeanor turned from restrained sadness to outright sobbing. The bond they all shared was palpable, and she was glad to know that even though her life had been turned upside down, she would at least be part of this team of people who cared so strongly about each other and about their mission.

It was now Thursday, and Maria felt like the days had been a blur since her arrival just over a week before. She was focused on her program, reviewing every line to make sure there were no errors, when Karen broke her concentration.

"Time for lunch!" Karen said, standing from her seat at her desk. Maria got up too, the graphics disappearing from around her as her station closed and saved her work. Last to disappear were Karen's octopus costume and Maria's rubber

duck costume. They walked out the door and to the nearest stairway, chatting as they climbed the stairs to the third
floor.

"So, are we ready to tell Vincent?" Maria asked.

"I think so," Karen replied. "I think my part is finished,
and yours is done, right?"

"Yep," Maria said. "I want to look it over one more time
but I should be finished doing that this afternoon."

"Great!" Karen replied excitedly, clearly looking forward
to moving on to the next stage. They had run a few tests of
their programs, Maria having reconstructed snippets of the
security code protecting SEER from memory and reasoning
through it. So far everything seemed to have worked okay, her
program was able to break through the dummy code she had
made, allowing Karen to run her program.

Maria was excited to be moving on to the next stage, but
also terribly frightened. There could be no wireless signals
sent during the mission, so she would have to go with the field
team in case there were any problems with her program. The
thought of breaking into a high-security compound terrified
her, especially after seeing the footage from Tiron's mission.
But the fear of breaking into the compound paled in compari-
son to the terror she felt when she thought about hacking into
the system. What if her program failed? What if they spent
all this time and effort to break into the compound and hack
into the system and she had messed it all up? She could be
putting everyone on the team in danger. If that happened, the
best-case scenario would be that it just failed without alerting

anyone. But if it failed and did raise an alarm? They would all be captured or killed.

She shoved the thought from her mind. All she could do was the best she possibly could; she must not allow herself to get in a panic before they even leave for the mission.

The delicious smell of chili hit her nose, pulling her out of her apprehension. They were nearly to the lounge, the smell wafting out the door and into the hallway as they approached. Karen walked through the door in front of her into a room with a large table in the middle, big enough to seat the entire team. Toward the side of the room was a counter with stools. Behind the counter was a closed door, which led to the kitchen. The rest of the team was already there, with the exception of Antonio and Zu. Karen sat down in the open seat next to Vincent. Maria followed and sat across from her, next to Min, who smiled at her as she sat down.

"Hey Maria, how's it going?" Min asked cheerfully.

Maria smiled back at her. "Oh pretty good, how are you doing?"

"You know, just sitting around twiddling my thumbs while I wait for a couple of slackers to finish their programs," Min replied, grinning playfully.

Maria laughed, retorting with fake exasperation, "Maybe I could work a little faster if you got off my back once in a while."

The door to the kitchen pushed open and Zu walked out, a large pot of chili in his hands. Antonio followed him through the door, carrying a bowl of tortilla chips, plates, and silverware. "Help yourselves," Antonio announced as they set the items on the counter.

They all got up and shuffled through the line, scooping the chili into their bowls and chips onto small plates. It smelled fantastic, and Maria was grateful for the good food they served, even better than what she had been used to at home. "Thanks, guys," she said, smiling at Zu and Antonio as she shuffled by.

"Another satisfied customer," Zu said, grinning and playfully punching Antonio's arm.

"Are there any other kind when we're cooking?" Antonio boasted, punching Zu back.

Maria chuckled at their banter and returned to her seat. Zu and Antonio helped themselves to the chili once everyone else had received some and then joined the group at the table.

"So when's Maria going to stop hiding out in her office and take a turn cooking, huh?" Clarissa called out from down the table. It took Maria by surprise. She hadn't talked to Clarissa much, other than meeting her and seeing her security office and a couple brief chats here and there. Maria at first thought she was voicing an actual complaint, but then the corner of Clarissa's lips curled up into a subtle smile.

Maria grinned and retorted, "Hey, someone's gotta get some actual work done around here." After a few laughs and playful protests from the rest of the group, she continued. "And speaking of getting work done, Karen and I are just about done with our programs."

Choruses of surprise and praise echoed from around the table, and Vincent, who had been quietly listening and smiling at the group's antics, leaned forward. "Ah, so the tests you ran this morning were successful?" He was now fully engaged, an eager look on his face.

Maria looked to Karen, not wanting to steal the credit since Karen had been working on this project much longer than her. Karen seemed to understand the look Maria gave her, and she answered Vincent's question. "Yes," Karen replied, "our tests were successful. Based on our best guesses of what SEER's defenses and database look like, our programs were able to break into the system and insert our fake data."

"That's fantastic," Vasu said, speaking up from farther down the table. "But Maria has only been here a week, how were you able to get it done so quickly?"

Maria felt her face redden slightly, embarrassed to be receiving praise for her brief work instead of Karen. "Really, most of the work was already done before I got here," she replied. "Since Irina had stolen my program from the office, all I had to do was modify it. I just had to add a few more possible weaknesses for it to look out for and then change what the program did once it found a vulnerability."

Vincent had an excited grin on his face, and he placed his hand on Karen's shoulder, giving her a gentle shake. "Well done, you two. We can move on to the next step thanks to you."

Maria's appetite vanished as Vincent's words reminded her that the entire operation was hinging on her program.

The confidence in his voice did not comfort her, and made the idea of failure even worse.

Vincent spoke again, snapping Maria out of her unpleasant rumination. "There, Min, now you can stop twiddling your thumbs and do some work again." He laughed, looking across the table at Min.

But Min did not laugh. Min was not even listening, and instead looked as if she had seen a ghost, her face ashen. She *had* seen a kind of ghost, one projected onto her vision by her personal virtual display, a projection only she could see.

"Lock—" she whispered, cutting off as she choked on the rest of what she was trying to say.

"Min?" Vincent asked questioningly. The room had quieted, and smiles were being replaced with looks of worry.

"Lockdown!" Min shouted, bursting up from her chair. "Lockdown, lockdown!"

There was a brief pause, and then the room erupted into chaos.

Chapter 5

The rest of the group sprang up from the table almost as one, a few knocking over their chairs. Min rushed to the door, calling over her shoulder as she opened it, "Incoming drones four miles out, closing fast!" Clarissa followed close behind her, running out into the hallway.

Zu grabbed the pot of chili and scurried through the kitchen door. Antonio reached for the bowls, but Vincent stopped him. "Zu will shield the food and stove, you follow the rest of the procedure."

At first Maria could hardly believe they were bothering with the food at a time like this, but then she realized the food would be a dead giveaway if the drones were scanning for heat signatures.

Antonio gave Vincent a single nod and ran out of the room. The rest of the group began to leave too, crowding toward the door. Lily stayed behind with Zu to help cover the food.

Maria followed the group out the door. They had told her what to do in case of lockdown, but the suddenness of it left her disoriented and hesitant. Thankfully, Karen moved next to her and reassured her. "Just follow me," she said, her voice strained, taking off down the hallway with the others. Maria stuck close behind her. Henry split off from them as they reached the stairs, going upstairs while they went down. When they reached the second floor, Irina peeled off and continued down the stairs to the first floor.

The group was eerily quiet as they ran. The only sounds were the clapping of their feet on the smooth floor and their breathing. There was no panicked chatter or shouted orders, just a group of people who knew what they were supposed to do in this situation. This helped calm Maria, but only slightly. Her chest was tight, afraid an attack could come at any second.

After what felt like forever, they reached their destination on the second floor, Clarissa and Min's office. Clarissa and Min were standing by their desks, eyes staring at images in the air that Maria could not see. They both had weapons strapped to their backs, what looked like machine guns.

Clarissa walked to a cabinet against the wall. "Over here, everyone grab a weapon. Min, share the virtual display with them. Vasu, close the door behind you."

Vasu closed the door. Min gestured a few times until several virtual displays appeared. One was a satellite map of the area, centered on what Maria assumed was their building. She had not been allowed outside since her escape attempt, so she could not recognize it by sight, but it was rectangular-shaped like she expected it to be. Overlaid on the map were three red dots, spread out in a row and approaching at a steady pace.

The other displays showed video feeds, what looked like views around the perimeter of the building, some looking at entrances and others looking out from the building toward the surrounding area. A few showed the hallways inside the building on each floor.

"Stay focused, Maria, we need everyone alert," Clarissa said gruffly, startling her. She turned away from the images to see Clarissa in front of her, a smaller pistol-type weapon held out in her hands, grip towards her.

"Sorry," Maria replied, taking the outstretched weapon, keeping it pointed at the ground. She could tell Clarissa was on edge; her usually friendly demeanor was gone and replaced with a curt, military-like attitude.

Maria stepped around the others to stand beside Karen, whose eyes were glued to the displays. Maria watched them too, and after a second she saw movement on one of them. It was Zu and Lily, running down the hallway on their floor. Clarissa stepped to the door, shifting her weapon so that she could easily raise and fire if they were being followed.

"It's just them," Min said. Clarissa opened the door and let them in. Zu and Lily walked over and grabbed weapons for themselves. Clarissa shut the door behind them.

"We have three drones incoming, they're a mile out and closing at sixty miles an hour," Clarissa said.

"That's pretty slow, they must be running a deep scan, right?" Vasu asked.

Min nodded. "Yeah, we're picking up strong signals coming from them, seems like a thorough scan."

Maria relaxed slightly. They had not been found yet. But the drones were coming right for them. It was possible they knew their group was in the area and were coming to find and eliminate them.

Clarissa spoke again. "Henry, Irina, Antonio, do any of you see anything?"

"Nothing yet," replied Irina, her voice clear, as if she was in the room with them. Henry and Antonio echoed the same. Three displays enlarged, two showing what looked to be corners on the roof of the building, the other showing windows on the inside of the building on the first floor. Maria squinted at the displays, then frowned. There was nothing on them worth showing as far as she could tell. Then a slight shimmer caught her eye near the corner of the rooftop on one of the displays.

"What's on those displays?" she whispered to Karen.

"That's Irina, Henry, and Antonio," Karen whispered back. "They're hiding under Camofoil."

Karen noticed the blank look on Maria's face, so she continued. "It's like a metallic blanket that takes an image of the ground it's lying on and replicates that image, so then you can lie under it and you blend into your surroundings. We have a few defensive positions set up with Camofoil, weapons, and hardwired communications line. All our video feeds and coms are hard wired so we don't transmit any signals that could be detected."

Maria nodded in understanding and they returned to nervously watching the displays in silence. After a few seconds, Karen leaned back over to her and whispered. "Do you know how to use that thing?" she asked, gesturing to Maria's weapon.

Maria had shot a rifle before, but the handgun was different. She thought she could figure it out, but just to be sure she shook her head. Karen set her weapon down on a nearby table and grabbed Maria's pistol. Keeping it pointed at the floor, she held it out so that Maria could see. "Here's the safety, switch it this way for safe and this way to shoot. Then just aim and pull the trigger. It's semi-automatic so you have to pull the trigger for each shot. This button here releases the magazine. It's a large magazine so you have thirty rounds."

Karen pulled an extra magazine out of her pocket and handed it to Maria. "Here, if you run out of rounds you just switch magazines and you're ready to go again, you don't have to do anything else."

Maria took the clip and stuffed it into her pocket. "Thanks," she whispered to Karen.

"I see something," came Henry's voice, whispering. "Looks like a drone, I can just barely make it out through my visor."

Clarissa replied, "They're about a quarter mile out, the middle drone is coming right toward us and the other two are a half mile on each side. You're probably seeing the middle drone. Stay concealed and don't engage, hopefully they'll pass by."

The next minute was excruciating. There was total silence in the room, everyone seeming to hold their breath. All eyes were glued on the three red blips on the floating display. The blips slowly traced their way over the top of the building, the center one passing directly over it. Maria's heart nearly stopped, imagining briefly that the drone had stopped moving. But then it passed, the distance between it and their building increasing millimeter by millimeter.

Maria could hear the sound of their collective breath being released in a relieved sigh. But everyone remained on edge, keeping quiet for several more minutes.

At last Clarissa broke the silence. "They're three miles past us and continuing at sixty miles an hour. Everyone sit tight, we'll remain on lockdown for the next hour."

They settled into the limited space, Min and Clarissa sitting at their desks and the rest of them taking one of the two remaining chairs or a spot on the floor. Maria had no preference so she took the floor, offering the nearby chair to Vincent, who thanked her and accepted. Maria took a spot near the wall, leaning against it with her eyes closed for a few minutes, taking deep breaths and trying to calm her nerves after the dread of the last few minutes.

The group was quiet as they recovered from the panic. No one spoke, seeming to want to avoid the question that was on everyone's lips. Maria wanted to avoid it too, so instead she asked a different question, breaking the silence. "What kind of scan are the drones running?"

Min answered her. "Vasu has checked out the hardware of the few drones we've been able to take out and recover, and it looks like they're capable of scanning the entire useful electromagnetic spectrum and are very sensitive at detecting pressure variations, or sound. They're also capable of using a type of radar system that can see inside buildings. Basically if it moves, emits heat or light, or makes noise, they can probably detect it."

"So how did it not detect us?" Maria asked.

Vasu answered her. "We built this room to be a signal dead zone. All communications and video feeds in the building are hard wired so there are no signals broadcasted, and this room is lined with material to block the drones' radar signal. Min and I identified the signals we needed to block, and then modified this room to be virtually invisible."

Maria nodded, impressed. "What about Irina, Henry, and Antonio, how do they avoid detection?"

"Their Camofoil masks their electromagnetic signature," Vasu replied, "and they also wear special suits and masks to cancel any sounds they make, such as breathing. Zu and Lily also used something similar to the Camofoil to conceal the heat of the stove and food."

Maria nodded again, satisfied with the answer. The group again sank into uneasy quiet, still not wanting to voice their fears.

Finally, Vincent broke the silence. "I know what you're all thinking. Are they on to us? Did they track us back here, and is it only a matter of time until they find us?" He paused, standing up and walking closer to the displays. "I don't know the answer to that. Min, Clarissa, what do you think?"

They looked at each other, unsure. Min thought for another moment before replying. "The fact that they're sweeping this area is troubling. Especially with more than one drone, and at such a close proximity. They could have done a stealth run and just surveyed the area and we never would have known they passed by. But since they ran a full radar scan, that leads me to believe they suspect we're in this area, and they're doing a very detailed sweep."

Clarissa nodded, and then added, "And it's possible that we may continue to see increased frequency of sweeps. Continued lockdowns could hamper our progress and effectively incapacitate us. That may be part of their strategy."

Vincent nodded in agreement. "I think you're both right. We need to act. We won't let this scan change our plans. The longer we wait, the greater the chance of discovery."

He turned to face Maria and Karen. "You said you're done with your programs, right?"

They nodded, but Maria cut in before he could continue, "I think it's done but I did want to look it over one more time."

"Good," he replied, "pull it up and look it over. Everyone else stay alert and do what you can to prepare for the next phase. As soon as this lockdown is over, we need to get everything ready to move out. We're still on target for our first window and now we have to hit it. We leave tomorrow morning."

Min gave Maria access to a virtual station on her machine and Maria pulled up her program from their server. From her spot on the floor, she began reading through every line of the program, looking for any possible mistakes. It was hard to focus at times because Vincent started asking the other team members for updates on their contribution to the next phase. She was dying to know how they would proceed from here, and she noticed her attention frequently shifting to what the rest of the team was discussing. But when she caught her attention wandering, she forced herself back to the task at hand.

After close to a half hour, she had finished her read through. She had found no issues and had not made any changes. The program was done. She closed her virtual station and leaned back, eyes closed, feeling the fate of the team weighing heavily on her.

Vincent noticed her change in posture and interrupted her anxious meditation. "Is it finished, Maria?"

She nodded. "No changes, it seems complete."

Vincent seemed to pick up on her anxiety, his attitude changing from excited to comforting. "Try not to worry. You've done the best you can. We're a team, this is not your responsibility alone. And try not to worry about the mission either. Our field team will get you where you need to go, all you'll have to do is follow their orders."

She gave him a slight smile, grateful for his comforting words but unable to shake the sick feeling in her stomach. She leaned her head back against the wall again and tried to relax, pulling her legs up to her chest. But she could not calm down, her foot tapping anxiously against the floor, her thoughts traveling too fast.

She heard the sound of footsteps and opened her eyes to see Zu sit down beside her. "So where are you originally from?" he asked.

Maria knew he was trying to take her mind off her worries, and she was grateful for it. "I'm originally from the state of Chiapas, in southern Mexico," she replied. "My parents owned a farm when I was little, nothing much, just enough to provide for the family. When they saw how good my sister and I were doing in school they decided they wanted us to have the best opportunities, so they sold their farm and used the money they had to move us to the US. I was nine when we moved to Arizona. We stayed put after that, until I left for college at Carnegie Mellon in Pennsylvania. When I graduated from college I got a job in Arlington, Virginia and I've been working there since then."

Maria's face flushed as she finished talking, realizing she might have gone into more detail than Zu was expecting. She quickly returned the question back to Zu. "Where are you from, and how did you end up here?" she asked, with genuine curiosity.

"I was born and raised in Tanzania," he replied, "and I came to the US during high school as a foreign exchange student. I liked it a lot and wanted the best college education I could find, so after graduating back in Tanzania I applied and was accepted into MIT, and was able to attend thanks to some scholarships. I got a master's degree in electrical engineering there. I went back to Tanzania after graduating and worked for a few years until Vincent found me. Tanzania has a pretty weak surveillance presence so Vincent didn't have to abduct me. He found me and convinced me to join, and I've been working on setting up and maintaining our base here since then."

Maria nodded, conveying her interest. "How long has that been?" she asked.

Zu thought for a moment, a startled look on his face. "You would think I would know off the top of my head," he replied, laughing. He thought about it some more. "I think it's been around six months," he said. "When I think about how long I've been here, it feels a lot shorter than that, but when I think about everything I've worked on it feels a lot longer." He grinned at the strangeness of his statement and added, "That probably doesn't make any sense though."

"No, it makes perfect sense, I feel the same but on a smaller scale," Maria replied, laughing. And she did understand that feeling. It had only been a little over a week since she had arrived and it had flown by. But at the same time so much had happened and she had gotten so much done that she felt like it had to have been much longer than that.

"So what work did you do in Tanzania when you graduated?" Maria asked, following up on what Zu had said.

"I worked for a power company there," Zu replied. "I was in charge of updating our design processes with the automation tools I had learned about in college. Tanzania isn't far behind on our actual solar and wind infrastructure, but we are pretty far behind on our automation. What the US has with SEER and other software cuts the time to design and maintain new plants and electrical grids by at least a factor of five. Tanzania doesn't have anything like SEER, but I was able to implement some new engineering software at the company that saved a lot of time and money."

Maria was impressed, nodding her approval. "That's pretty exciting," she replied. She thought for a second, a look of confusion crossing her face. "I thought you said Tanzania has a low surveillance presence since Vincent was able to recruit you there. If you aren't too far behind on infrastructure and technology, why is the surveillance presence still low?"

"Good question," Zu replied, smiling at her. "While Tanzania has had pretty rapid modernization, there are still a lot of rural farming communities without internet access and with limited technology. My parents actually live in one of those communities. They have a good-sized farming operation there. Vincent waited until I was visiting my parents until he approached me about all this."

"Gotcha," Maria replied. "That's so great that your parents are farmers, I thought I would be the only one here who has parents who played in the dirt for a living."

They laughed and chatted for a while about the crops their parents grew and some of their childhood farming memories. Maria's worries faded into the background and she felt more relaxed than she had since she had arrived here.

But her calm was to be short-lived. Clarissa spoke up after several minutes to announce that the lockdown was over. Thoughts of leaving in the morning flooded back in and her chest tightened, but she did feel a bit better than before. She gave a tight smile to Zu, to thank him for taking her mind off things. He smiled back, seeming to understand.

Vincent wasted no time in taking command. "Okay everyone, I want everything prepped and ready to go before dinner tonight. After dinner we'll check over everything and then we get to bed early. We're moving out before dawn tomorrow."

They all stood up and moved toward the door. Maria went to follow, unsure of where to go, until Vasu approached her.

"Maria, Karen, come with me please," Vasu said. "We need to get you fitted for your gear."

Maria followed him out the door and down the hallway, with Karen walking beside her. They turned a corner at the end of the hall and then entered a door on the left into Vasu's office. She had only been inside his office a few times, first when Vincent had shown her around and then a couple more times for some scuba-diving simulations. Frustratingly, no one had told her yet why exactly she would need to know how to scuba dive.

The first time she had been in his office, she had been surprised at its size. It was twice as large as the other offices, the wall between two of the original rooms having been removed. There had been cases of tools and equipment lining every wall, and several tables in the middle, each covered in wires and machine components.

The room was unchanged from her last visit, except for a large, black-fabric box filling the center of the office, the tables pushed to the side to make room. It was nearly as tall as the ceiling and around ten feet long and ten feet wide. Maria had no idea what it was for.

Vasu noticed her questioning expression and smiled. "You'll find out what that is in a minute."

He walked over to one of the cases against the wall and opened it. He pulled out two full-body suits, entirely black with a strange striped texture in the fabric. Vasu handed one to each of them.

"Put these on," he said, "they should be sized to fit each of you."

Maria took the suit he held out to her and examined it. The fabric was light, and now she could see that the striped pattern was actually thick strands, like those of a knitted wool sweater, woven throughout the entire suit. She squeezed one of the strands and was surprised to feel a hard surface underneath.

Meanwhile, Karen was turning the suit in her hands, confusion on her face. "Um, how does it open?" she asked.

"Oh right," Vasu replied, laughing. "That's important to know. Like this." He reached over and pulled on the waist of the suit, and with a soft sound of Velcro the suit separated into two parts, pants and a top. A thick strand stayed connected between the two pieces, unwinding slightly as they separated.

Maria copied him with her suit and separated it. She removed her shoes and put the suit on over her clothes. The strand settled back into its place as she pulled the top down and connected it to the bottom. Vasu handed her and Karen another piece with the same pattern on it, resembling a ski mask. They put them on and he showed them how to connect the strand from the shirt to the strand on the mask. He then gave them each a pair of boots, gloves, and a large backpack covered in the material, and showed them how to connect those things to the rest of the suit.

Maria looked at Karen when they were finished. She was covered from head to toe in the material, leaving only her face exposed. Maria was surprised at how light and cool the suit material felt. She did not feel much warmer than she had felt in her regular clothes. The backpack was the heaviest part of the suit; she guessed something like twenty or thirty pounds. It rested firmly but comfortably on her shoulders, distributing the load evenly and making the extra weight less noticeable.

"Alright, Maria, you're up first," said Vasu, leading her over to the large, black cube. He handed her a mask and she put it on. It covered her entire face, attaching to clips on the head of her suit. The mask had the same strand pattern as the rest of the suit, even over where her eyes were. It fit comfortably on her face, not restricting her breathing at all, although she could see nothing.

"Just a second," Vasu said. She heard him jog over to his desk, while she stood helpless and blind. Then all of a sudden she could see as if she were looking through ski goggles. "Your vision is via cameras on your suit and a display inside your mask, so I had to turn it on before you could see anything."

Vasu pulled back a flap on the large cube and Maria stepped inside. He closed the flap behind her, leaving her in the dark. She stood there unmoving, unsure of what to expect, until Vasu's voice sounded in her ear.

"Can you hear me?" he asked, his voice sounding clear and crisp through speakers built into the suit at her ears.

"Yes," she replied.

"Okay, I'm going to turn the lights on in there," Vasu said. "It'll get bright but your display should adjust so it doesn't hurt your eyes."

The room lit up, turning from dark to pure white on every wall and even the ceiling and floor, completely illuminating the empty room. It would have been blinding if not for her display darkening. On the wall in front of her, the outline of a person appeared, standing straight up and down, their arms outstretched to each side.

"Stand in the center of the room and make that pose please," came Vasu's voice. Maria complied. "Okay," Vasu continued, "I'm going to start the calibration. Just stand still, and every time you see a new pose on the wall copy it."

The outline of the body faded, and the room turned from bright white to dark again. Suddenly her suit lit up, every strand emitting white light with no gaps in the color, and then cycling rapidly through red, green, and blue. Then the room lit up again, this time with a bright pattern of colors mixed together in random splotches. With her arms outstretched, Maria could see out of the corner of her eye that her suit seemed to be making a similar pattern. A few more patterns appeared on the room, and then an image of a new pose appeared, a crouched position. She took that pose and the patterns continued in the room, now sometimes with moving colors and images.

From her crouched position she looked down at her bent legs, but could barely see them. They were nearly perfectly blended with the moving background of the floor.

"That's amazing!" she exclaimed. "How's it doing that?"

Vasu laughed, enjoying her surprise. "It is amazing, isn't it?" he replied. "The strands on your suit are made up of tiny LEDs and sensors, arrayed around the circumference and length of the strand. They're all connected and communicate with each other, the sensors see the light that hits you and the LEDs on the opposite side of you mimic that light. The calibration we're doing right now tells the small computer in your backpack which sensors correspond to which LEDs as you move around."

"Incredible," she replied, getting up as another body outline appeared on the screen. She jogged in place, mirroring the figure on the screen. It hurt her brain to think about the programming that would be involved to make the suit work. "And the battery is in the backpack too?" she asked.

"Yep," Vasu replied, "it's got enough juice for two hours of use. And not only does it camouflage you in visible light, but infrared as well, shielding your heat signature and emitting one that blends into the surroundings. Plus, it absorbs radar, so active scanning won't work either."

Maria whistled appreciatively. "Impressive. Did you come up with this?"

"No, no," he said, seeming amused at that. "I'm not nearly that talented. We 'acquired' these from the military, thanks to Irina. I just set them up and do the calibration, and make repairs and adjustments if necessary."

The scene in the room shifted to a forest area at dusk. Vasu told her to just move around as she pleased. She walked around a bit, looking down at her suit. She blended perfectly into the forest floor. She held up her arm, camouflaging as she moved it, until it disappeared into the canopy and the patches of sky. She might not have been able to see it if she had not known to look for it.

"Okay, we're all done, you can come on out," Vasu said. Maria exited, the suit changing to her surroundings as she walked out. "When you actually go on the mission there'll be some graphics in your display visible only to you that'll show you where your limbs and teammates are, but I don't have that running right now." She was glad it was off, seeing it in action was amazing. She held up her arm between herself and Vasu as he walked toward her.

"Why doesn't it seem as clear now?" she asked, noticing that Vasu looked kind of blurry and unrealistic through it.

"It doesn't do detail very well, matching the light across your body is difficult and not perfectly accurate," he replied. "If you're trying to stay hidden, you'll want to make sure your background is lacking in detail, sharp edges, or color changes that could make you stand out."

Vasu helped her remove the suit and he placed it back in its case. Maria waited patiently for Karen to complete the process she had just gone through. Ten minutes later Karen walked back out, giving Maria a full view of the suit in action. It was spectacular, only a faint human-shaped shimmer giving away Karen's location. Maria stood up and walked around Karen, amazed at the seamless transition from background to background, the illusion only faltering when it tried to display details such as Vasu and his cluttered desk.

Maria waited while Karen removed the suit. When she was done, Vasu walked them over to another case and opened it up. Inside was a short-barreled rifle with a boxy body, two barrels stubbing out a short distance from the front of the rectangular area. The top one was a regular-sized barrel and the one below it was larger, like a grenade launcher. It was mostly covered in the same material as the suits. "This is the weapon you're being issued," he said. "It hooks into your pack to blend in. It automatically feeds ammo from your pack too, no reloading. It also overlays a targeting reticle on your visor, tracking where you aim so you don't have to look down the sight. Ammo count and firing mode will show up in your display too. It shoots regular bullets, spread shot for taking out drones, blitz rounds for incapacitating, and the launcher allows you to manually load a variety of things."

Maria again found herself impressed. The tech they had was amazing, and she could hardly imagine how much each piece of equipment must cost.

"I know you've had some weapons training, Karen. Have you shot a gun before, Maria?" Vasu asked.

She nodded. Karen looked surprised, glancing questioningly at Maria.

"My mom taught me how to shoot back home in Mexico," Maria said, answering Karen's look. "We lived on a farm so sometimes we had to take drastic measures to keep the coyotes away from the chickens."

Karen nodded and appeared impressed, and then looked back at the weapon and frowned. "I don't know if I'll be very good with that thing," she said, seeming a little nervous. "It looks a lot more complicated than what I've trained with."

"Don't worry," Vasu reassured her, "I had never shot a gun before using this one and it's not hard to figure out. It looks intimidating but it's really pretty simple. Irina will give you a crash course on the trip tomorrow. Besides, you shouldn't need to use it if everything goes well."

Vasu's words reassured Maria too, since the weapon was a lot different from the simple rifle she had used as a girl. But his last sentence reminded her of how much the team was relying on her code to work smoothly, and the fear of failure swept over her again.

Vasu closed the case back up and then showed them how to operate the last few tools and gadgets that they would be carrying in their backpacks. There was a kind of compact grappling hook, a first-aid kit, and some Camofoil. Maria watched as Vasu went over the items, but she was not very focused. Her mind was elsewhere, in her office with her program.

After a short time, which seemed excruciatingly long to Maria, Vasu told them they were all done and that he would see them at dinner.

Maria walked out into the hallway next to Karen. "We've got about an hour until dinner and I have my program loaded up already, want to go play a game and relax a bit?" Karen asked.

Maria thought for a minute. The offer sounded really nice, and she wished she could accept. But her anxiety was pulling her toward her office. She felt like she had to check it again.

"That sounds fun," she replied, "but I need to go copy my program onto some drives and put it with my gear."

Karen smiled and nodded. "See you at dinner then," she said.

Maria smiled back at her, and then turned and walked quickly down the hallway, her smile immediately fading. She walked into her office and sat down in her chair, turning on her station. For a few minutes she shut her eyes and rested her head in her hands, trying to clear her mind. It helped less than she was hoping it would.

She spent the first few minutes loading her program onto several portable drives. It was important that she had plenty of backups in case she lost one or one became corrupted. One she clipped to a wristband, another around her neck, and a third for her pack. She would give one to Karen in the morning too, in case she lost hers or something happened to her.

All at once, the implications of that last thought hit her and a wave of nausea washed over her. What if she froze with fear at the first sign of trouble? She was not brave, not like the field team. Could she hold up under pressure if her life was at risk? How many more would end up like Ana if she failed?

Thoughts of fear, death, and failure plagued her as she spent the remainder of her time poring over the code, searching for any mistakes and trying to think of ways that it would fail. She found nothing. She was simultaneously confident that it would crack SEER's security undetected and mortified at the thought of a tiny error slipping past her and ruining it all. She ran test after test, and it worked perfectly every time. This did little to reassure her.

She found it odd that she never felt this kind of pressure when designing security for national systems that millions of people depended on, but the thought of failing and risking the lives of these ten people had her petrified. At work, their code was checked and tested through a rigorous process, but here she was just one woman. Karen was skilled but Maria's cybersecurity knowledge was far beyond hers. The success of the program rested entirely with her.

At six-thirty, Maria reluctantly pried herself away from her station and went to dinner. The group was quieter than normal, their nerves apparently running high like hers. She was not sure whether that made her feel relieved that she was not the only one, or nervous that they were feeling unsure. Did she want to be able to relate to the group or did she want them to be like machines, calm and confident? She decided it did not matter what she wanted, and she took comfort in the fact that she was not alone in her fear.

When they were finished eating, Vincent stood up and cleared his throat. "I just want to thank you all for your hard work getting us to this point," he said. "I'm confident in all of your individual abilities, and as a team I'm positive that we'll be successful. I suggest you all go and get some sleep. We're meeting here before dawn, at four, for a quick breakfast and then we leave."

They all stood up and filed out the door and to the stairs, heading up to their rooms. Maria resisted the urge to go to her office and continue scouring the program. She wished the group good night as they each went to their rooms. Once in her room, she changed and collapsed onto her bed. She tried to clear her mind of her worries and get to sleep. She was not successful.

Chapter 6

The next morning was a blur of activity, the stress of it all assaulting Maria's brain. She had finally managed to sleep, but it was restless and brief, full of nightmares of failure. But despite the early morning and the lack of sleep, she was not tired. Fear-induced adrenaline was keeping her alert.

The team met in the lounge first for a quick breakfast. Maria made sure she had the drives with her, and gave one of the copies to Karen. When they were finished eating, they all walked quickly together to the first floor. Maria had not been down to the first floor since her escape attempt, and at the time had been too preoccupied to observe it closely. It was like walking into a different world. Filth and water damage from previous flooding covered the floor. The musty smell of mold and neglect filled the air.

Irina was in the lead, and she brought the group to a set of double doors, opening them and letting them pass through in front of her. Maria followed Karen through the doors onto the concrete surface of a loading bay. The bay was large, with a single garage door, likely originally intended for deliveries of food and equipment for the building. The garage door was closed, the room lit by several large ceiling lights.

In front of the garage door, at ground level, was a large boat. Or at least she thought it was a boat. It was black and angular, with strange wing-like projections extending down and to the side. It was completely enclosed, the only windows were low in the front, tinted so as to be nearly opaque. It looked more like a fierce attack aircraft than a boat. It rested on four wheels that looked like they would fold back into it once it reached the water.

Irina stepped around the clustered group and down a set of concrete stairs to the floor. She reached for the underside of the hull and opened a folding door, the top half lifting up and the bottom half folding down into three steps.

"Everything's loaded up," she said, "come on in."

Maria walked with the rest of the group to the boat and climbed the steps, ducking slightly to clear the opening. The interior looked like it belonged to a submarine. There were chairs along each side with floating graphics in front of each, showing views of the outside of the boat and other information. Near the back was a ladder up through the ceiling. Maria walked over to it and looked up, to what looked like an upper deck area.

Everyone took a seat at the chairs along the side. Maria sat down next to Karen. Irina sat in the command chair and powered up the boat. Antonio and Clarissa sat in the seats on either side of Irina and pulled up their displays.

"Alright, here we go," Irina said, nerves evident in her voice. This would be the most exposed they had been since arriving. Maria was not sure how they planned to stay hidden other than driving the large black boat down the road in the dark, but she would ask later — if they made it.

The lights inside the bay shut off, casting it into near total darkness. Maria could not see or hear the bay door opening, but she knew it must have when a dim light illuminated the loading dock, cast by the moon and stars. She felt the boat begin to move backwards, and she watched out the front as they traveled away from the elevated platform. They passed under the door out into the back lot of the building. Irina turned the boat around and they pulled out onto the road, moving at a silent crawl.

No one spoke, and the tension was heavy in the air. Maria tried to distract herself by observing their surroundings out the front window and through the virtual display at her station. The front window and virtual display compensated for the low light, and she could see the abandoned and crumbling buildings she had seen on her brief venture outside. The boat rode smoothly despite the potholed road. Several times, Irina had to swerve around large sinkholes where the high water table and frequent flooding had undermined the pavement.

After only driving a few minutes, the ocean came into view in the dim light, swallowing up the road in front of them. Irina continued on her path, driving the boat straight into the water. Their firm ride turned into a gentle rocking as the tires left the ground. There was a soft mechanical sound and the boat rose in the water. It accelerated, pushing her back into her seat until they were at speed. The ride was surprisingly smooth. With a few gestures, Irina turned off the night-vision mode for the front window. Maria could no longer see any distinguishing features out the front, just the soft glint of light reflecting on the water and some stars in the sky.

Irina made a few more quick gestures and then released the controls, the boat now locked into its course. "Okay," she said, "we've got nineteen hours until we approach our landing spot. When we arrive, we'll be under the cover of darkness."

Antonio spoke up. "That means we'll all need to be awake and alert late tonight. So we're going to start off with a mission brief and then weapons training. Then the rest of the day you'll be free, but I suggest you use that to get some rest before the mission."

Antonio gestured and a display appeared in the air in the aisle. It was playing body-cam footage of Tiron's mission, his black-gloved hands occasionally reaching into view to push branches aside as he walked through the woods.

"We'll start with some intel from Tiron's mission," Antonio said, his voice catching as he said his name. On the display, Tiron approached the edge of the woods and the compound came into view. Antonio made a slight gesture and paused the video when the compound was clearly visible.

"Most of you have seen this footage," Antonio continued, "and as you know these buildings here are entirely empty. It's a decoy, so that if anyone does discover it and manage to break in, they can't easily find what's being guarded. But we were prepared for that, and Tiron was carrying a ground scanner with him."

The display changed from the video still to a three-dimensional aerial view of the forest. "Here's the satellite view of this spot, but you can't see the compound due to some clever shielding," Antonio said. "Here," he continued, "is data from the scan Tiron performed." A black and white image appeared on the ground in the aerial view, showing the outline of the underground structure. The image was incomplete, with gaps where Tiron had not walked.

"We aren't positive where the entrance is, but since it's likely to be heavily guarded, we don't want to go that way anyway. Instead, we're going by river. We believe the SEER servers are cooled with river water. Being underground and considering the amount of heat they have to generate, this is likely the only feasible way to cool them. Tiron's scan and previous data we've stolen seem to confirm that."

A portion of Tiron's scan brightened on the screen. It projected out from the rest of the underground structure slightly, appearing to continue on past where Tiron had imaged.

"We think this part of the structure is some buried pipe used for bringing river water to the servers and expelling the hot water. Infrared scans of the area seem to confirm this." Antonio gestured and the aerial view zoomed out, showing the nearby river, some roads around the forest, and some buildings. Then the colors shifted into a thermal gradient, red signifying hot and blue signifying cold. There was a noticeable hot spot near the edge of the river.

Something struck Maria as familiar about this aerial view. Then she realized what it was. "Wait," she said incredulously, "is that Quantico?"

Antonio smiled. "Good eye, Maria," he said. "Yes, that's Marine Corps Base Quantico, and the river is the Potomac.

We're going to boat into Chesapeake Bay and then up the Potomac River. From there, the infiltration team will scuba dive into the cold water inlet."

"Won't the boat be pretty exposed in the river?" Zu asked.

"Yes," Antonio replied, "but we should still be well-hidden. The boat has a submersible mode, so we can stay hidden below the surface. On top of that it has electromagnetic cloaking. Basically, the surface acts like Camofoil or our stealth suits. The profile of the boat is designed to minimize its radar presence, and it also has active radar cancellation. It'll intercept incoming radar signals and send back signals that make it look like the boat isn't here. With all these stealth features, we should be pretty well hidden in the river under the cover of night, and out on the ocean in boat mode during the day."

Yet again Maria was impressed by the tech they had. "What about security on the water inlet?" she asked. "They've got to have some kind of security there."

Antonio nodded. "That's one of the riskier parts of the mission," he said. "We don't know exactly what they have there. We can only try to predict what a really good security system would look like there. We are fairly confident that what we have prepared should get us through."

"Makes sense, but why can't we just send in a drone?" Maria asked.

"We know they'll be monitoring for signals," Antonio replied, "so we wouldn't be able to steer the drone, and our scan of the underground servers is vague and incomplete. We don't have enough information about the base layout and what kind of capabilities the drone would need, in order for us to program a drone to complete the mission autonomously."

Maria nodded, satisfied with the answer, although their lack of solid information worried her. Antonio continued with the briefing, showing on the diagram where they expected to exit the pipes and where they believed they could access the servers.

"Once we're at the servers," Antonio said, "Karen and Maria hack in and upload profiles for each of us with fake information in them, making it look like we're from foreign countries and that we've had limited internet access. Right now we're all assumed missing or dead, so any sign of us on SEER's surveillance network would make alarm bells go off. But once we have our fake data uploaded, we can go out in public again and fly into the US. SEER will think we're just regular tourists. That's how we get close to the SEER terminal at the DARPA headquarters. We can't take control of SEER from the servers because they're isolated from the control terminal, no commands can be issued from the servers. And this server farm is one of several duplicates around the country. Even if we try to control the way the server data is used, they have other copies of the data and they would just shut this server down and use the others. So our best shot of getting to the terminal is successfully faking our data on the servers. Once the job is done, we leave the same way we came in and go back down the river in the boat."

Antonio asked if there were any questions, but no one had any. Maria knew that the field team had already been training for this plan, and she and Karen already knew what they needed to know. The field team would get them in, they hack the system, and then the field team brings them back out.

Next was weapons training for everyone not on the field team. Everyone but her had already had some weapons training, but this training was more involved. They put on visors that simulated the display shown on their suit helmets, and which also showed moving targets to aim at in virtual reality. They used their actual weapons with no ammo and simulated firing them in all modes. The simulation accurately modeled sounds and projectile physics and seemed to Maria to be as close to the real thing as you could get without firing a weapon in real life. She picked up on it quickly, and was soon able to consistently hit the simulated target drones as they flew around her. It reminded her of the video games she liked to play at home.

They trained for over an hour, practicing how to switch between modes on their weapons until they could do it quickly under pressure. Irina and Henry had been giving them advice, and they seemed pleased with their progress.

"I wouldn't call them an elite squad," Henry said, smiling as they removed their visors, "but I think they should be able to hold their own."

"Not that they should need to anyway," Irina added, smiling reassuringly at Karen and Maria.

Vincent removed his mask and walked over to place it in its spot in the case. "Now, please remember," he said, turning to face them all. "And this goes for everyone, but in the unlikely case that we come under fire, try your best not to kill any people. The people at the base are just doing their job, they're soldiers and guards who are protecting a vital piece of American infrastructure. I would be surprised if any humans were involved in an emergency response, but if they are, do what you can to avoid harming them. You have blitz rounds, so incapacitate them if you can. Only use lethal force if there are no other options. Enough Americans have died because of SEER already, we don't want to add to the body count."

They all nodded in agreement. Maria was pleased that Vincent had said this. She did not want to be part of a blood-thirsty group, and she certainly was not comfortable killing anyone, let alone someone who was just trying to protect their country. She hoped that Irina was right and that they would not need to fight.

They were only a few hours into their long trip and had a lot of downtime ahead of them. Zu, Lily, and Henry went up to the upper quarters to sleep. Vincent took a seat at the corner station and started reading something on his display. Maria was not tired, but she was not sure what to do. She considered reviewing her program again, but the thought gave her even more anxiety. She needed to relax.

While Maria was contemplating what she should do, Karen took a seat at one of the stations and pulled up a familiar game.

"No way," Maria exclaimed, "is that Trajectory?"

"You bet!" Karen said. "Wanna play?"

"Absolutely!" Maria took a seat at the station next to her. Her station lit up and she was in the game, controlling her character with subtle hand gestures.

"How about you Min? Vasu?" Karen asked, turning around to look at where Min and Vasu were sitting, just watching her play.

"Sure," Vasu replied, smiling mischievously. "I wouldn't pass up such an easy win."

He took a seat next to Maria. Min sat down on the other side of Karen, their displays appearing and their characters joining in the simulated battle. It was a shooting-style game with quirky weapons, all of which fired large projectiles that traveled in strange patterns instead of straight lines. Some fired in parabolas, useful for shooting around obstructions, some made zigzags, some bounced, and one even orbited around a target, drawing closer until it hit the target or the target found an obstruction to collide with the orbiting projectile. It was one of Maria's favorite games, easy to learn but requiring good strategy and skill.

Apparently the others were familiar with the game too, which surprised Maria a bit. Karen won most of the games they played, with Vasu and Min fighting Maria for second place. They quickly became comfortable trash talking and teasing each other, frequently cracking jokes and bursting into fits of laughter. Occasionally Irina, Antonio, and Clarissa would take breaks from monitoring the boat to come over and heckle them or join in for a round. Maria even noticed Vincent sometimes looking back from his reading to watch them, an amused smile on his face. It was the most relaxed Maria had been since being kidnapped, and she felt almost as comfortable playing with them as she did with her friends back home.

Eventually Karen decided she was hungry, and the rest of them concurred. Maria glanced at the time and was shocked to see that it was nearly noon. She followed the others up the ladder to the upper deck. She had not been up there yet, and was surprised at how much room there was. Based on the way the boat looked from the outside, she had expected it to be much smaller. There were cots along the wall on either side, eight total in sets of two, one mounted on the wall above the other with a ladder up to it. The cots had curtains hung around them that could be closed for privacy. At the rear was a small kitchen with a fridge, microwave, and a sink. A small table and benches were bolted to the floor next to it. Toward the front of the boat was a closed door leading to what she guessed was the bathroom.

Henry and Lily were sitting at the table eating some sandwiches. Maria's group made some food for themselves and joined them at the table. Maria noticed one of the bunks was hidden behind a curtain and kept quiet, not wanting to wake Zu.

Lily noticed Maria being careful not to make any noise and laughed. "Don't worry," she said, "Zu could sleep through a drum solo."

They ate lunch and chatted for a while, and then they parted ways, or at least as much as they could part ways in the small boat. Maria used the restroom and then climbed up to one of the upper cots and pulled the curtain shut. She closed her eyes for a short while but was not tired enough to sleep, especially with the sounds of conversation from the rest of the team clearly audible. Instead she decided to watch one of the movies they had on their downloaded storage. With a wave, she turned on the visual projector attached to the wall next to her. It was similar to the drone version, except stationary and less immersive. She watched nearly half of the movie before her restless night caught up to her and she drifted off to sleep.

The sound of her name being whispered woke her. As she slowly remembered where she was she, recognized Karen's voice, gently rousing her.

"What is it?" Maria replied groggily.

"We're a half hour from Chesapeake Bay, it's time to get ready," Karen replied, speaking at a normal volume now.

Maria became fully alert, the pressure crashing back in on her. "Wow, I can't believe I slept that long," she said, pulling the curtain back and seeing Karen standing by the cot.

"Yeah, guess you needed to catch up," Karen replied, smiling.

Maria climbed down the ladder to the floor. She and Karen were the only ones on the upper level.

"Grab something to eat if you're hungry, our gear is on the lower level," Karen said, climbing down the ladder to the lower deck.

Maria nodded. She walked to the kitchen and tried to eat some crackers, but could only manage a few. Her stomach was too upset from nerves. She left the kitchen, used the restroom, and then climbed down to the lower deck. The rest of the team was there, sitting in the chairs or standing nearby. Vasu was bringing cases out from a floor storage panel at the rear and setting them down near the group. Maria walked over and stood next to Karen.

"Okay, that should be everything," Vasu said, setting a fourth case down next to the other three. He opened them up and began distributing the contents. He handed Maria the suit they had calibrated earlier and he pulled a backpack for her out of the floor storage area. Vasu passed out the rest of the suits and packs to Karen, Clarissa, Henry, Irina, and Antonio. Maria had not thought about it until now but she realized that only she, Karen, and the field team would be going. It made sense, more people meant higher chances of being noticed, and the rest of the team was not necessary.

They all put on their suits and then attached their weapons, which Vasu distributed from the second case. Maria noticed that the field team had somewhat bulkier packs than what she and Karen were wearing. She did not envy them. Hers was not uncomfortable, but another ten to fifteen pounds on her back and it might start to be. Maria made sure her portable drives were easily accessible on her suit. Vasu opened the third case and handed out objects resembling small oxygen tanks.

"These should fit in your packs," he said. "They're good for two hours of oxygen, which should be plenty. The hose clips into the side of your facemask. This is a fully closed-circuit scuba system, known as a rebreather. What you exhale is captured and stored, and what can be reused is reused. Keeping the system closed prevents bubbles which could give you away. When you're out of the water, it'll automatically switch off and back to outside air to conserve oxygen." He used Karen's gear to demonstrate how to place the tanks in the pack and clip the hose to the facemask. The rest copied him.

Vasu opened up the fourth case. "Finally," he said, "here are your DPVs." He pulled a black object from the case. It was cylindrical and about two feet long, almost resembling a larger version of their oxygen tanks.

Maria had been given a few scuba training simulations back at their base, during which she had been taught how to use a DPV. The initialism stood for diver propulsion vehicle, and they were basically a battery-powered propeller with handles. A throttle on one handle controlled the propeller speed and it took you where you pointed it. Theirs was a stealth model and it was fairly slow, but still faster than swimming.

"You won't have flippers or anything like that," Vasu continued, "so these will be how you get through the pipe."

Maria took one of the DPVs from Vasu and examined it. She figured out how to clip it to her suit, letting it hang from the front of her. It weighed around ten pounds, a pleasant surprise as she had been expecting it to be heavier.

Antonio spoke up. "So everyone knows what they need to do right? Karen and Maria, you have your programs, correct? Okay good. Anyone have any questions? I want everyone on the same page, if you're even a little unsure I want you to ask." He looked around at every person. No one said anything.

Antonio looked like he was about to accept that there were no questions, but then Karen spoke up. "I just thought of something," she said. "If we're all wearing suits and nearly invisible, how will we see each other?"

"Good question, Karen," Antonio replied. "Vasu has planned for that. Vasu, would you like to explain?"

"Sure," Vasu said. "I think I mentioned this before but just never explained it. I programmed in a pattern of slight light shifts at various points on the suits. Your suits have been programmed to recognize this pattern and associate it with a person. It's subtle enough that any security system wouldn't notice it, but since your suits know what to look for, they'll see it. Your suit will identify the pattern and show you an outline of a person, but you won't be able to see details, other than important things like the location of someone's com line if you need to connect to it. Every suit has a different pattern, which your suit will recognize and it'll overlay the person's name into your display."

Karen nodded, satisfied. Maria was glad Karen had asked; it was something she had wanted to know more about. Antonio looked around at the group for more questions, but there were none. He nodded and they continued on in silence.

The silence continued for the next fifteen minutes. Maria sat in a seat and fidgeted as she looked out the front window, watching the sun disappear behind the now-visible coast, which was growing larger as they approached. The rest of the group was pretty much doing the same, five of them covered from head to toe in black material and equipment, their facemasks pushed up on top of their heads, the other five just in regular clothes.

Irina spoke up from her seat at the controls. "Switching to submersible mode," she said. Maria heard a soft mechanical sound and felt the boat begin to drop down from its elevated position, dipping beneath the water. They dove down fifteen or twenty feet below the surface, the view out the window becoming nearly black. Then the front windows illuminated in an eerie night-vision mode with a faint green tinge, the rock formations on the ocean floor now faintly visible farther below them.

They continued in silence again for some time, the seafloor slowly rising below them as they approached the bay. Maria had never been in a submarine before, and she would have been enjoying the experience if it were not for the circumstances of the trip. It was a strange mix of claustrophobia at being under the water combined with the calm and beauty of their alien surroundings. Occasionally she could see fish swim by, the green-tinted shapes hard to see as they moved in the distance or through the tall strands of seaweed at the bottom of the ocean.

Eventually Irina turned her head slightly to call over her shoulder. "We're about to enter Chesapeake Bay," she said. "Under five hours until we reach Quantico. Stay alert, this is the riskiest part of our trip so far and I want everyone on hand if things go south. Mission team, keep your gear on and be ready in case of emergency."

The next two hours dragged on, seemingly taking forever. Irina had slowed the boat down significantly since they had entered the bay, choosing stealth over speed. The only interesting part was passing under the bay bridge, a massive algae-covered concrete pier emerging from the murk before disappearing out of view. That was at the mouth of the bay, and since then Maria had seen nothing but plants waving gently from the bay floor.

Finally, they reached the mouth of the Potomac and began their trip up the river. The river bed inched closer and closer as the channel grew shallower, until it seemed like they would nearly scrape the boat along the bottom. The silty water reduced their visibility as well, giving Irina a more challenging task as she could not use any active scanning equipment to navigate. In several spots the water was too shallow and they had to move toward the surface and breach, exposing the upper portion of the boat. Nobody moved during these episodes, tensing up as if the slightest motion would give them away. But the day had given way to night by the time they reached the river and it was unlikely their boat would be seen.

After two hours of traveling up the river, Irina broke the silence. "We're a half hour out from our infiltration point," she said. "If you need to use the bathroom, now would be a good time."

"Okay, Mom," Min retorted, earning a nervous chuckle from the others.

"Don't make me come back there," Irina warned, shooting her a fake glare before breaking into a smile and turning back to face the front window. Maria felt the tension in the air ease, and she enjoyed the brief respite. Several people climbed the ladder to use the bathroom. Maria decided it would be wise to do so too, and she removed some of her gear before climbing up after them.

When she was finished, she came down and put her gear back on. She stared out the front window at the muddy water and took deep breaths, trying to relieve the tightness in her lungs. Most of the rest of the team were doing the same thing she was, just staring stoically toward the front.

"Ten minutes," Irina called out from the front, startling Maria and twisting her stomach into knots. She checked her pack and wrist clip for the thousandth time, her mini drives with copies of her program still there.

"Okay mission team, with me," Antonio said. He walked over to the rear of the boat. The black-clad members of the team followed. Irina handed control of the boat over to Min and joined them.

"Remember," Antonio said, "we get in, do our jobs, and get out. If we get separated, we meet back here at the boat. We can't risk sending signals so we communicate with hand signals only. If you need to speak to someone, you have to connect your com wire to theirs and talk through the hard line like we showed you earlier." He paused, then looked at Karen and Maria and added, "And stay calm, take deep breaths. We've trained for this, we'll take care of you."

He hit a button on the wall and the rear doors slid open to each side, revealing an airlock. The six of them walked inside. Antonio hit another button to close the doors behind them. Maria watched as Zu, Min, Vasu, Lily, and Vincent disappeared from view.

"Okay, turn on your gear and your respirators," Antonio said when the doors were shut. They all placed their masks over their faces and turned on their equipment. Maria felt a slight shift in temperature inside her mask as the oxygen from her tank filled it. One by one the rest of the group disappeared from sight, replaced by a barely visible shimmer.

For a brief moment she felt alone, but then Vasu's overlay kicked in and outlines of the rest of the team reappeared as ghost-like bright-green figures. Their names hovered over their bodies like something out of a video game.

Antonio went around to each person and connected his retractable wrist com line to theirs. Maria extended her line when he approached her. Antonio extended his, and she could see its green outline with much more detail than the rest of his body. "Can you hear me? Is your air working?" Antonio asked after connecting his line, his voice clear over her mask com system.

"Yes to both," Maria replied.

"Good, in a minute we'll arrive and the airlock will fill with water. Just stay calm. Irina, Henry, Clarissa, and I will get you in and out." Maria could not see his face, only a green blur, but the confidence in his voice reassured her. He disconnected and moved on to Karen.

He completed his check of the group and stood by the wall control. After a minute, Min's voice sounded over a speaker in the airlock. "We've reached our stop. You're clear to proceed," she said, and then added, "be safe."

Antonio hit a button and the airlock began filling quickly with water, seeping up from below them. Maria had never scuba dived before; her only experience was the simulated diving they had practiced back at the base. But this was real, and she suddenly realized it frightened her quite a bit. The water chilled her as it climbed past her knees, though the insulation in her suit kept most of the cold at bay. As it reached her chest, she instinctively started to tread water, her breaths coming fast and shallow. The others remained still, and her panic embarrassed her, but she was fully in its grip and could not break free.

A hand grasped her right arm. She looked over to see Irina's bright-green figure near her. Irina gave her a reassuring squeeze, putting her other hand on her own chest and making slow, exaggerated breathing motions. Maria got the message and closed her eyes, taking deep breaths and letting herself sink back down to the floor, her head dipping under the water.

She opened her eyes again and looked around. Her feeling of claustrophobia had dulled and the fresh air in her mask eliminated her irrational fear of suffocation. Breathing air while having water pressing in on all sides still felt strange, but she pushed the fear to the back of her mind and resolved herself to carry on.

The rest of the group was around her, green specters floating in the water. They turned to face the doors, and Antonio moved to the control panel. The lights went out, plunging the room into complete darkness. The door lifted open and the water began to swirl around her, beckoning her out into the river.

Chapter 7

The darkness slowly lifted as her mask compensated for the light, filtering in the available wavelengths until her vision was as near to normal as possible. The result was seeing as if it were daytime, except with a slight green tinge. The rest of the team floated in front of her, and she could see past them a short distance beyond the edge of the boat, but the water was too murky and there was too little light to see much farther than that.

One by one the team pointed their DPVs and steered themselves out of the airlock and into the river. Maria grasped the handles of hers and squeezed the throttle, gently accelerating after them. The current tugged at her as she moved away from the boat, threatening to pull her downstream. Henry floated nearby, waiting to make sure she did not fall behind. Maria turned upstream to find the rest of the group and accelerated toward them. Despite training with the DPV during simulations, her steering was clumsy, and she found herself frequently overcorrecting.

Maria drew closer to the others, who had traveled upstream from the boat a short distance before slowing down. When she and Henry caught up, Antonio continued on, this time moving slightly upstream but mostly toward the bank. They followed him, continuing for several minutes. Maria opened a map window in her mask. A small dot showed her location on the map, and a programmed set of coordinates showed the approximate location of the boat. The river was broad here, over a mile wide.

It took nearly ten minutes before they neared the bank. The river grew shallower to the point that the rocky riverbed was visible through the murk. Closer to the bank the water was only a few feet deep, the rocks transitioning to thick reeds. The team avoided the reeds, staying in the deeper water where it was easier to navigate. They shifted course slightly to head upstream. The water grew warmer as they continued, and she switched her mask to the thermal setting. A red glow appeared ahead of them near some larger rocks, close to thirty feet out from the bank in the deeper water. The hottest area was concentrated amidst the rocks, fading to a fainter red farther away as the exhaust water intermixed with the chilly river water. From Maria's position, it looked like the outlet was hidden beneath the rocks.

Antonio peeled off from the group to investigate. He approached the hot-spot, looked at it for a moment, and then continued upstream, gesturing for the rest of them to follow. They continued after him, staying near the bank but in the deeper water.

Maria switched her thermal view off. They would have to find the cold water inlet by sight or by feeling for current. Surprisingly, it was not hard to spot after knowing what the outlet looked like. Up ahead there was a similar area with a grouping of larger rocks. As they neared, Maria could feel a gentle downward current from the water being drawn into the inlet.

They stopped a few feet above the rocks, using their DPVs to stay in place in the current. Antonio gestured to stay put. He and Irina propelled themselves down closer. They connected com lines and examined the area. Maria could see the large rocks on the riverbed floor, but she could not see the inlet itself. She watched as they moved around the rocks, searching for where the suction was strongest.

After a minute, Irina reached between her back and her pack and removed some kind of scanner. She waved it slowly over the surface of the rocks near her for a few minutes. Returning the scanner to its place, Irina next removed a small device shaped almost like a pistol, which was connected to her pack by a wire. She held down the trigger and dragged it along the surface of the rocks, the rocks glowing and melting as the tip of the device touched them. Maria was surprised to see the rocks melting, until Irina finished cutting a large rectangle and lifted the panel off the ground. They were not rocks at all, but a cleverly shaped metal panel made to look like rocks, with tiny holes throughout to allow water to flow through.

With the panel removed, there was now a large hole in the river bed, but Maria could only see darkness inside.

Antonio reached under his pack and removed a black case. He unlatched and opened the case, and a group of small green objects swam out and floated in front of him. They were drones, five small spheres each about the size of an apple. Antonio pointed into the open hole and the drones swam in, one after the other.

When the last of the drones had disappeared into the darkness, Antonio turned back to the rest of the group and waved for them to come closer. They propelled themselves down to him and maintained their position. Antonio went around to each of them to connect com lines. When he connected to Maria, he talked quickly and calmly. "We're going into that pipe. It'll be a little tight but we should be okay. It should only be ten minutes. If we can't get through, we'll turn around and come back out. And if you see one of those drones fold into a ring, make sure you go through the center of it. Their job is to intercept any laser detection systems."

"Okay," Maria replied nervously, and then Antonio disconnected, his ghostly, green figure moving on to speak to Karen. When he had finished, he gave them all a thumbs up and squeezed the throttle on his DPV, diving into the opening and waving for them to follow. Irina went in after him. Clarissa waited by the entrance and waved for Karen to go next, Maria following close behind her.

It was dim inside, her surroundings turning a more noticeable shade of green as her mask tried to compensate for the darkness. She was in a box-like area that had been dug into the river bed, about the size of a small bedroom. The box had smooth metal walls, except for above her at the river bed where it was porous and bent into a rocky shape. Henry and Clarissa passed through the opening that Irina had cut and then turned around to cover the hole with the removed piece of metal.

Maria turned back to the bottom of the box in time to see Karen's legs disappearing into a large opening. Maria followed, feeling the water flowing around her, pulling her into the pipe. It was even darker inside, and now Maria could hardly see anything except the green figure of Karen up ahead of her. She could just make out the walls of the metal pipe around her, large enough that she would easily have room to turn around if she needed to. She was relieved at the size of it, having feared that it would be a tight fit and cause her to panic from the claustrophobia. Despite its size, she shivered as the thought of the walls closing in forced itself into her head.

The pipe initially went straight down but curved back up toward horizontal after a short distance. After the curved portion, it maintained a slight downward slope, likely to allow gravity and hydrostatic pressure to do the work. The water flowed fairly quickly, and Maria mostly just used her DPV for staying centered in the pipe, letting the water pull her along. She kept pace behind Karen who seemed to be doing the same thing.

The light had faded fast as they entered farther into the pipe, making the night-vision mode ineffective without ambient light. But Vasu seemed to have planned for this, as an overlay showed up in the dark, highlighting the pipe around her in a light grey. To stop herself from thinking about being trapped in the pipe forever, she occupied her mind trying to figure out how the grey outline worked. Since they were unable to emit any signals, her best guess was that it used some ambient waves outside the visible spectrum to show where the pipe walls were.

After only a minute or two inside the pipe, Karen's green figure slowed down ahead of her. Maria used the reverse throttle on the DPV to slow down too, the flow of the pipe pushing against her. She looked back to see Clarissa pull up behind her.

Up ahead Maria could now catch glimpses of Irina past Karen, traveling slowly. She shivered, suddenly worried that something had gone wrong. Karen was only a few feet in front of Maria, and Clarissa a few feet behind. If something was wrong there was nowhere to turn, no room to escape. She closed her eyes and breathed deep, willing her fear away, with some success.

When she opened them again, she could see the reason for their slowed pace. One of the small drones was ahead of Irina, the overlay displaying it as bright green in Maria's visor. It was no longer a small sphere, instead having opened itself up into a large ring, big enough to fit a person through.

Irina passed slowly through the center of the ring, and Karen followed her through. As Maria came closer to the drone, she could see many faint red lines, just visible in the cloudy water, extending from the edges of the pipe to the surface of the drone. It was intercepting the lasers and replicating the pattern on the opposite side of its ring, allowing the sensor that received each laser to see an uninterrupted signal.

Maria carefully inched through the ring, with close to a foot of clearance all around her. Irina and Karen were still drifting ahead of her, waiting for Clarissa and Henry to pass through the drone. A minute later they had, and they resumed their previous pace, letting the water push them along. A green sphere sped past them after they set off, startling Maria until she realized it was the transformed drone moving ahead to look for more security features.

They encountered two more laser grids within the next five minutes, passing through them just as they had the first. Each time Maria could not see Antonio ahead of Irina. She assumed he was scouting ahead.

After the third laser grid Maria's body began to tremble. If they had to turn around now, it would be a long time before she would be out of this pipe. Too long. She wished she could talk to someone to distract her. Instead, all she had to listen to was the muffled sound of water moving around her.

To her relief, it was only another minute until Karen slowed, drifting out into a larger space. Then Maria was out of the pipe, the current slowing around her as if she had just exited a water slide. She looked around, trying to figure out where they were. There was no light, she could only see the grey outline of her surroundings thanks to the computer-generated images in her visor, the same way she had been able to see the pipe walls. As far as she could tell, they were in a large tank.

Behind her, Clarissa and Henry spilled out of the pipe, one after the other. The green shapes of Antonio and Irina floated at the surface, maybe fifteen feet above her. The drones were no longer visible, probably back in Antonio's case.

Maria followed Karen up to the surface to join the others. When Maria broke the surface she could see the grey outline of her surroundings more clearly. They were in a holding tank. She guessed it was the size of an Olympic swimming pool, but much deeper. It was box-shaped, the concrete sides of the tank extending up from the water and forming a ceiling. Above them was a catwalk, hanging from the ceiling in the shape of a cross. Each arm of the cross stretched to the four walls from where they intersected in the middle. On the walls of the tank near the catwalk ends were pipes, coming out of the water and extending up through the ceiling. Maria could hear the hum of pumps as they sucked water through the pipes.

Where the catwalks crossed was a ladder, leading from the walkway up to a hatch in the ceiling. The group was floating below the center of the cross, but the catwalk was out of reach, ten feet above them.

Antonio turned to the nearest wall and propelled himself toward it, gesturing for them to follow. As they neared the wall, Maria could see rungs protruding from it, leading up to an access on the catwalk above. When Antonio reached the ladder, he removed his DPV and clipped it to a rung below the water. The rest of the group did the same before climbing up.

They hurried to the catwalk center, the soft soles of their feet muffling the sound of their footsteps. The only other noise was the quiet drip of water from their suits, barely audible over the thrum of the pumps. Antonio paused by the ladder while Irina removed the scanner from her back. She ascended and scanned the hatch. Satisfied, she returned her scanner to its place.

Irina climbed down the ladder and then reached into her pack, removing a rectangular object. She activated it and it unfurled itself, flying up to the hatch. It looked like a blanket with tiny drones around the edges. It appeared green in Maria's mask, the same color as the rest of her teammates.

Stretching itself out, the blanket encircled the hatch like a cone, blocking it from view. Maria realized this must be like an automatic version of the Camofoil. The way it moved reminded her of a magic carpet. Without the carpet, any cameras watching in the room would see a hatch opening by itself, the people opening the hatch being invisible thanks to their suits. The magic carpet would mimic the background and show a closed hatch.

Irina removed a second carpet from her pack but kept it folded. Next she removed her weapon from her back, attaching it to the front of her suit. The rest of the group readied their weapons too, and Maria quickly reminded herself how to operate hers.

Maria's heart raced as Irina climbed up the ladder. The magic carpet opened for her and swallowed her up in the green blob as she passed through. There was a faint click as the hatch unlatched, and the muffled sound of hinges barely opening. It was quiet for a brief moment, and then she heard the soft protest of hinges again.

After a moment, Irina emerged from the bottom of the carpet, motioning for them to climb up after her. Maria followed Antonio and Karen up the ladder as quietly as she could. She emerged from the hatch and stepped through the second magic carpet, which had formed itself in a cone around the top of the hatch, with a door flap like a teepee. She found herself in the corner of a control room, the walls and ceiling made from solid concrete. A single light fixture protruded from the concrete ceiling, casting a dim glow throughout the room. Physical screens were arrayed around a long curved control panel in the center of the room, showing diagnostics, diagrams, and video feeds of various pumps. On the panel were buttons, levers, knobs, and keyboards. Maria had only seen pictures of control rooms like this. Modern control rooms used virtual displays for everything. She wondered if it had been used by humans at all recently. SEER could easily maintain its own systems, so the control area would never need to be updated.

She joined Antonio, Irina, and Karen by the entrance to the room. Irina was scanning the metal door while waiting for the others. Clarissa joined them next, and then Henry stepped from the carpet, bringing with him the carpet from below, now refolded. He touched the corner of the teepee and it folded itself up too, revealing the closed hatch. Henry joined them at the door.

Irina was apparently satisfied with her scan, finding no electronic sensors. They proceeded through the door, again using the magic carpets to shield the opening door from view. They were now in a long hallway, several ceiling lights emitting a dim glow down the length of it, revealing the plain concrete construction. The group hurried down it, passing several doors on each side.

Near the end of the hallway they came across a door with the symbol for stairs on it. The process of scanning and entering using the carpets was repeated. After several flights of stairs, they reached a door, though the stairs continued on up past the door as well, maybe leading to another level or to the surface. Antonio and Irina conferred briefly over their com lines and seemed to decide that they should try this door, again repeating the process of scanning and entering through the magic carpets.

They emerged in the corner of a massive room. Maria guessed the corridor ahead of them stretched for at least a hundred yards, passing by row upon row of servers. To her right, she could see down the first row of servers, stretching almost as far as the corridor. Halfway down the row was a gap for a central corridor. Strips of lights on a dim setting ran the length of the corridor and down each row, providing enough light to walk around, but not enough to pierce the shadows that covered the walls of servers. Thousands of multicolored lights blinked from the dark server racks.

They moved to the nearest server rack in the first row. Antonio, Clarissa, Henry, and Irina took up positions around Maria and Karen, facing down the row and down the corridor, weapons at the ready. Irina squeezed Maria and Karen's shoulders reassuringly before taking her position. Maria took deep breaths, her heart pounding and her palms sweaty beneath her suit.

Maria connected her com line to Karen's. "Are you ready?" Maria asked.

"Yes," Karen replied. "Go for it. We got this."

Maria breathed a little easier, comforted by the sound of another human voice. The total silence of their infiltration had been unnerving. Being surrounded by green, featureless figures with only name tags for identification had not helped with that feeling. Despite being invisible, she felt exposed, like every security system in the compound knew they were there. Even her exchange with Karen over the coms felt loud. She had been told that their suits cancelled all noise, but the only proof of it working had been that she could not hear the others without com lines and alarms had not sounded.

Maria examined the server. She found the access port and removed the small portable drive from her pack. She extended a cord from the rear of the drive and plugged it into one of the ports on their com line connection. New graphics appeared in her vision, next to the suit status displays, showing information about the drive and its contents. Maria enlarged the graphics, inhaled slowly, and then winced in fear as she plugged the drive into the server access port.

After a brief wait, a login screen appeared in her graphics window. She exhaled. No alarms went off and no drones appeared. So far so good. She tried to stop the trembling in her hands but quickly gave up. With a shaky finger movement, she executed her program.

Her eyes watched the readout from her program in anticipation, text scrolling rapidly on her display. Next to it, the login screen was still and untouched. Her program cycled through the potential weak points, looking for something to exploit. Minutes passed, her anxiety increasing with each passing second. She felt a twisting in her stomach as the number of failures mounted. If she was unable to get in, all their efforts would have been for nothing. Or worse, if the program was detected, they would all be as good as dead.

The scrolling text came to a sudden stop. Success! The login screen changed and the scrolling resumed, but now her program was in, it had found an exploit. Relief washed over her and she grinned ear to ear, knowing that no one could see it. What used to be the login screen was now jumping to different pages, moving through the authorizations and various levels of security. She felt something squeeze her arm, startling her, until she turned to see Karen giving her a thumbs up.

"Nice work," came Karen's voice over the com line, whispering even though she did not have to.

"Thanks," Maria replied, as the program broke through the final layer of security. "You're up, you got this." Maria found herself whispering too, which still seemed too loud for the dead silence around them.

A weight lifted from Maria's shoulders as Karen took over. She remained tense about being found, but her fears about letting the team down had vanished. She watched the readout on her display as Karen spent some time navigating through the data, pulling up user files and examining them, checking out the format. The data was extensive. Anything you could know about a person was there. Birth date, family members, identification numbers, health records, psychological profiles, political affiliation, travel patterns, people they were close to, even what they had eaten at their recent meal, it was all there. And that was just what she could understand. There were thousands of entries for behavioral traits, voice profiles, desires, fears, thoughts, and every aspect of human identity, all collected in files and formats that Maria could not hope to read. But SEER could sort through the data with ease, using it to predict that person's every move. Or to control what moves were made.

On Maria's display, she could see Karen selecting the version of her program that best fit the data. She executed it, lines of output stacking upon each other. A few minutes later, the program returned one last line. Complete. Karen went back to the server data, pulling up a user file. Karen's picture appeared, a headshot like one used for ID. It had a fake name next to it, and other fake details, including origin country and other background. It was sparse compared to the other files they had seen, but that was what they intended. Her program had worked.

It was Maria's turn to pat Karen on the shoulder and give her a thumbs up. "Way to go," Maria said.

Karen nodded, and Maria disconnected her drive, stowing it in her pack.

"Talk to you on the boat," Maria said, and then disconnected their com line. The others noticed their movement and regrouped to leave, giving Maria and Karen thumbs up and clapping them on the back. Maria smiled, filled with joy. They just had to go back the way they came in and they would be home free.

"GET OUT! RUN!"

Maria's heart stopped. Their heads snapped around to the central aisle in the middle of the row, where the shout had originated. Maria caught a glimpse of a black-clad figure before it disappeared. A cold sweat broke out on her forehead, and she felt like she needed to vomit. She looked to the rest of the group. What should they do? They all seemed unsure, glancing hurriedly from person to person.

The far end of their row erupted, consuming the servers in a fiery cloud and spraying chunks of concrete and metal toward them. The compound shook with the force of the blast, knocking Maria off her feet. The explosion was deafening, or at least it would have been if Maria's suit had not deadened the sound and saved her hearing.

"We have to go, switch your coms on!" Antonio's voice came over her com system, sounding shaken but authoritative. "Follow me!"

He took off, sprinting down the corridor near them at the edge of the room. Henry helped Maria scramble to her feet and she ran after Antonio, away from the stairs they had entered through. As much as she wanted to just go back the way they had came, she knew it was hopeless. Moving through the pipe was too slow, and even without that problem there was no telling how much of the pump level had collapsed from the explosion. They would have to find another exit.

An alarm sounded, the blaring siren drowning out the sound of Maria's manic breathing. She gripped her weapon tightly as she ran, hoping she would not have to use it.

A blast behind her shook the building, and she felt the shockwave reverberate in her chest. A wave of heat flooded across her back, accompanied by a shower of debris. The debris stung her back where it had missed her pack, but thankfully none of it was large enough to do any real damage. A larger chunk of rubble flew past her head, striking Antonio in the leg. He tumbled to the ground, and Maria stopped to help him up. As she did, she looked back, seeing Henry and Clarissa close behind, moving fast. What had been rows of servers behind them was now a mass of rubble, dust, and fire.

Antonio staggered to his feet and ran on, limping at first but recovering as he moved. Maria fell in behind him next to Karen. They continued running down the corridor, two by two. She could hear more explosions coming from other parts of the compound, the structure shaking with each blast. Another bomb detonated, this one far down the row to their right. The lights flickered, but stayed on.

"Drones!" Irina shouted, bringing Maria's attention back to the front. Two drones had zoomed out from among the servers, ten rows in front of them. They hovered five feet from the ground, the whisper of their rotors drowned out by the alarm. Their bodies were the size of a basketball, round and coated in black sheet-metal armor. Four shielded rotors spread outward from the top of the sphere, making them as wide as a person's shoulders. Menacing weapon barrels protruded from their bodies.

The group was still invisible, but they knew from Tiron's mission that the drones could target them by sound and by the imperfect image of the suits if alerted to their presence. Irina and Antonio did not wait to find out if the drones would notice them. The six of them continued sprinting ahead while the two in the lead raised their weapons and fired. A barrage of automatic fire flew down the corridor, each round exploding into a spread of anti-drone shrapnel. The two drones went down in a shower of sparks.

The group leapt over the smoking carcasses as another explosion battered them from behind. This time they had outpaced it, only a few tiny chunks striking their backs.

They raced on, reaching the end of the corridor. On the left wall near the corner of the room was a steel door, a symbol for stairs posted on it. They opened it and rushed through one by one.

The room was larger than Maria expected, with a metal staircase in the center. There were also three other doors, one opposite the one they entered through and two more doors on the other side of the stairs. The scale of the compound really hit her then, despite the chaos, as she realized that each door probably led to another server room the same size as the one they had just left.

They sprinted to the stairs, rushing up them as one of the doors rocketed off its hinges, fire and smoke flooding in after it. The stairs shook violently. They made it to the top and found themselves in an identical room, with another flight of stairs next to them leading up. They bounded up to the next level as the concrete floor crumbled away below.

At the top, they were stopped in their tracks, unable to move. They had emerged in a similar room as before, but this time there was not another flight of stairs, and instead of four doors there were five. The fifth door was on the wall in front of them, and it looked formidable. It was a high-security door, solid-looking metal with various electronic security measures by the handle.

But the door was not what paralyzed them. Ten drones were hovering in front of them, guarding the door. The drones were motionless, waiting for anyone not authorized to be there.

"Back, back, back," Antonio said, his voice a hurried whisper. But they could not go back, the floor below them was collapsing, and Maria expected the stairs to go any moment. Antonio had barely spoken when the drones darted toward them, picking up his com signal.

"Deploy drones!" Antonio shouted, backpedaling and raising his weapon. Shots blasted out from his and Irina's weapons, the noise of the gunfire drowned out by the thunder of the explosions below them and the screech of the alarm. The drones dodged as they came at them, faster than Maria's eyes could register, covering half the distance to them in an instant. One crashed to the ground but the other nine kept coming. The drones began firing, their barrels emitting puffs of smoke as they sent blitz rounds hurtling toward them. Maria instinctively closed her eyes and turned away, expecting to feel electricity coursing through her any moment.

The rounds never landed. She opened her eyes to see a swarm of smaller drones fly out in front of them, intercepting the incoming blitz rounds with small shields that projected from their bodies, made from a non-conductive material. The swarm danced around to block the enemy projectiles, moving so fast they were little more than a blur. More drones joined the first group, launching upward out of Irina and Antonio's backpacks. A spring-loaded device was jettisoning metal blocks several feet into the air out the top of the packs.

The sides of the blocks then unfolded into four rotors at the top of the drone, uncovering a round, softball-sized body with a flat shield on one side and a small barrel protruding beneath the shield. More flew out from behind her, coming from Henry and Clarissa. Maria guessed there were around forty of them total, ten from each of their packs.

The shield drones returned fire, emitting quick bursts of small metallic projectiles at the larger security drones. The two groups of drones merged together, diving, chasing, and evading each other at lightning speed. One of the security drones was struck by a barrage of pellets, which exploded on impact, sounding like gunshots. The explosions ripped through the body of the drone and sent it crashing to the ground.

"Duck!" Clarissa yelled. They dropped, and Clarissa fired a cylinder over their heads from the launcher mounted on her weapon. It sailed toward the door and detonated just before impact, sending out a powerful blast that launched the massive door down the hallway away from them.

"Go!" Clarissa yelled. They obeyed, sprinting toward the mangled frame where the door used to be. Behind them the stairs disappeared in an eruption of fire and dust. The wall to their left blasted open as they neared the hallway, showering them with chunks of concrete. The large security drones swooped at them, blitz rounds streaming out from their barrels. But the smaller shield drones guarded the team, intercepting the shots and firing bursts of the deadly pellets, forcing the security drones to change course and engage the smaller drones.

Maria felt as if she was running through a swarm of angry bees. The throng of drones swirled about her at high speed, exploding pellets and blitz rounds landing all around her. She instinctively raised her arm over her head, as if warding them off. Her other arm held the weapon clipped to the front of her, keeping it from bouncing around. Chunks of concrete and the wreckage of drones, both big and small, littered the ground, threatening to twist her ankle as she sprinted over them.

They reached the doorway, dashing through it and entering into a wide hallway. They sprinted down it as fast as they could, leaping over the crumpled remains of the steel door. Up ahead was another door, similar to the first. Antonio raised his weapon and fired another door-buster. The door smashed open.

Four more security drones swept in through the newly destroyed door, unleashing a barrage of blitz rounds at them. A squad of defense drones swooped in from behind the team and intercepted the projectiles, firing back at the incoming drones. The mass of drones behind them had caught up, enveloping the team within the dogfight.

The team dashed through the door. They passed through a scanner and a security station before the hallway turned into a flight of stairs. Explosions continued to shake the ground beneath them, but for now the team seemed to be out ahead of them. At the top of the stairs they found another door, which Antonio quickly blasted.

They passed through the opening into a pitch-black room. A stream of light from the hallway behind them pierced through the darkness. Maria's mask adjusted, revealing the inside of a large warehouse. They were above ground! The warehouse was completely empty, except for the concrete box which they had just exited, protruding from the ground in the corner of the room.

"Look out!" Clarissa shouted. The warehouse was not entirely empty. Twenty more security drones swooped down on them from above. A salvo of blitz rounds rained down. Behind them, the swarm of drones from below poured out of the doorway. The small defense drones tried to block the incoming rounds but there were too many. Maria dove out of the way, blitz rounds smacking into the ground where she had just stood, the defense drones blocking the rest. She scrambled to her feet and ran, holding down the trigger of her weapon, spraying shells into the air at the new force of drones.

A scream pierced through her coms before abruptly cutting off. Maria looked back to see Henry convulsing on the ground, a blitz round stuck to his shoulder. The shock had shorted out his suit, turning him from the green of Vasu's overlay back to black. He was no longer invisible.

"Henry!" Antonio shouted, raising his weapon and sending a stream of shells at the drones swooping in on his stunned teammate. Maria joined in, the team laying down a wall of cover fire. Drones exploded in the air, crashing down around them. Henry hobbled to his feet, pulling his mask off.

"Just go!" he shouted, raising his weapon and blasting the air around him. Clarissa darted back to help him but it was too late. He was an easy target. Three rounds smacked across his chest. He did not make a sound, his heart stopping instantly. His twitching body collapsed to the floor and was still.

"No!" Clarissa cried, still continuing back toward him.

"Clarissa, come on," Irina yelled, her voice cracking. "We have to go!"

Clarissa reluctantly turned away from Henry. They ran and the drones followed. Maria's stomach churned. It took all her effort not to just lie down with her hands over her head and submit to her fate. But she continued on, adrenaline powering her legs, pushing her to ignore the burning in her lungs. She did her best to shove the thought of Henry out of her head. But it seemed hopeless. There were so many drones, how could they make it out alive?

Ahead of her Antonio fired two door-busters in rapid succession, this time at the concrete wall near them. The explosives punched a large hole and they leapt through it. They emerged onto the central road of a group of buildings. Maria recognized it from Tiron's footage. Except now there were gaping craters scattered throughout the compound, smoke billowing out of them. Floodlights were beaming from the buildings and perimeter guard towers, casting bright light all along the main road and alleys. Several of the buildings were partially collapsed, and a few had been entirely destroyed. And the explosions continued. The building two down from them erupted upward in a geyser of debris and fire, lighting up the night sky. The ground shook as it collapsed back into itself, leaving nothing but a smoking hole. Beyond the building, she could see small objects in the air, coming their way fast. More drones.

"This way!" Antonio shouted, and Maria turned to follow him. Clarissa was the last to appear from inside the building, firing shells behind her as the drones streamed out after them. She fell in behind Maria and they rushed down a side road, in between two of the buildings. The drones enveloped them, blitz rounds impacting all around and pellets exploding in a rapid staccato.

Maria fired her weapon into the air as she ran, the drones easily dodging most of her shots. She managed to land one, causing a diving security drone to spiral out of control and smash into the building next to her with a crunch. There were nearly as many security drones as the smaller shield drones now. Maria guessed that there were just over twenty of each. And in a few moments the security drones she had seen in the distance would catch up and the shield drones would be outnumbered. Already the shield drones seemed to be having trouble blocking the shots from the security drones, some of them coming uncomfortably close to her and the rest of the team. The near invisibility provided by their suits was probably the one thing keeping them from certain death at this point.

The team had made it nearly halfway down the alley between the two buildings. Up ahead beyond the buildings the wall of the compound loomed. Down the wall to their right, a tall security tower projected upward from just inside the wall. A sudden barrage of heavy machine gun fire rang out from the tower, blasting chunks from the concrete building beside them. Several drones from both sides fell from the sky, their bodies pierced by the large rounds. Maria flung herself to the side, continuing to run but staying close to the building to her right where she would be shielded.

"Automated sentry gun!" Irina called over their coms. "Stick to the wall, I'll handle it." As the sentry's bullets continued to smash into the wall across from them, Irina dove out into the open, rolled, and lifted her weapon to her shoulder. She fired three shots in rapid succession, large cylinders launching out from the big barrel mounted below her weapon's main barrel. A second later, three explosions echoed from the tower. The hail of bullets from the sentry gun came to an abrupt stop.

The team reached the end of the buildings and turned the corner, sprinting along the perimeter wall toward the disabled guard tower. The top of the tower was now just a jagged, smoking mass.

"Ready your grappling shot," Antonio yelled over the coms. "We're using the tower and going over the wall."

Maria reached to her gear and loaded the grappling round, clipping the attached spool of wire to her suit. Antonio and Irina fired at the tower, their rounds sailing up through the cloud of drones around them, wire trailing after them. The grappling rounds slapped against the side of the tower near the mangled mess at the top, sticking to it. The wires drew taut and then lifted them gracefully off the ground as they pushed off toward the wall. They swung out over the wall, firing their weapons at the surrounding drones as they soared through the air.

Karen was in front of Maria, and she copied them, attaching herself to the tower and swinging up toward it. Maria pointed her weapon up at the tower, the targeting overlay showing her where her shot would land. She squeezed the trigger and her grappling round arced up and smacked right onto her target, above Karen's. Another round sailed over her head and Clarissa's grappling shot stuck to the right of Maria's on the tower. Maria activated the retracting line and it grew taut. She was jerked off her feet hard, lacking the grace of Antonio and Irina.

Maria had nearly reached the top of the wall when another explosion ripped through the compound right below them. A concussive wave of concrete chunks and earth blasted upward, enveloping the perimeter wall and the end of the building. Intense heat washed over her legs. The flames and debris swallowed up some of the drones that had been battling closer to the ground. The explosion had obscured Karen from Maria's view, but she caught a glimpse of her landing near Antonio and Irina outside the wall.

Maria clung fearfully to her line as tight as she could. She was disoriented from the blast, and she felt as if she was falling instead of continuing to rise. Then she realized she actually was falling. The base of the tower had suffered heavy damage, and the tower was now leaning inward, picking up speed. Some of the composite camouflage that stretched over the compound had still been embedded into the ruin of the top of the tower. Now it pulled free with a metallic snap. The tower began to topple into the compound toward the building next to it. With Maria still attached.

The ground below her had fallen away, collapsing down into the subterranean structure below. Her twenty-foot drop to the ground had now turned into a fifty-foot drop onto broken concrete and twisted rebar.

"No-no-no-no," Maria repeated as the tower fell and she fell with it, swinging down toward the pit.

"Maria! Swing under it!" shouted Clarissa. Maria glanced back to see Clarissa swinging farther behind her, drones fighting all around her. Maria looked ahead and saw what she meant. In the path of the tower's fall was the edge of the crater. If they could swing underneath and past the falling tower, they could reach the ledge of the pavement and land on solid ground. Too short and they would fall down into the crater. If they were too slow, they would land on the edge, only to be crushed by the falling tower.

"O-okay!" Maria shouted, her voice betraying her fear. She retracted her line, tightening the arc of her swing. The tower loomed as she sailed toward it. It was now at forty-five degrees and gaining speed. She reached the bottom of her trajectory and passed beneath the tower, swinging fast. She hit the release and her grappling round detached. Her untethered body flew through the air toward the lip of the crater. She landed hard, beyond the edge, rolling to a stop. Jumping to her feet, she turned back to see Clarissa sailing toward her, clearing the crater and landing just past the edge. Clarissa scrambled on all fours, the massive tower falling right toward her.

The top of it smashed through the remaining wreckage of the adjacent building and broke off. Clarissa dove out of the way just as the remainder of the tower hit the lip of the crater with a resounding boom, rocking the ground. But the tower did not stop. It crashed through the concrete lip, breaking off a large piece of the edge and falling through into the depths of the underground structure. Maria dove away as the ground beneath her crumbled. She landed hard on the solid concrete, just barely reaching safety. A scream rang out over the coms and Maria turned to see Clarissa falling, the ground beneath her carried down along with the tower. She disappeared, engulfed by the falling rubble all around her.

"Clarissa!" Maria yelled, reaching out at nothing as the tower and pavement hit the ruins below with a resounding boom. She was gone, buried beneath dust and broken concrete. Grief washed over her and she could not move, oblivious to the chaos around her.

"You have to go, Maria!" Antonio's voice shouted over her coms. "She's gone!"

Maria looked up, snapping back to the danger around her. Across the red, smoky glow of the chasm, she could see three green figures running outside the compound, parallel to the remains of the wall. Their weapons blasted at the group of drones that had followed them out, the security drones and the shield drones still fighting around them.

A smaller group of drones appeared around Maria, the security drones now outnumbering the shield drones. She rolled out of the way, three blitz rounds smacking into the ground where she had just been. She opened fire, spraying rounds at a group of security drones that were dive bombing her. Two were blasted to pieces and crashed down. Three more kept coming, unleashing a volley of blitz rounds. She had no time to move.

Two shield drones swept in front of her at the last moment, blocking the incoming shots and retaliating with a stream of pellets. Two of the incoming security drones were torn to shreds as the pellets exploded against their metal bodies. The third evaded them, swooping to the side and turning its fire on the small drones. Maria leapt to her feet and ran.

"We're coming, we'll meet you over the wall!" Antonio shouted, his voice in her ears just loud enough to cut through the constant scream of the alarm and the destruction of the compound.

"No, I'll be okay," Maria replied, trying to sound braver than she felt. "Just get out of here!" She kept running, moving along the wall toward the next tower.

"We're not leaving you behind!"

"You have to! More drones will be here any minute, you can't jeopardize the mission just for me." She knew she was right, but deep down she hoped Antonio had a plan. Something, anything, that would get her out of here and get them all back safely.

He did not. "Okay," he said, his voice heavy and reluctant. "You're right. But you're gonna make it. You get out of there. We'll meet you at the rendezvous."

Maria turned her coms to listen-only mode, hoping that she would be harder to locate if she was not broadcasting signals. Drones swirled around her as she ran hard for the next tower. She watched in horror as the sentry gun on top of it spun to face her, preparing to turn her into red pulp.

The top of the tower exploded, debris spraying out in a cloud of smoke. "I got your back," Irina's voice came over the coms. "Now get your ass over the wall, we'll be expecting you at the boat."

Maria mouthed a silent word of thanks, not letting up on her sprint toward the tower. She blasted short bursts at the surrounding drones followed by quick side-steps, trying to avoid being targeted by their shots. She passed another building, just before it vanished in a thundering flower of fire and debris.

The compound was in ruins at this point, and most of the area she could see was either a pit of rubble or scarred with craters. The air was thick with a haze of smoke and dust, the smell strong in every breath she took. The wall was still mostly intact, marred in a few places with collapsed sections. But these were too far away from her to use as an exit.

She reloaded her grappling round as she neared the tower. Her legs and lungs were burning and her heart pounded in her chest with a mixture of fear and fatigue. She pushed through it, launching her grappling round at the tower. It stuck in place and she retracted her line. This time her feet left the ground much more smoothly, and she launched up and over the wall and the electric fence on top.

She opened fire on the drones surrounding her as she sailed through the air. Shots whizzed by her. There were too many security drones and too few of the defense drones. She watched as two security drones ganged up on a smaller drone, bombarding it from both sides. Its shield blocked a few shots while it tried to evade the pursuers, until a blitz round struck it on the body and it fell from the sky, sparking and trailing smoke.

The security drones turned their attention to Maria and she fired her weapon at them. They easily evaded her wild shots and sent rounds hurtling toward her. Maria hit the release on her line and she fell the last ten feet to the ground, the shots sailing over her head.

She rolled to her feet and dashed for the tree line. If she could get out of the artificial light from the compound and into the dark woods, she might have a chance! The last few small drones shielded her as she ran, keeping the most accurate shots away.

She reached the trees and dashed into the woods, not slowing down. All around her, blitz rounds smacked into tree trunks as the security drones gave chase. But she could no longer hear the crack of the explosive pellets. There were no drones left to defend her; she was truly on her own.

Maria checked her GPS location and adjusted her heading, running hard toward the river. Branches slapped across her face and hands as she pushed through the brush. The drones did not seem to slow down, simply darting through the gaps in the foliage. One pulled up near her and sprayed a volley of rounds at her. She returned fire, holding down the trigger and sending a wave of shells at the drone. The blitz rounds missed behind her, the drones having a hard time targeting her now that the illusion of her invisibility was aided by the dark woods. Maria connected with one of her shots, blasting the drone away in a shower of sparks.

The river was not far from her, and she watched her GPS dot near it on the display in her mask. The terrain was hilly, but luckily she was running downhill. She kept up a punishing pace, ducking around trees and branches and hearing the smack of blitz rounds all around her. She could no longer hear any explosions from the compound, and she was far enough away that the alarm was a faint echo.

Her breaths were sharp and ragged, and a pain burned in her side. But she was almost there. According to her GPS, she was only a few hundred feet from the river. She gained a second wind, sprinting fast and barreling through the underbrush. But then her heart sank.

Up ahead was a tall chain-link fence, with a clearing fifteen feet wide on each side of it. They had been told that there was a fence here in the briefing, but they had not planned on going this way, and in all the chaos she had forgotten it. The only way to reach the river was through it. That meant leaving the low-visibility woods and running through the open. She had no choice. Reaching for her belt, she loaded a shell into the launcher on her weapon. She brought the weapon to bear and fired, just as she reached the clearing. The round sailed toward the base of the fence, exploding on impact. A plume of fire and dirt sprayed upward, shaking the chain-link violently.

Maria tore out from the tree line toward the fence, giving it everything she had. She reached it in under a second, ducking through a hole in the mangled chain-link. Regaining her stride, she pushed hard for the woods. She reached the welcoming embrace of the tree line just as a barrage of blitz rounds smacked into the trunks all around her. And one found its mark.

Pain shot through her body and her limbs froze. Agony laced its way through her nerves, her muscles convulsing. Her

mouth formed a scream but there was no sound. She hit
the ground hard, her momentum carrying her arched body
forward. She skidded through the grass and leaves, coming to
a stop fifteen feet into the woods.

As suddenly as it started, the pain stopped. But her vision
was black. For an instant she panicked, thinking she was blind.
Then her hands reached for her mask, ripping it off, and she
could see the dim outlines of the trees around her. Her suit
had burned out. Which meant she was no longer invisible.
The drones would be on her any second, and she would be
lying plain as day on the ground in their robot night vision.
She had to hide, but how?

It came to her in an instant. Her muscles protested as
she fumbled in the pack on her back, removing the Camofoil.
She spread it on the ground and dove beneath it. Then the
drones were on her, their whirring rotors now audible over
the music of insects, the distant whine of the alarm, and the
babble of the nearby river. She could hear them passing right
over her, and she braced for the inevitable pain. But it did not
come. It had worked! Beneath the Camofoil, she looked just
like the surrounding foliage on the ground.

The drones must have known that she could not have
gone far, and she heard their rotors slow as they searched
around her. It sounded like maybe three or four of them. She
silently willed them to move away.

The drones did not obey her wish. Light flooded the
woods, startling her. She could see it through the edges of the
Camofoil, beams of light piercing the darkness. The drones
were shining it, conducting a thorough search of the area.

Maria was out of options. Any second now the light would illuminate her hiding place, and the combination of bright light, close scrutiny, and the imperfect illusion of the Camofoil would expose her.

Maria leapt to her feet, hurling the Camofoil off of her body. Rounds spewed from her weapon, aimed at the sources of the lights. The drones reacted fast, but not before two of them were shredded. Maria ducked and rolled behind a nearby tree, leaning out to take down the last two drones. But she was too slow. The drones shut their lights off and sped toward her, dodging her shots. Maria ducked back behind the tree as shots whizzed past, right where her head had been a moment before. In an instant, the drones would be around the tree with a clear shot at her. She was doomed.

Gunfire erupted, chewing up the tree around her. Maria heard the sound of crunching metal as the two drones sailed past her tree and crashed into the ground, rolling to a stop. She scrambled to her feet and peeked around the trunk.

"Irina?" she called. There was no answer. She raised her weapon toward the origin of the gunfire. "Who's there?"

A figure materialized out of the darkness. It was dressed all in black, just like she was, and holding a weapon similar to hers, pointed at the ground. The person raised their hands from their weapon, signaling peace, and removed their mask and hood. It was a woman, a bunched ponytail bouncing free. But it was not Irina or Karen.

"Who are you?" Maria demanded, nervous.

"I'm a friend," the woman responded. "I want to help you."

"Who are you with?" Maria asked, not buying it.

"I'm with a group fighting against SEER, just like you," she responded, at ease. "Except we have different goals. And we don't keep secret goals that we hide from our team, like those your leader keeps. Come with me, Maria, I'll get you out of here and explain what's going on."

Maria's mind raced. Who was this person, and how did they know her? What did she mean about Vincent? "W-what goals?" Maria stammered. "How do you—"

But she was cut off by the sound of spinning rotors. Maria ducked back behind the tree as shots smacked into it. The woman dove for cover, her weapon roaring back at the on-coming drones. Maria took the opportunity provided by the cover fire and bolted for the river.

"Don't trust Vincent!" the woman called after her over the sound of the gunfire.

Maria crashed through the underbrush and dangling branches, beelining for the river. She could see it up ahead through the trees. The last few lines of branches gave way and she leapt through the air, diving toward the water.

Something struck her pack in midair and electricity coursed through her. She cried out in pain, her limbs spasming. The electricity stopped and her limbs went limp. She slapped into the water with a splash. She sank beneath the surface and was pulled downstream, her helpless limbs unable to fight it. The world faded to black, and the last thing she felt was something pressing onto her face and tugging her further down into the water.

Chapter 8

Maria's eyes lifted open, blinking away the fog blurring her vision and revealing a strange wire grid in front of her face. Her hands lifted to rub her eyes, confused by what she was seeing. She winced. It felt like she had just finished the hardest workout of her life. Every muscle in her body ached.

Her surroundings became clear as her eyes regained their focus. She was looking at the underside of a cot, back on the boat. Why was she here? Then it all came back to her. The compound. Passing out in the water. Henry and Clarissa's deaths. She held her face in her hands, tears in her eyes. Images of Henry convulsing and Clarissa disappearing into the pit flashed through her head.

"Hey, it's okay," a voice said softly, a hand touching her shoulder comfortingly. It was Lily. "Does anything hurt?" she asked.

"Yes, everything," she said, her voice dry and raspy.

Lily handed her a glass of water. "Here, drink this slowly."

Maria thanked her, groaning as she sat up in the cot. She

took the glass and sipped it. After her head cleared, she noticed she was no longer wearing her suit. Instead she was dressed in loose, comfortable pants and a soft shirt. "What happened?" Maria asked, and before Lily could respond, added, "And how did I get here? Who blew up the base and why?"

"Antonio was watching to make sure you escaped," she replied. "He was waiting under the water when he saw you get hit and fall in. He pulled you under and back to the boat." She paused, and then added, "And you were lucky. That blitz round hit your pack, which shielded you from most of the shock. Your suit can lessen the shock from the first hit, but with your suit already dead, if you had been hit anywhere else we probably wouldn't be having this conversation."

Maria nodded. "I was lucky," she said. Clarissa and Henry had not been lucky. The thought brought more tears to her eyes, and she quickly wiped them away. Gathering herself, she asked, "What about my other questions?"

"That's something we'll all talk about together, when you're feeling strong enough." Lily stood up and walked over to the ladder. "Get some rest if you need it and join us when you're ready," she said, climbing down below.

Maria checked the time. "Wow," she muttered to herself. It was eight in the morning. She felt like she had just landed in the water a few minutes ago, but their mission had started near midnight. It had all happened so fast, so she must have been lying in the cot for close to seven hours.

Her mind was restless, and she sat up the rest of the way, ignoring her protesting muscles. She stood and slowly walked around the room, trying to stretch her limbs. No one else was on the upper level. There was no sound from the lower level either, the only noise was the soft hum of the boat engines. She ate a snack from the kitchen before painfully descending the ladder to the level below.

Maria found the team sitting in various states of somber reflection. Min was staring at the ground, sniffling softly. Karen had lines of code on her display, but they were untouched as she stared into space. Irina was at the helm of the boat, facing away from Maria. Next to her was Antonio, his head in his hands, distraught.

Maria glanced toward Vincent. He was sitting at a station at the rear. Near him was Vasu, who was busying himself examining the gear the team had been wearing. Vincent was looking toward Vasu, staring blankly at him as he worked. Maria felt anger swell up, the words of the strange woman in the woods ringing in her ears. *Don't trust Vincent.* She did not know whether to believe this woman, but clearly there was more that he had not told them. And it may have cost two people their lives.

Vincent's gaze turned toward Maria as she stepped off the last rung of the ladder. For a moment he just stared blankly at her, lost in thought, not registering her presence. Then he seemed to snap back to the present. Maria forced her anger to the back of her mind for the time being. She decided not to tell anyone about her encounter with the woman. At least for now.

"Ah, Maria, I'm so glad to see you up and moving," Vincent said. He sounded genuine, and Maria could tell that he was more restrained, his usual energy dampened by sadness. The others looked up, giving her small smiles. She took a seat between Karen and Zu.

"I'm glad you made it out," Karen said softly as Maria sat down. "When you got separated, I thought you'd never make it back."

"Me too," Maria replied. "I was just lucky, I guess."

"I would bet it was more tenacity than luck," Zu said, "but whatever the reason I'm glad you escaped." He gave her a smile, his sad, bloodshot eyes brightening for a moment. She smiled back at him, before turning her attention to Vincent.

"Antonio, Irina, and Karen have told us about the mission," Vincent said, standing and walking to the middle of the group. "We're all devastated by the loss of Clarissa and Henry. Unfortunately, we'll have to wait until this is all over before we can give them a proper farewell. Just know that they sacrificed themselves for the cause. I hope no one feels at fault here, we couldn't have anticipated the mission becoming disrupted. There was nothing that could be done about that." Vincent glanced over at Antonio, who still sat with his head in his hands.

Lily chimed in, echoing Vincent's hope that no one feel accountable. "He's right," she said, "we had no way of knowing someone else would try to destroy the servers, and especially while we were there. It's not anyone's fault."

Maria's eyes narrowed. So it was not just her, everyone else had no idea this other group would be there either. Her anger flooded back and she could no longer restrain herself. "I think Vincent could have done more," she growled, staring at him. "I think you knew this other group existed. And I think you've been keeping information from us, information that could have helped us be more prepared for this possibility!"

Irina nodded her head and joined in. "I think Maria is right. The other group warned us about the explosion. First of all, how did they know we were there, and why were they there at the same time? And why warn us? This seems too coincidental."

"Come on," Antonio interjected, "Vincent couldn't have known. This was my mission and I was unprepared. Henry and Clarissa's deaths are on me. I'm sorry for letting you all down." His voice broke and he returned his head to his hands.

Vincent was silent, staring at his feet, looking remorseful. "It's not your fault, Antonio," he said, looking up at him. "They're right." Antonio lifted his head from his hands, his eyes wide. The rest of the group was a mixture of confusion and anger. Maria clenched her fists, feeling both vindicated and betrayed.

Vincent continued before anyone could batter him with angry questions. "I knew the group existed," he said. "In fact, I used to be part of that group."

Eyebrows raised around the room. Irina opened her mouth to chastise Vincent, but Vincent raised his hand. "Please, Irina, let me speak. I'll explain everything," he said. He began to pace in a small circle in the middle of them and continued. "Their leader is a woman named Reyah. I first met Reyah when I worked for DARPA. As I told you all before, I was a researcher in human behavior and working to improve SEER. Reyah was a programmer, who worked with the researchers to implement the improvements to our human model into SEER's human profiles. She and I worked together frequently. But as time passed and we learned how SEER really worked and what it was being used for, we began to get worried. Some of our friends who had been less careful in concealing their feelings about SEER began to disappear. Reyah and I realized we had to do something, so she began to modify our profiles, making sure that SEER was never suspicious of us. She also mined SEER's data for information about how it manipulates us. That's how I got those files that I showed you back at the base."

"Wait a minute," Min interjected, "if Reyah had access to SEER's programming, why didn't she just cripple it from the inside, or change the commands that caused SEER to control the population?"

"Reyah only had access to the data portion of SEER," Vincent replied. "Just like how we couldn't access SEER's command module from the servers, neither could Reyah. Her position only gave her access to the code behind SEER's data. She was able to modify our personal data and gather some of SEER's data by disguising the code as an improvement to SEER's programming. All of the code that modified SEER's programming had to be checked by two other people. Anything more extreme than her disguised code would probably have been noticed by the checkers. And SEER did well at selecting employees, most were loyal to the cause."

Min nodded, satisfied, and Vincent continued. "Reyah made my profile and hers look like we were immigrants with little background living in the US, and we abandoned our jobs and traveled out of the country. The data Reyah had gathered included a set of key people who had skills and backgrounds that we would need in order to take down SEER's control. We traveled around outside the reach of SEER and convinced people to join us. It wasn't long before we had a team put together."

Vincent stopped his pacing for a moment, looking forlorn. Then he sighed and continued his story, sitting down at a station by Vasu. "The problem was that although Reyah and I knew we needed to take down SEER, we disagreed on the appropriate solution. I believed that SEER had achieved so much good and had improved our lives immensely, and that we should capture it, eliminate the commands that made it control our lives, and transfer the power and knowledge back to the people. And I still believe that to be the correct solution. But Reyah saw it differently. She believed that the people couldn't be trusted with this kind of power, that the majority would use it to crush the minority, using it even more heinously than how it's currently being used. She believed that it must be destroyed, regardless of how far it sets society back. I had foolishly thought that we would gather the rest of the team, and with their help I would be able to convince her that SEER must be preserved. But Reyah had used her data to run a personality analysis of potential recruits without my knowledge, and the people we were recruiting were the ones most likely to agree with Reyah. It didn't take long for me to realize that I was the sole voice of reason on our team. I left, taking with me some of her resources and a copy of her data she had taken from SEER. I used that data and her analysis of personalities to create a new group, one that recognizes that the destruction of SEER would cause death and chaos in the United States. That's how I found all of you."

"I don't understand though," Vasu said. "Why would she bother to blow up the servers if she knew there were copies of the data in other places? Isn't it a wasted effort?"

"Not to her," Vincent replied. "Reyah is committed to destroying SEER any way she can. The easiest way would be to wipe it all from the SEER command terminal. But I don't think she has a cybersecurity expert with the skill to hack into the command terminal. Reyah was a good programmer, but she didn't have much experience with cybersecurity. So I think she must be trying to destroy all the servers one by one. Once all the data is destroyed, SEER would be effectively crippled. She must have followed us all the way up the river and through the pipe and then planted the bombs while you were hacking in. It would've had to be quick work, but with a few people and maybe some drones to help, I don't doubt that she could do it."

Maria listened with rapt attention, amazed that he had kept all this hidden from them. But her amazement quickly turned back to anger. "Why would you not tell us any of this? Why keep us in the dark when another group could strike at any moment?" Maria blurted.

Vincent looked at the ground, his cheeks reddening. "I thought there was no danger," he said, his voice quiet. He continued, his voice regaining strength. "I thought we would take back SEER before we ever heard from Reyah and her group. I had taken some critical resources with me when I left, and I gathered all of you quickly. I thought about telling you, but Tiron got us the layout of their compound and we were within weeks of taking back SEER. It seemed like unnecessary information."

Maria's eyes narrowed, but Antonio spoke before she could. He was no longer withdrawn and remorseful; now he sat with his fists clenched, his lower lip quivering. "You're avoiding the question," he said, his voice barely above a whisper, as if he would lose control if he spoke any louder. "What purpose did you have for keeping this from us?"

Vincent was silent, his face twisting as he wrestled with his thoughts. After a moment, his shoulders slumped, his face taking on a defeated expression. "I didn't want to risk any of you sympathizing with Reyah's view. I thought the knowledge of the existence of her group would lend credibility to her position. I thought it would be easier to keep us on track if you were only aware of one group resisting SEER, since the only option for resistance was our option."

Maria felt her face contort into a sneer. She was angry, not just at Vincent, but also at herself. His plan had worked up until now. She had recognized that destroying SEER would disrupt society and likely cause pain and death. But since the group seemed uniform in their belief that SEER had to be changed and not destroyed, she had not fully weighed each option. The illusion of one group resisting SEER, united in their goals, had convinced Maria that it was the most sensible option. Maybe it still was, but now she would no longer blindly believe that.

"Well your plan has blown up in your face," Maria snapped. "So why don't we have an open discussion then? Some of us have lost family to SEER. My sister was put through hell to the point that she killed herself, all because she was deemed a problem by the people in control of SEER. Knowing that, how can we let SEER continue to exist? How can we tell everyone about SEER and trust the public to make a responsible decision? How can we trust that we won't end up with the exact same situation, or worse?"

Lily had been sitting quietly up until this point, listening with amazement. "Maybe the public can't be trusted," she said, "but our entire society is based on SEER. It would set us back so far in so many areas, and quality of life would drop significantly. Think of the hospitals. SEER runs many of their systems, and its health records are used constantly for diagnoses. If it went dark the hospitals would be incapacitated and thousands would die. Even once they adapted to a world without SEER, the quality of care would severely drop without that data. Those are people's lives, lives that could have been saved or improved. And destroying SEER means shutting it down all at once. The entire country would shut down. The machines that harvest and grow our food would stop. Transportation would shut down so even the imported food couldn't get where it needs to be. People would be stranded. The economy would halt. Our police forces would be incapacitated. Even once we recover, everything would be less efficient, and less efficiency means lower quality of life. Everything relies on SEER. Who knows how many could die in the chaos."

They listened to Lily somberly, letting her words sink in, some nodding in agreement. After considering for a few moments, Vasu spoke up. "But think about what could happen if we don't destroy SEER and turned it over to the public like we originally planned," he said. "If a power-hungry group managed to get elected, they could use it to identify people who disagree with the majority party and imprison them or execute them, and use SEER to make everyone else conform to their worldview. That would be far worse than any losses from SEER being destroyed. And even if the public did elect responsible leaders, the positions at the NSA and at DARPA are mostly out of the public's control. A small group of people could shape this country however they pleased. That's likely what's happening now, based on the commands we stole from SEER, it looks like even Congress and the president have no idea what SEER is capable of and what it's really being used for."

Karen spoke up. "He has a good point, and think about all the other countries too. They do okay without SEER, and they have separate systems in place that track health records and diagnose patients, or run their vehicle systems. And they have private companies who operate knowledge and search programs. The main difference with SEER is that it's the sole source of all this information, and having all that information in one place makes it dangerous."

It was quiet for a minute. Vincent had been silent during the conversation so far, and he remained that way. Maria guessed that he knew his input was not wanted after the revelation of his dishonesty. Antonio had calmed somewhat after Vincent had revealed the truth, perhaps understanding Vincent's concern on some level.

Antonio broke the silence, taking the side of change over destruction. "But look at the direction that other countries have been going. It won't be long now before they realize that there are benefits to shared data across systems. I mean, just look at the nearly nonexistent crime rates and the massive economic output of the US. Look at any sector. Health, transportation, efficient use of resources, education, infrastructure, you name it. SEER has enabled us to be the best in every category. We can't destroy SEER without also falling significantly behind. And it's not being the best that's important, but the real impacts on human lives. Losing that data means lowering quality of life, like Lily said. That's more than just an inconvenience to people, it translates to worse health, education, and income for everyone. With the lost productivity, we would fall into a massive recession. Incomes would have to drop, people would lose their homes. We can't just force that on people."

"He's right," Min added. "And like he said, it won't be long before other countries have systems like SEER. Even if we destroyed SEER in the United States, it would only be a temporary reprieve. SEER was created before, and it'll be created again. What if we destroy it and a private company creates something similar? Then it becomes much more difficult to control it democratically. That's why SEER was a government program in the first place. People didn't want so much data about themselves held by private companies, they wanted it somewhere they could control it and have at least some power over how it's used. Like it or not, SEER is the future. The best we can hope for is to put safeguards in place to prevent it from being abused."

They fell into silence again. Maria looked around at their faces. Some were lost in thought, staring into space or chewing lips. Karen and Vasu seemed to nod in agreement when Min finished speaking, despite their concerns. Maria still believed destroying SEER was wrong, but guilt kept nagging at her. It had been used to kill her sister. How could she allow SEER to continue existing after that? Any tool was dangerous in the wrong hands, but was SEER too dangerous?

Irina had been silently contemplating. Now she spoke. "What about privacy and free will? We've only been talking about the dangers of power. But is the violation of our privacy and our freedom something we should tolerate? As long as SEER exists, there is no privacy. As long as it exists, can we really have free will? We know that our actions are able to be predicted, SEER proves that. But should we tell people how easy they are to predict? People like to believe that they can take any path they choose. But SEER shows us that the path you choose is entirely based your genetic makeup and on external stimuli, a mixture of influences from parents, friends, strangers, or just random influences from nature or from artificial environments. Some people may already believe their paths are determined, but can the general public handle that knowledge? How can anyone be responsible for anything if they can just say that their choice was inevitable? Look at us for example. We're sitting here discussing whether we should destroy SEER or hand it to the people for them to do what they want with it. But the data Reyah gathered and Vincent used shows that the question is already decided. We were chosen because we're more likely to favor handing SEER to the people. Despite my concerns, I still lean that direction. Discussing it is futile."

Maria frowned. "I don't think it's futile," she said. "SEER can't predict the future beyond a short time. It can't predict pollen in the air, the wind, a falling branch, the movements of trillions of insects, or the infinite combinations of external stimuli present on each of us at every moment. That means we're still difficult to predict further in advance of the moment that's being predicted. So much can change in that time, it's very possible for people to change their minds, or to change each other's minds. So I think it's important to always discuss things and use the best info we have to make decisions. And don't forget that the data Reyah copied from SEER is over a year old. Plus, SEER didn't have complete data on us in the first place since we've lived outside the country. Any new information since the data was copied could change our minds. Like discussions with team members. Or being lied to by someone we had trusted." She shot a look at Vincent, who had been listening to the conversation with a growing expression of hope. His face fell, and he refocused his gaze on the floor.

Maria looked back at Irina. "And about free will," she continued, "maybe someday SEER will be able to model all the various interactions that take place in the world. Then it would be able to determine the future decades or centuries in advance. But even if that happens, people would have to recognize that they have a duty to make the best decision they can. Just because your actions are inevitable doesn't mean you can ignore reason and use lack of free will as an excuse. Punishment can still be used as a deterrent. Not having free will just means having more sympathy for people whose lives have been shaped under hardship or bad influences. Our judges can take that into account. Dangerous individuals can still be separated from society, but understanding the things that caused them to act the way they did can help us try to tailor sentencing to focus more on rehabilitation and less on punishment. Maybe the knowledge of predictability can help us make the choice to be a positive impact on others and become part of the influences that factor into their decisions. The knowledge that future decisions are the result of previous interactions makes it even more important to learn from others and change our minds when presented with new information."

Maria paused to collect her thoughts, and then continued. "I think the questions of privacy and free will are serious questions," she said. "But the people have already chosen to sacrifice privacy for the many benefits SEER provides. They know that their privacy is invaded by an unthinking machine instead of by the prying eyes of judgmental humans. That's good enough for them. My sister died advocating for the right to privacy, but turning SEER over to the public doesn't mean denying her goal. All it means is that we believe in democracy and we think the public needs to know what's going on and that everyone gets a say in what happens to SEER. Whether they choose to destroy SEER and prevent future incarnations of it or to preserve SEER and modify it, it's a decision best left up to the public instead of a few people."

Irina nodded slowly, her expression thoughtful but showing agreement. They fell into silence. When it appeared that no one had anything to say, Vincent spoke. "I'm truly sorry for deceiving you," he said, looking around to each of them, his voice sincere. "It was the wrong decision, and I'll be honest with you all from here forward. Are we in agreement then that the fate of SEER should be left up to the public?"

His eyes scanned the room. Some still seemed unsure, brows furrowed and lips twisting thoughtfully. Yet they each gave a slow nod as Vincent's gaze passed over them. He reached the end of his circle and his eyes stopped on Zu, who was motionless. His usual cheery expression had been somber throughout the whole discussion, and he had not said a word.

"Zu," Min said, "you've been quiet the whole time. Do you have anything you want to add?"

Zu contemplated another moment, staring at the floor. Finally, he spoke. "Growing up in Tanzania, I learned about the country's history in school and from my parents. As Tanzania developed and began to grow richer, most of the new wealth became concentrated among the wealthy. There were protests and riots as the poor demanded a chance to share in the new wealth. Foreign countries took advantage of this unrest, trying to support leaders who would be friendly to their causes. They positioned themselves so they would have an advantage as Tanzania developed, giving themselves better access to its resources. This made the people distrust their leaders and increased the unrest, setting the country back and slowing its development. Only when the citizens rose up and threw out foreign influences did we resume our progress. We created elections that were truly free, and which resulted in elected leaders who had the interests of all of the citizens of Tanzania at heart."

Zu looked up at Vincent. "The people of the United States must have the power to choose."

Vincent seemed momentarily surprised by Zu's words. "Well said," he replied, regaining his composure. "Then we continue on with the plan. But we need to discuss something else that Irina mentioned earlier. Reyah's interference at the servers can't be a coincidence. She must have known we were going to break in. I think it's likely that her group followed you in, letting you find the entrance for them. But how?"

"Could Reyah have known anything about your plan from when you were with her team?" Antonio asked.

Vincent thought for a moment. "Hmm, only rough information," he replied. "We had discussed breaking into the servers and changing the data of our team so that it would be easier to operate. But we didn't find the location of the servers until after I left. Tiron's mission was to verify that we had found a data center and to find an entrance. Reyah couldn't have known its location."

"Could she have been spying on us? Following our movements the whole time?" Min asked.

"Seems unlikely," Vincent replied. "The Nova Scotia base was established after I left her team, and the boat should have been too well-disguised to track when we headed for Quanti—"

He cut off, his eyes widening. "The boat!" he exclaimed.
"We had stolen the boat from the government when I was
part of Reyah's team, and I took it when I left!"

Min understood what he was implying immediately. She
swiveled in her chair, the graphics on her station popping up
as she turned to face them. A few quick hand gestures and
the display changed to a camera view from a drone, ascending
into the air from on top of the boat. When the boat was
entirely in view, the drone held its position, showing the ocean
with a shimmering patch where the boat was camouflaged.
Min gestured several more times and a text overlay appeared,
scrolling rapidly.

Maria quickly caught on to what Min was doing, and the
quiet from the rest indicated that they did too. It only took a
few minutes.

"Aha!" Min exclaimed, as the graphics changed to show
a still frame of the ocean with a green outline of their boat.
There was a filter applied, turning the picture darker than normal. One spot near the rear of the boat had a small pinprick
of red light.

Vincent slapped his palm to his forehead. "How could I
have been so stupid," he moaned.

"It's a beacon," Min said, "set to emit a flash of light inter-
mittently. To detect it you'd have to know to look for it, otherwise you'd miss it. Reyah must have a drone within a few miles
following the signal. She wanted to track us, but without sending signals that could be intercepted and tracked by SEER."

"That means she either knew I was going to leave," Vincent said, "or she put the beacon on there in case the boat

went missing. We checked it for trackers when we stole it from the Army but I never thought to check it again once I took it." He paused, remorse filling his face as he cast his eyes to the floor. "I'm sorry everyone, I endangered all of you and I got Clarissa and Henry killed. I would completely understand if you no longer wanted to be part of the team."

"No," Antonio said, "you should've been honest with us but their deaths are not your fault. Even if we knew Reyah's team existed, we wouldn't have expected them to show up. And you couldn't have known she'd be tracking the boat. We're fighting for the people's freedom and I'm not quitting now."

Vincent looked at him and bowed his head in gratitude. "I'm glad, Antonio," he said. "Does everyone feel that way? If anyone doesn't want to participate they don't have to. Your identity is erased, you are free to go anywhere, except back to your old life, unfortunately."

His eyes scanned the room. Each person voiced their assent or nodded in solidarity with Antonio. Maria nodded as his eyes paused on her. Despite her earlier frustration and the warning she had received about Vincent, the goal was too important to abandon. And she still did not know if the warning was accurate. Maybe Reyah had just wanted to make her distrust Vincent and create conflict. Or it could have been referring to Vincent lying about the existence of Reyah's team. Or the warning was real and there was something else Vincent was hiding. There was no way to be sure, but she intended to find out.

After resolving to continue on, Vincent asked Maria and Karen if they were sure that the fake data they had placed inside SEER's servers had survived the destruction. They assured him that it had. Part of Karen's program had been to force the servers to do a backup of the fake data, copying it to the other servers hidden around the country. This had been a tricky thing to code, as SEER's servers performed a data check any time data was updated in order to make sure there were not any large differences during backups. If there were, it would indicate an error, or that someone was trying to fake the data. But with some help from Maria, the two of them had been able to account for this in their programs, circumventing the check.

That concern resolved, the team decided that it would be best to remove Reyah's beacon before doing anything else. Zu went out onto the surface of the boat and removed and deactivated it. They had briefly considered trying to place it on a decoy drone or a piece of garbage floating in the ocean. But they dismissed that idea, as Reyah's team had to have a drone watching the area of the boat to see the signal. She would be able to see Zu climb out on the boat, and she would know that her tracker had been removed.

When Zu had come back inside the boat, they discussed the next stage of their plan. It was somewhat frustrating to Maria that they had been unable to reach the DARPA headquarters in Arlington, less than an hour away from their mission in Quantico. But she understood why. As they had told her before, they would have had to somehow deactivate hundreds of the surveillance drones that watched from the sky, and even if they could have done that, there were still cameras all over in Arlington. They would have never made it to the DARPA headquarters, even with their stealth suits. The illusion would have failed at some point. Plus, they had gear they needed to get to the headquarters that would have been difficult to disguise. One small slip up and the Army would be on them before they could hope to react.

Even though they had successfully inserted fake data for each of them in SEER's servers, they could not just suddenly appear in the States either. Anyone who lived in the US, even for the briefest period of time, would already have a significant amount of data in their profile. Their DNA, foods they liked to eat, behavioral traits, speech patterns. It would have been too much to try to fake. Their fake profiles had to look like people who had never set foot in the US. With their fake profiles, they would be able to fly into the US as tourists from other countries, places that had limited surveillance and would therefore have little information about each of them.

So their next step was to drop each of them off in several different nearby countries, where they could then fly into the US without drawing suspicion. They would be separated, each to a different area, so that there would be no need for them to have to fake relationships and risk SEER picking up on the lies or on any strange behavior.

Their first stop would be Haiti, a full day away, where they would drop off Vasu and Zu at different regions along the Haitian coast. From there they would continue on to Jamaica, where Min would be dropped off. After that it was another half day to Honduras, where they would move along the coast, dropping Maria, Karen, Lily, Irina, Antonio, and Vincent near various Central American airports. They would each travel to nearby cities, cities that had been programmed as the last known destination for each team member in their fake SEER profiles. Going by new names, they would board planes traveling to Arlington, Virginia. When they arrived they would pretend to be tourists, using the cover of participating in Labor Day festivities to make their way to the DARPA headquarters, break in, and take control of SEER.

That gave Maria the duration of the day and a half boat ride to Honduras to make sure her program could get them inside the DARPA headquarters and give them access to SEER. She also had to create commands to shut down SEER's manipulative directives and transfer control to her team. As Vincent had promised, Maria would be in charge of the commands they entered into SEER. Of course, she did have to show them to Vincent for approval, but she would still be the one in control of the system. This was especially important now, with the question of Vincent's honesty at the forefront of her mind. She would have to add some extra security to her program to make sure he could not take control.

Maria only had a day and a half to find out if Vincent could be trusted and what his plan was before she would be on her own in Honduras. Except she had no idea where to start. Could she trust the rest of her team? Was it only Vincent she had to worry about? They had all seemed angry and betrayed by Vincent's secrets. Maria was inclined to believe that if Vincent had hidden motives, they were his alone.

After reviewing the plan, they separated to prepare for the next phase. Maria went to work at one of the stations, reviewing her program she had used to hack SEER's servers and modifying it for the next phase. Next to her sat Karen, who was reviewing and creating fake documentation for each of them, to match what they had put in SEER's servers. Maria worked for several hours before she had an opening. When the rest of the team was on the main level of the boat with them, she sent an encrypted message to Karen's station: "Meet me upstairs, privately."

Maria stood and walked to the ladder. The rest of the team was preparing for the next phase. Min, Vasu, and Zu were in the back, cases of drones splayed out around them. Min was adjusting some of the code while Vasu made mechanical adjustments and repairs. As Maria approached the ladder, Zu opened a small door in the rear that Maria did not know existed, leading to a covered walkway on the rear exterior of the boat. In one hand he held a drone, apparently going out to test it. Zu noticed her and gave her a brief smile as he closed the door behind him.

Maria ascended the ladder and walked to the kitchen, pretending to look through the cabinets for some food. After only a few minutes, Maria heard the soft clanging of someone climbing the ladder. Karen appeared in the kitchen next to her and pretended to scroll through the fridge options.

"What did you want to talk about?" Karen whispered, her voice barely audible.

Maria was quiet for a minute, her heart pounding. Was this the right call? Could she trust Karen? Of all the people on the team, she knew Karen the best, to the point that she would call her a friend. If she had to confide in anyone, it would be her. And she needed to share her concern. If it turned out that Vincent had plans to betray them and she had done nothing to prevent it, she would never forgive herself.

"I'm worried that Vincent has ulterior motives," Maria said, as quietly as she could. Sweat broke out on her brow as the words escaped her lips. She studied Karen's face for a reaction.

Karen's eyes widened slightly, then her face changed. Her mouth formed into a small smile of relief. "Oh good, then it's not just me," Karen replied. "I've been suspicious of him for a while. I'm worried that he intends to keep control of SEER and never return it to the people."

Now it was Maria's turn for surprise. Relief flooded over her. It felt like Karen was now sharing the enormous weight of the secret Maria had carried. "What makes you think so?" Maria asked, glancing around the upper level, paranoid that someone could hear their hushed words.

Karen thought for a moment. "It's nothing concrete, but just some subtle slips over the last few months. Sometimes if he gets carried away he makes comments about how the public can't be trusted, or that we can't transfer the power back to the people until the people prove they can handle it responsibly." She paused, and then added, "And his comments about the public make me think he'll never consider them responsible. Was it just our discussion this morning that made you not trust him?"

Maria shook her head. "No," she said, "during our mission something happened to me that I didn't tell anyone about." She quickly explained her encounter with the woman from Reyah's team to Karen, who was listening with wide eyes. "I couldn't tell if she was trying to spread distrust among our team or if she was telling the truth," Maria said, "but learning about Vincent's lies this morning made me wonder if he really was hiding other things. I'm glad I asked you. So what do we do? Should we talk to the others?"

Karen considered for a minute. "I don't think so," she said. "I don't know if Vincent is conspiring with any of them. And the more people we talk to, the more suspicious we'll seem. No, I think you and I can handle this. We know about it and we can plan for it."

Maria thought about it and then nodded. "So what do we do?"

Karen was quick with a response, already having a plan. "You're the one who'll enter the commands into SEER right? Make sure your program has some kind of security, so that once you've hacked in, he can't enter commands without your approval. He would have to threaten you to get you to do what he wants. If he does that, I'll back you up."

"Back me up how?" Maria asked.

"I'll come up with something," Karen replied. "Maybe I'll program a few drones or—"

She froze. Someone was clanging up the ladder. Maria turned away from Karen and rummaged through a cabinet, grabbing a granola bar. Karen busied herself at the sink, filling a water bottle.

"How's your updated program coming, Maria?" came Vincent's voice. A chill spread over her body. Had he heard anything? She wiped the fearful expression from her face and turned to respond, trying her best to look relaxed.

"Pretty good," she replied, "I've prioritized the exploit that worked on the servers. They shouldn't know we hacked them so it should still be open. I think the security at the command terminal will be similar so it should work. I don't have long left on that and then I'll dig into SEER's command code and create some commands."

"Great news," Vincent said, smiling at her. "Let me know when you have the commands worked out and we can go over those."

"I will." She smiled back and walked past him, taking a bite out of her granola bar and climbing down the ladder. She let out a breath she had been holding in. That was much too close for comfort. Still, she now had an ally and a plan. It would not take long to add some extra security to her program, and she hoped that Karen would be able to come up with a plan in case Vincent turned on them. It was too risky to discuss the matter on the boat much more, so she would just have to hope that Karen could handle it.

Maria returned to her station and began revising her code, trying not to think about the fact that the security she was adding may be the only thing standing between Vincent and complete control of the United States.

Chapter 9

The remainder of the day passed by quickly. Maria spent the first half working on her program, occasionally getting up to pace and stretch her sore body. She was feeling much better, but her aching muscles still plagued her. While stretching, she would look out the front window, seeing only the blue of the ocean and the bright, cloudless sky all around.

A few times during the morning an alarm sounded, indicating that something was scanning the area. The first of these events happened soon after Maria's discussion with Karen. Irina or Antonio would send the boat down beneath the waves, making them harder to spot. During the alarms the team became eerily still, each stopping whatever they were working on and watching out the window with bated breath. The alerts would only last a few minutes before the signals would disappear. They would remain under the water for a few extra minutes before returning to the surface. The frequency of these events decreased the farther they got from Chesapeake Bay, until seeming to stop altogether after they were over twelve hours away in the early afternoon. At that point, they must have passed beyond the range that was being scoured for whoever was responsible for the server farm destruction.

Despite these occasional distractions, Maria was able to complete her program by early afternoon. Her breach of the servers at the compound greatly helped with this, as she had also recorded data about SEER's security structure. She had used that information to tailor her program to target likely weaknesses, hopefully making it faster than it had been at the compound.

In fact, most of the work she did on her program involved adding extra layers of security. Once the program hacked into SEER, it had to ensure that Vincent would not be able to input commands. The difficult part was figuring out the best way to do that. Should she make it only accessible to herself? The thought gave her pause. That was a lot of power for one person to wield. But she could see no alternative. She could not allow Vincent to have the power. Control would have to belong to her alone. When the thought crossed her mind, she laughed inwardly at the absurdity. In order to prevent power from falling into the hands of someone who wanted to keep it for himself, she would have to keep the power for herself.

Her other concern was difficult to think about. What if she died during their takeover? The thought made her ill. But it had to be considered. Even if she were to die, she could not allow what happened to Ana to happen to anyone else. Someone would still need to be able to access SEER if things went wrong. She decided the best plan was to use an access code, one she would share with Karen if needed. But having an access code meant if Vincent tried to force her to give him access, she would run the risk of giving it up. There was no way around it. If Vincent threatened her she would just have to hope that Karen could protect her.

There were just so many ways it could go wrong. Maria briefly considered not breaking into DARPA at all. She was Vincent's key to SEER, so why unlock it for him? It was a question of lesser evils. But, she realized, it was not a very difficult question. The evil that SEER was being used for now was cause to act, and she would have to risk the potential evil that Vincent could inflict.

In the afternoon, she worked on creating commands for SEER. She pored over the data that Vincent had shown her in Nova Scotia, documenting the commands that had been input into SEER and learning their meaning through context. It was difficult work. Some of the commands were vague, and she did not want to end programs that could potentially be serving non-nefarious purposes. She decided to err on the safe side, writing commands to end programs she was positive were infringing upon personal freedoms and which would not cripple any important systems. The remainder would have to be researched on a case-by-case basis once they were in control of SEER and had full access to its data.

The most critical part of her work was creating a command to disable the drone defenses. When they broke into DARPA, they were likely to raise alarms everywhere. They would have security forces all over them. There was no way their little group could hold out for long against an army of drones. They would have to hack in fast, and she would have to turn the drones to their side as soon as possible.

But doing this was easier said than done. She had difficulty finding commands that would turn off the security at DARPA. Probably because no one had ever needed to do that before. In the end, she found her answer in a few commands that she had originally glossed over. There was a PROTECT function built into SEER that seemed to be used for people of high importance and visiting diplomats. Using that command and feeding their fake identities to it should make the drones stop their attack.

Her work on SEER's commands carried on well into the evening, only pausing for a break to have dinner with the team. They ate a somber meal of microwaved noodles, bringing their food to the lower level to eat together. The absence of Henry and Clarissa weighed heavily on them all.

It was nearly dark when she finally finished. Vincent was eager to go over her commands immediately. She had been dreading this conversation, worried that her distrust would show through. Surprisingly, talking to him became easy after the first few minutes, like the times they had talked in Nova Scotia when she had trusted him more. His passion for righting wrongs disarmed her, and they vigorously discussed which commands should be entered immediately, which might need tweaking or more research, and which ones she may have forgotten. He spoke like a man who wanted the best for the US and its citizens. How could someone who spoke so passionately about freedom and choice have hidden motives of power and control? She had to frequently remind herself to maintain her distrust while simultaneously acting at ease.

When they had finished going over her commands, she returned to her station to make the changes they had discussed. Thankfully, there were not many. A few commands needed tweaking and Vincent had pointed out some other SEER programs that they should stop immediately. It took her an hour to make the changes, and she spent another few hours reviewing her program and the commands.

By the time she was finished, it was after midnight. She stood and stretched, joining Antonio and Irina at the front to look out the window. The window was set to normal vision, and the ocean was shimmering in the dark, reflecting the quarter moon and the thousands of stars dotting the night sky. It was an awesome sight. Maria had never seen the stars so clearly; the light pollution in the city usually hid most of them from view.

"It's beautiful," she murmured, transfixed at the sight. The two at the front were also staring up at the sky, taking in the view.

"Yes it is," Antonio and Irina replied dreamily, in unison, earning a laugh from the three of them.

"We're almost to Haiti," Irina said, nodding toward the horizon. Maria had not noticed it in the dark but a strip of land was just visible in the distance under the dim light of the night sky. "We're about a half hour from the first stop, that's Cap-Haitien up ahead."

Maria stood with them at the front, enjoying the view in shared silence as their destination grew nearer. The strip of land on the horizon grew larger and more defined, trees and buildings taking shape. Soon they could see lights, spread across the landscape. Their boat was entering a bay, the shore curving around them on each side. To their right, the beach made a sudden transition into a large hill, the face of it covered with buildings. Some were large apartments and offices made from concrete and glass. Many were smaller, a mix of wood and steel construction for the small businesses and houses. The hill was dotted with lights, some stationary from street-lights, buildings, and billboards. Others were mobile, created by the headlights of pods, a surprising number still on the roads so late at night.

Directly in front of the boat was a different scene. It was like a snapshot from a history book. The land was flat, packed with dilapidated and neglected buildings, stretching for miles along the coast. Most were merely shacks, small and in various states of collapse. Others were larger, what had once been bigger businesses. Most of the sheet metal had been blown off of these, exposing the skeletal steel framing. The ocean swallowed up the bottom few feet of the closest row of buildings, the small waves splashing up against the sides of their remains.

"Wow," Maria breathed. The abandoned buildings were fascinating, but they also sent a shiver down her back. They would be creepy enough in the daylight, but in the dark of night they looked like the prime location for a horror movie.

"No kidding," Irina said. "I've seen pictures of the impact of sea-level rise before, but it's different in person."

"I've seen it up close in the US," Maria replied. "I'm not too far from the coast. But it's nothing like this. Most of the buildings that flood get torn down. With these, it's like the people just disappeared all at once."

"They probably did," Vasu said from behind her. Maria turned to see him walk up, his eyes fixed on the view. "There are some areas on the coast of India like this. Only the homes in the first few hundred feet are actually flooded at sea level, but the entire area is usually abandoned at once when a bad storm hits. The whole area floods in the storm surge and people leave and never come back. Sometimes it takes a few storms, but they happen more often now and the flooding keeps getting worse." He gestured to the more modern city sprawling across the hill. "People move to higher ground and start over. It's sad, but look at how far they've come now. Developing countries have made pretty huge advances in the last century, all while having to contend with climate change."

Maria nodded. It was true. Progress had been lightning-fast in many developing countries throughout the world. A good portion had become almost indistinguishable from the countries normally considered fully developed, like the US, China, or all of Europe. A good example was her birth country. Her parents had told her second-hand stories of the crime and gang violence her great-grandparents had lived through nearly a century ago. But the crime had peaked then, and had been steadily dropping ever since. Safety and well-being increased as the government regained control of the country, and prosperity followed. Mexico was now only a short distance behind the leading countries in technology, research, and automation capabilities. Poverty was unknown to most citizens, and Maria and Ana could have been successful there if their parents had stayed. But the US was still the best place to be for learning, and it was likely that her parents' decision to move there was responsible for letting her reach the top of her field.

"It's good that our parents' generation finally cut emissions," Antonio said. "The old fossils had done enough damage with their addiction. Even now that we're maintaining sustainable carbon emissions, the oceans will keep getting higher and the Earth hotter for at least another fifty years before things level off."

Maria smiled at the nickname he used. Fossils was one of the nicer nicknames commonly used for the older generations who had continued to use fossil fuels even though less destructive alternatives were available, ignoring the damage they were doing. "I wonder how much more advanced some of these countries would be without the deaths and expense that climate change caused for these people," Maria said, taking a somber tone.

"Hard to say," Vasu replied after thinking for a moment. "But I would bet it's been significant. Droughts and floods led to mass displacement, territory disputes, and death for many people. I bet it set developing countries back several decades at the least. Yet most seem to have made progress despite it all. Sometimes you wouldn't know it by the sensationalism in the news but the trend of increased wealth, safety, and peace has continued unceasing for a long time."

Maria nodded. There were always setbacks, solutions to previous problems causing new unexpected problems for the next generation to solve. But while new problems were always created, they usually did not seem as bad as the ones that were solved. She thought of the advent of mass transportation long ago, horses and buggies giving way to planes, trains, automobiles, and massive ships. With the change had come increased efficiency and higher standards of living globally, opening the doors for trade around the world. Yet this new technology and standard of living had also brought with it increased pollution, leading to climate change and other environmental damage. But this was a manageable problem, one they had overcome, and one that should have been overcome long ago, when people had learned the danger but instead ignored it or pretended there was nothing they could do about it. Despite the hardship caused by climate change, would anyone truly want to go back to a time when streets were mud and rock and a trip across a city would take hours or even days instead of minutes? When people in developing countries died of malaria, AIDS, tuberculosis, and other now rare diseases at astounding rates? When food and clean water were scarce in parts of the world and hunger and malnourishment kept children from achieving what they otherwise would have been capable of?

They fell back into silence and watched the approaching shore. The boat was approaching the abandoned buildings, where Vasu would be the first to be dropped off. They could not get too close for fear of debris, so he would raft to dry land and act like he had been in Haiti the last few days. Vasu would be the first because he had an important task. He had to send their drones and weapons ahead on a cargo plane so that they could recover them when they arrived in Virginia.

A loud rumbling noise disturbed Maria's thoughts, and a large shadow appeared in the night sky over the top of the abandoned village, speeding toward the boat. Her heart skipped a beat, afraid that their boat was under attack. Then she recognized the familiar shape of a large passenger airliner, having just taken off from the Cap-Haitien airport. That was where Vasu would be shipping his cargo as soon as possible, and then boarding a passenger plane a day later. His was the riskiest part of the mission, and they were relying on a contact of Henry's to help pull this off. Henry had arranged for a contact at the airport to meet Vasu near the shore and help him smuggle his stuff inside a cargo plane. Then Vasu would stay the night in Cap-Haitien until he took off on a commercial airliner in the morning.

"What, you can't get me any closer?" Vasu teased Irina as the boat slowed, coming to a stop a few hundred feet from the nearest row of flooded buildings.

"Keep that up and we'll make you swim the rest," Irina replied with a grin.

"Okay, okay," Vasu held up his hands in mock defeat, "don't make me walk the plank, Captain Barkova."

The team said their goodbyes and wished him luck. Min helped him carry his boxes of gear out the rear door, loading them onto the inflated raft. They all watched from the rear walkway as he climbed aboard and started the electric outboard motor, propelling his raft toward the shore in near silence. He gave one last wave before he disappeared around the side of the boat, leaving them standing in the warm ocean air.

The next few hours passed slowly as they traveled around Haiti, staying a few miles from the coast until they reached the northwest edge and traveled south toward the tip of the Tiburon peninsula. There they would drop off Zu near the Jeremie airport before traveling toward Honduras. On the way to Honduras, they would stop at Jamaica to drop off Min. Originally, before leaving Haiti, they would have traveled around the tip of the Tiburon to drop off Clarissa near the Les Cayes airport. But now Clarissa was gone. The thought brought an ache to her heart, and the image of Clarissa disappearing down into the chasm flashed through her mind. It had become a familiar episode that day, taking turns in her mind with the memory of Henry's body convulsing. Each flashback left her with trembling hands, moist eyes, and the feeling that there must have been something she could have done to prevent it.

Maria had considered trying to rest, hoping it would ease the pain in her heart and the soreness in her body. She was tired, but decided against it. She wanted to be awake to see Zu and Min off. If things went wrong, it could very well be the last time she saw them.

She spent the trip to Jeremie sitting near the front, looking out the window and chatting with Irina and Antonio. The rest of the group came up to join them after an hour, after they finished going over Zu's schedule. They talked quietly, the mood shifting to and fro, from lighthearted teasing to somber thoughts about lost teammates. All the while, Maria could not shake the nagging voice in her head telling her not to trust them. Her eyes watched each of them carefully for any sign of dishonesty, but found none. They were all so friendly and kind, and she could not keep her guard up against the comfort she felt around them. Even Vincent, who she knew to be deceitful, seemed so sincere and passionate that it was difficult to reconcile his talk with his true intentions. She was grateful that Karen had confirmed her suspicion or she might have let down her guard or convinced herself that he was trustworthy.

It was shortly after midnight when the Tiburon peninsula came into view, marked by little dots of light along the distant coast. It took another half hour until they could make out the city of Jeremie illuminated by streetlights and the nearby airport with its warning lights. Here the land was more elevated, and there were no abandoned cities. The ocean swallowed the bottom of the first row of ruins, but beyond them, the land sloped gently upward, leaving the next-closest buildings a few feet above the water. The city was smaller than Cap-Haitien, but looked just as modern. There were ads playing on electronic billboards intermixed with tall office buildings and apartments. Maria could make out a few quiet neighborhoods on the outskirts with evenly spaced homes throughout. Pods traveled silently through the city and neighborhoods picking up and dropping off passengers, hundreds on the road even at two in the morning.

They gathered to wish Zu farewell. He went around to each of them and gave them a hug. When he reached Maria, he smiled at her, his face cheerful with no sign of fear.

"It's up to you to keep these city-slickers in line for now," he teased. "I don't know what they would do without us farm-folk."

"Probably starve," she laughed, and gave him a hug. Her voice turned more serious. "We'll see you soon, be safe."

He nodded, smiled, and moved on to Karen. Then he was boarding his raft and gliding toward the shore, his outboard motor whirring softly.

Maria realized then just how tired she was, and she made her way to her bunk. Her sore muscles struggled to pull her up the ladder, and she wobbled unsteadily with fatigue. She only had enough consciousness left to set her alarm before her head hit the pillow and sleep overcame her.

It seemed like only an instant until a light was shining on her face and a soft chime began to sound. She lifted her groggy head from the pillow and shut off the simulated sunlight and alarm, taking a moment to remember where she was. It came back to her and she rolled out of bed, glancing at the time. Five in the morning.

She hurried down the ladder, hoping she had not missed Min's departure. Min was still there, carrying her bag to her raft. Antonio climbed down the ladder behind Maria, startling her. She had not noticed him, but he must have been up there resting as well.

The group followed Min out onto the catwalk, watching as she climbed down to the raft.

"If you want me to show up in Virginia, you had better plan on giving me a raise," Min said, narrowing her eyes at Vincent.

Her comment surprised Maria for a moment, but then a
smile crept across Min's face. Vincent laughed. "Ten percent,
how's that sound?"

Min smiled. "Make it twenty and you have a deal. Heck,
make it a hundred percent, a hundred percent of nothing's
still nothing. But it's the principle of the thing."

"I don't get why you're complaining," Vincent said, grinning. "We're sending you on an all-expenses-paid trip to Jamaica, that's a pretty swell deal."

She laughed and started up the propeller. "I needed a
vacation from you people anyway. If I don't show up it's
probably because I decided to stay here and drink daiquiris
on the beach. See you soon. Maybe."

Maria chuckled, waving back at Min as she pulled away
and disappeared around the side of the boat. She walked back
through the door of the boat and toward the front window,
where Min's raft appeared into view. It glided across the
shallow rolling waves toward the shore of Boscobel, Jamaica,
where she could see the glowing lights of luxurious beachfront
resorts nestled between palm trees. Here she could not see
any evidence of sea level rise at all, as if this part of the coast
had been unaffected. But she knew that was not the case, and
instead what she was seeing was the impact of sea level rise on
a place fortunate enough to be able to cover the costs without
batting an eye.

The whine of plane engines sounded overhead and a massive passenger airliner coasted down from the sky and disappeared below the palm trees. Min would be taking off from
there in the next day or so.

"Did you know that airport is named for the guy who created James Bond?"

Maria had not heard Karen approach, and she jumped.

"Sorry," Karen laughed, "but yeah it's the Ian Fleming International Airport."

"I didn't know that," Maria replied, and grinned at her. "Why do you have that ancient bit of movie trivia floating around in your head?"

Karen feigned offense, and then looked surprised. "Movie trivia? I'm talking about the author!"

Maria raised an eyebrow. "James Bond came from a book? I thought it started as a play back in ancient Rome," she joked. The latest reboot had come out a few years ago, and she had liked it, but other than that, all she knew about it was that it was a movie franchise that had started over a hundred years ago.

Karen snorted with laughter. "Yeah it was a book first," she said, "almost two hundred years old now. It was actually a series of books. I've read them all, they're my favorite. The author, Ian Fleming, was a British guy who owned an estate near here. He wrote all the books there, so they named the airport after him. Fleming was actually a naval intelligence officer back in World War II, and he named his Jamaican estate Goldeneye after one of his wartime operations. After he died and they ran out of his books to turn into movies, they named the first movie that wasn't based on his books Goldeneye as a reference to his Jamaican estate."

Karen blushed, looking self-conscious. "Sorry," she said sheepishly, "probably more than you cared to know about it."

Maria laughed. "Nah," she assured her, "that's actually really interesting. You just increased my James Bond knowledge tenfold in ten seconds. That'll be important to know next time I go to a James Bond convention." Maria playfully punched her arm, and Karen pretended to grimace in pain.

Karen moved away to work on something at her station, leaving Maria alone to reflect on how her life had become like something out of a James Bond movie. Just over a week ago, she had been living comfortably, with plenty of time for family, friends, and hobbies. Now she was on a boat in the middle of the Caribbean, fighting against a nearly omniscient computer program controlled by a power-hungry group of government officials. She had never wanted any of this. Her thoughts turned to her parents back home, grieving over the loss of yet another daughter, both of their children now gone. Here she was, still alive but unable to tell them she was okay. And there was no telling if she would still be alive for much longer.

The sky was just starting to brighten, which reminded Maria how little sleep she had gotten. She climbed the ladder to the upper level and another one up to an empty bunk, drawing the curtains shut around her. The climb had drained the last bit of energy she had gained from her nap, and she was unconscious as soon as her head hit the pillow.

Chapter 10

She was awoken by the sound of a soft voice calling her name, and a gentle shake on her shoulder. Lily's kind face came into view as Maria's sleepy eyes opened. She had slept heavily, and could not remember dreaming at all.

"What time is it?" she groaned.

"Around one in the afternoon," Lily replied, "and it's your turn soon. You had probably better get ready."

Maria nodded, her stomach twisting into knots. She jumped up, wanting to have time to double and triple check that she had everything she needed and was up to speed on the plan.

She grabbed a snack and threw on fresh clothes, being careful to be quiet for Vincent and Irina, who were sleeping in their bunks. Descending the ladder, she found Karen and Lily seated along the side of the boat, each preoccupied with something on their displays. Antonio was at the front watching the travel data. Karen and Antonio each wished her good morning when she stepped onto the floor, and Antonio left his post to help her finish preparing.

Maria went through her bag, making sure she had everything she needed. It was not much. More importantly, she made sure that she did not have anything she was not supposed to have. She had a new identity now, and she could not bring anything with her that would tie her to her old identity or that would not fit with her new one.

"What's your name?" Antonio asked her.

"Alexa Palomo, born on a rural farm in Honduras with limited internet access and parents who were kind of privacy freaks."

"Good," he said, "and why are you flying to Virginia?"

"I've always wanted to visit the United States, and I wanted to take a trip and see the famous Labor Day celebrations and visit the capital."

He nodded approvingly. Maria had looked over her file the night before. Her new life was simple enough to remember, and most importantly, it was crafted so that the little amount of data in SEER's system would make sense. No internet, rural area, and privacy freak parents explained why only basic information about Alexa Palomo was available in SEER's system, placed there by Karen after Maria had hacked into the system. SEER was technically only active in the US, but it tracked any information publicly available online and analyzed any transaction data, audio, video, or images it could find. From that, it built profiles on as many people as it could in every corner of the world, identifying potential threats to the United States. Anything Maria said or did while in Honduras had to be consistent with what SEER already knew about Alexa in case it ended up online and in SEER's data servers.

"Have you ever been to Honduras?" Antonio asked, and Maria realized he meant in her real life, not her new identity.

"No," Maria replied, "we didn't travel much when we lived in Mexico, and when we moved to the US, we never traveled outside the country. Have you?"

"I was born here," he said.

Maria's face flushed. "Oh right, Vincent told us that when we met, I just forgot. Sorry."

He grinned at her. "No worries, it was a pretty stressful day for you, I wouldn't expect you to remember that."

She smiled back. "What part of Honduras are you from?"

"Right here," he said, pointing his thumb in the general direction of the shore. "I was born in La Ceiba and raised here until we moved to the US when I was in high school."

Maria raised her eyebrows. "That must be hard, being so close to home but unable to visit."

Antonio nodded.

"When was the last time you were home?" Maria asked.

"I've only been back once, and it was within a year of leaving." He looked hesitant, as if not sure he wanted to share the rest, but then the look passed and he struggled on. "My... my brother was sick. He had an aggressive form of cancer, and his best shot was coming to the US. So we moved. We became citizens and got him treatment. But it didn't work. He passed away about a year after we moved." He stopped again, his face twisting up as he fought back tears. "It wasn't until I was kidnapped by Vincent that I learned his death wasn't natural. SEER gave the doctors bad treatment data. Data that would cause his death. All because he had a large social media following and was critical of the fact that US citizens can't refuse having their DNA on file. Before he died, he told us he wanted to be buried here, back home, so we brought his body back. But we liked living in the US, so after the funeral we went back there to stay."

"I'm so sorry," Maria said, his story eliciting a familiar pain in her heart. His brother was just like Ana, killed for expressing a belief. "Was he older or younger?"

"It's okay," Antonio said. "I've had time to cope with it. It was a little more than ten years ago now. I had come to terms with it, accepted it. But learning that he was killed by SEER has brought it all back, and it's given me something I can fight, something I can do to really give him closure. He was two years older. I was a freshman in high school when we moved and he was a junior. My parents came back to visit family and his grave every few years after he died, but I never came with them." A look of embarrassment passed over his face, as if he thought she would judge him for not visiting his brother's grave. "It was just a patch of dirt to me," he explained. "And seeing it won't help me remember him any better. The memories play in my head every day."

He gave her a sad smile, which she returned. They were silent for a moment, until Maria spoke again. "So, since you're the expert on La Ceiba, is there anything I have to see before I fly back tomorrow?"

"There's lots to see in La Ceiba," Antonio said, and then thought for a moment. "With how much time you have, I think you could check out two of my favorite things. The first is the El Bejuco waterfall. It's a beautiful hike, three hours round trip, and the waterfall is gorgeous. And the other is Vive Virtual, a local arcade. My brother and I spent a ridiculous amount of time there, and I haven't found any arcades that come close."

Maria was actually surprised at how great both of those sounded. She was expecting regular tourist stuff. See this beach, check out some boring landmark. But these were right up her alley. "Those sound great, I'll be sure to check them out if I have time," she said. She smiled mischievously and added, "And I'll make sure I beat all your high scores at Vive Virtual."

He grinned back at her. They finished checking over her stuff, and then she grabbed her bag and loaded it onto her raft. The rest of them followed her out, and she wished each of them an awkward goodbye while they wished her good luck. It was easier to say goodbye to Antonio, Irina, and Lily, and she shared a subtle knowing glance when she said farewell to Karen. But she had to try hard to keep her smile from looking forced and her voice from sounding flat when she got to Vincent. She was not sure if she succeeded, but it was over fast enough and she hoped he would just think it was nerves.

She climbed down the ladder into her raft, unhooked the mooring line, and pushed the raft clear. No witty parting lines came into her head, so she settled for a smile and wave as she opened the throttle and accelerated around the side of the boat. The team waved back at her and then they were gone, blocked from view by the black hull of the boat.

Maria held up a hand to shield her eyes from the bright, early afternoon sun and looked around. Close to a quarter mile from her was the shore, stretching into the distance along the horizon. She could see buildings all along it, placed behind a sand beach and a road with pods speeding to and fro. Further back into the city was a motley assortment of densely packed buildings, some barely peeking over the first row and some reaching high above. Towering over them all was Pico Bonito, the forest-covered mountain and namesake of the national park within which it resided.

Scanning the coastline, she spied her destination and upped her speed, bouncing over the rolling waves, the ocean spray on her face. She felt both exposed and free all at once. This was the first time she had been out in direct sunlight since agreeing to join the team. But that also meant it was the first time she was plainly visible. There was no Camofoil to protect her, just her and a raft and the open ocean. She was now supposed to be an average citizen, a resident of Honduras, blending in with the locals. Her only protection was the anonymity provided by her new identity.

She adjusted her course and headed for the mouth of the Cangrejal River, where Antonio had said she should go. It was the only part of the coast that was devoid of buildings, a natural preserve slicing through the city. More frequent and severe storm surges had pushed development back from the river, and the rising sea had made it impossible for wells to be dug anywhere near the mouth for fear of salt contamination. The lack of development made it the ideal place for showing up in a boat.

Other small watercraft were puttering around near the mouth of the river. Some of them were larger fishing boats, some smaller boats with people relaxing or fishing. Two boats sped past her as she approached the mouth, electric motors whining. They were driven by girls who looked like they were in high school, with a few more riding along, cheering and laughing as they each tried to beat the other boat to wherever they were going.

Another small boat cut across the mouth of the river in front of Maria, heading along the coast. The smell of exhaust caused Maria to wrinkle her nose. She was surprised that such an old boat was still in operation, and she wondered if gas was as expensive here as it was in the US.

Maria entered the river and traveled upstream. It was wider than a football field and lined on each side with trees and overgrowth. She continued up the river for a quarter mile until she got to a relatively empty part of it, where she steered her raft to the side. Her feet splashed into the chilly water as she jumped out to pull the raft ashore. A quick press of a button and it began to deflate. She stowed the shrinking raft underneath some bushes there, sad at the thought of dumping her garbage where it did not belong. But it was unavoidable, her fake SEER data said she was last tracked taking a pod to a walking trail on the river, and nothing about renting a boat.

She set off through the trees and brush, checking the map on her tablet to get closer to where she had supposedly been dropped off. The tablet felt strange to use, having used a virtual display her whole life. But it fit with her new persona, and the information on the tablet had been carefully crafted to look like it belonged to Alexa Palomo, a 26-year-old woman who lived in rural Honduras with limited internet access and who had just bought herself a tablet for her adventure to America.

Soon she was near enough to her fake drop-off point to leave the woods, passing between a few concrete buildings and emerging onto the sidewalk of a quiet road. A few pods passed by, but none of them pulled over to give her a ride. It took a moment before she remembered that SEER was not active down here, so the pods would not know to automatically pick her up. She waved her arm at one passing by. Someone was already in it, but it would alert the pod system that she needed a ride.

A minute later an empty pod pulled up and she got in. As the door shut, she remembered the last ride she had taken in a pod and her chest tightened. A quick check above her knees confirmed that the emergency stop lever was there and appeared untampered with. Letting out a sigh of relief, she said the name of her hotel and allowed herself to just enjoy her trip through the city.

She watched the scenery pass by, vibrant, colorful, and bustling with a mix of locals and tourists. Palm trees lined the streets, perfectly spaced, adding a taste of nature to the sea of concrete and masonry. The buildings behind them did not look old, but had the architectural flair to fit with the history and culture of the city. Many had red, orange, or tan clay roof tiles and multicolored painted stucco or textured concrete. There were a variety of different solar panel types on many of the buildings, some made to look like clay tiles, some just flat sheets of solar glass, and some were the more traditional rectangles jutting from the roof.

It was not long before she arrived at her hotel, a quaint building with inexpensive rooms that fit the budget of Alexa Palomo. She checked in with her new identity, the room already reserved and prepaid thanks to Henry. The thought brought the image of his death to her mind and her mood darkened. The excitement of the new experience was replaced with a reminder of her lost teammates and the feeling that her true identity was on display for the world to see. She hurried to her room and spent half an hour talking herself into going back out to see the city. Not only did she not want to waste the experience of a new place, but she needed to see the sights to appear like a regular tourist.

Finally, her fear subsided enough for her to emerge from her room and get in a pod. She decided she would first do the hike to El Bejuco while there was still daylight left. As the pod sped through the city, she told it that she wanted bug spray, snacks, and water. It searched the city for the best deals and placed an order, using the money chip she had scanned to pay for the ride to purchase them. Ten minutes later a pod pulled alongside and connected to hers. The windows rolled down and an automated tray extended with her items on them. She removed them and the other pod detached, off to complete more deliveries.

The buildings outside grew sparser and the scenery began to shift from city with a dash of nature to rainforest with a dash of development. To her left were trees, vines, and fronds all tangled together, densely packed into a lush, green landscape, only held back by the asphalt road. To her right was the Cangrejal River, separated from her by a few rows of trees. The river meandered through a strip of rocky terrain that formed banks and shoals, the only area she could see that was devoid of green aside from the road.

She passed several lodges and attractions before arriving at the visitor's center. She grabbed a map and headed to the beginning of the trail, dousing herself in bug spray on the way. With the spray and granola bars slipped into her pocket and the water bottle clipped to her belt, she headed across the road to the bridge over the river. A heavy cable ran across the river on each side of the bridge, supporting smaller vertical cables which were attached to the composite wood plank deck. A cable mesh guardrail protected each side, preventing falls into the river. The bridge was wide enough for two people side by side, and felt sturdy.

She paused at the center of the bridge, watching the water, before continuing on into the jungle. The sound of rushing water faded behind her and transformed into the sounds of the jungle: bugs and birds and the rare hoot of a monkey. There was no one in sight, and she enjoyed the isolation after being cooped up on the boat.

Her pace was ambling, taking her time to examine the mossy trees, ferns, and bushes pressing in around the path. She passed two other groups in the first half hour, both going the other way. One looked like a group of tourists; the other was a man and a woman who looked native to Honduras. Both groups smiled at her as they went by, and Maria returned their smiles.

Shortly after passing the second group she saw her first toucan, black with a yellow chest and a large colorful beak. It landed in a tree overhead and began scratching its beak along the branch, as if sharpening it. She stopped to watch it for a while, until it looked around and flew off. Continuing down the trail, she tried to just enjoy herself, but the bird brought to mind questions she had, questions she had not had enough time to process.

The knowledge that SEER could predict her every decision left her feeling strange, like anything special about her was now gone. She was an animal, just like the toucan, but supposedly separated by the ability to reason and choose her path. The toucan was not capable of human levels of thought, and therefore had a simpler decision-making process. Hungry? Find food. Reproductive instinct? Find a mate, build a nest. Its instincts were shaped by millions of years of survival. Those that did not groom died of disease or poor flight ability, or did not find a mate and did not pass on genes. Those that did not feel a mating instinct did not pass on genes. Those that were not wary of predators did not pass on genes. And the toucan was the result. If it was dirty, it groomed. If it was hungry, it ate. If it felt a reproductive instinct, it mated.

If it sensed danger, it moved. Environmental stimulus followed by instinctual response, a response based on previous stimulus and the outcomes of previous responses. They were entirely predictable creatures if you had the data that made each toucan what it was.

So then where was the difference? Humans liked to see themselves as more complex, and they were, but if humans were ultimately predictable how were they any freer than a lower animal? They were more capable, they had more reasoned thoughts and created better tools, and they had a more advanced sense of self. But all of that was only the result of larger brain capacity. There was more room in her head for learning and observations about the environment she lived in. As a result, she could piece more information together, and use that information to create complex thoughts and tools. But it was the same stimulus and response mechanism that made her do what she did; the only difference was how much information her brain could store and use for her responses. Her thoughts themselves were a response to stimulus. Still predictable, still a product of circumstances.

Maria furrowed her brow, deep in contemplation and out of breath from the incline of the trail. At first, she did not notice the sound in the background that grew from a low hiss to a dull roar. Then she entered into a clearing and saw it. Water cascaded down the side of a tall cliff, flowing and crashing into jutting rock formations, creating a beautiful pattern. The cliff face had a green forest of moss radiating out from the flow of water, damp with mist. She climbed up one of the boulders near the foot of the falls, refreshed by the cool spray. The water crashed into the rocks at the bottom, loud but soothing. She looked down and could see where it flowed outward from the base of the falls, down a nearby rock face and disappearing into the forest.

She was the only one there, and she sat atop the rock to rest. Despite her warmth, the afternoon sun felt nice combined with the wet air, and the rocky clearing and sheer cliff height allowed the sun to create rainbows in the billowing mist. She took a sip of water and pulled out her snack, watching the falls as she ate. It flowed in a constant path, slightly wavering but never changing, a path carved by thousands of years of flowing water. Despite the seemingly random action of the billions of water molecules swirling within the water, the outcome was predictable. She could take a three-dimensional scan of the topography and recreate this exact waterfall in a computer model. The effect of wind and amount of water could be modeled too. But being able to predict or model it did not decrease its value. It was still beautiful.

The temptation to just stay in Honduras and be done with it all swelled up in her. It was so nice here, so much simpler than their problems with SEER. She wondered at the futility of it all. Perhaps it did not matter if SEER was being used to control people. People were hardly in control anyway if they were only a product of genes and environmental influences. Why be concerned if someone was trying to change what those influences were? At the individual level, people would still have the perception that they were making their own choices. Did it really matter what was influencing them? A hidden group in the US government, Vincent, or the next power-hungry fool with a mind to fix things — did it matter who was in control as long as people still felt in control of themselves and the country had equality, safety, and prosperity?

She finished her granola bar, staring in silence for several minutes at the waterfall. She grimaced, repulsed that she could consider letting things be. It would be as if someone were to trench a new, man-made path down this cliff for the water to follow, claiming that it would be better that way. Less variation, more uniformity, a smooth and straight path where the water would not splash or waver. Taking something natural and beautiful and bending it to their will. The thought saddened her. These were people, with individual ideas and beliefs. It was not right to use a tool with superior computational ability to manipulate them, no matter how noble the cause.

Ana was proof of that. Killing and manipulating people to preserve someone's idea of a perfect society was not right, and would never be right. She could not stand by and let that keep happening to people. But neither could she support destroying something that had done so much good. SEER was only a tool, a tool more powerful and with more potential for good than any tool ever before. And ultimately, the fate of SEER could not be her decision alone. It impacted the lives of every citizen, and every citizen had a say. She would show them all how SEER was being used, and they would all decide together what must be done with it. She hoped they would choose to preserve it, to safeguard it and operate it with complete transparency. But if the consensus was to destroy it

and try to limit future incarnations of SEER, she would accept
that outcome.

She climbed down from the rock, pausing for a last look
at El Bejuco before returning to the trail. The trek back was
easier, going mostly downhill, and her mind was more relaxed,
making it easier to enjoy the forest. Close to an hour later,
she reached the bridge, the sun now low in the sky. She was
surprised how early the sun was setting — it was only a little
after five PM — and she was glad she made it back before it
got any darker.

The pod she had requested on her tablet arrived as she
walked into the parking lot, and it brought her back to the
city. She was not hungry yet and decided to check out Vive
Virtual while she had the chance. The sun was nearly gone
when she arrived, the sky red and gold, coloring the glass
skyscrapers. Vive Virtual was outside the downtown area,
on a quiet street with local shops in older-looking buildings.
It had a large screen on the front displaying the name and
cycling through the games it had inside. She smiled, recognizing some of the games and looking forward to playing
them.

A kindly old woman greeted her in Spanish from behind
a counter when she stepped inside. Maria walked up to the
counter, looking up at the video screen over her head displaying the available options.

"Have you been here before?" she asked, noticing Maria's
hesitation.

"No, this is my first time," Maria replied, her Spanish a
bit rusty.

She smiled, looking delighted. "You're in for a treat. We've got the best collection of games in all of Honduras, and the most immersive systems. And as a first-time customer you get a free half hour." She winked. "I can pretty much guarantee you'll want to play longer."

"Sounds great," Maria said, smiling back at her.

"Okay, let's get your name as you want it on the score-board, and scan your money chip so you can add more time."

Maria opened her mouth to say her name, and then choked on it. She had almost just given her real name. She kicked herself and tried to act casual. "Excuse me, something in my throat I guess. It's Alexa Palomo."

The woman entered her name into the system and scan-ned her payment. "Okay, just head back that way, you can use door four."

Nearly two hours later, Maria emerged from the room, absolutely blown away. The gaming rig had been one of the most advanced she had ever seen, consisting of a harness sus-pended from the ceiling with automatic restraints that would adjust to provide in-game feedback and positioning. Playing games back home had been plenty immersive under regular virtual reality, but this was like being an actual part of the game.

Walking on solid ground was a little odd at first, like walking on the deck of a boat being tossed around at sea. She headed down the hall and out to the desk, thanking the woman on the way out. Something on the wall next to the door caught her eye as she went to open it. She stopped to examine it. It was a memorial plaque. "In loving memory of

Raul Thomas," it read. A picture of a smiling young man was just below it, who looked just like a younger version of Antonio.

"Raul used to be in here all the time with his little brother Antonio," the woman at the desk said. "Great kids, they were a lot of fun to have around. Poor Raul got cancer and they took him to America for treatment, but it didn't work. I haven't seen the younger one since he stopped in after his brother died and asked if we could put up a memorial in his favorite place. Poor kid. I hope he's doing okay."

Maria could see the sad look on the woman's face. After a brief moment of hesitation, Maria said, "He is." She smiled at the woman and left before she could respond. Maria hoped her words had brought her a bit of happiness.

Maria got into a pod and headed back toward her hotel, ordering some food for when she arrived. The farther she got from Vive Virtual, the more her carefree feeling faded. Instead, the anxiety of the next day's mission crept back over her.

Chapter 11

The plane ride to Virginia was fortunately uneventful. At five in the morning she had taken a pod to the airport and boarded. Six hours and one transfer later and she had arrived at the Ronald Reagan Washington National Airport. After leaving the plane she had been ushered through customs, where her bag had been searched. She had been relieved when they had not searched her tablet or found the hidden compartment inside it where her two small portable drives with her code had been stashed.

On her way to the airport in the morning, she had checked the status of the other flights from a public computer in a local coffee shop. She had walked nearly a mile to get to it, and then walked back towards her hotel before catching a pod, just in case SEER had access to the pod data in Honduras and could connect that to the flight searches. To her relief, all of the flights would arrive in time. Zu's had been delayed, but only for a few hours, and his had been scheduled to depart last night. They should all be there at the scheduled meeting time.

Stepping off the plane, she had been immediately struck by the difference not having augmented-reality drones made. Normally there would be three-dimensional displays and advertisements everywhere, and pertinent information such as walking directions appearing wherever they were needed. Without her orb virtual display, the world was kind of blank and empty. Except for all the orbs flying around everyone else's heads. Normally they communicated with each other to cloak themselves, augmenting each person's vision with a drone-less view of the world. Since Maria did not have an augmented-reality system the orbs were plainly visible to her, swarming around everyone like large flies.

When she arrived in the US, she checked into a hotel near the airport, something that would make her look like a typical tourist. She left everything but her tablet and her portable drives in her hotel room and caught a pod outside. It carried her to downtown Arlington, where the Labor Day festivities were underway. The sidewalks were filled with people and roads were closed for the parade. She got out near one of the closed roads and walked along the parade route.

It was difficult for her to act like a relaxed tourist. A shiver traced down her spine at every camera she saw. Her stomach turned in a mixture of fear and apprehension. But she had to play her part, so she did her best to watch the parade and pretend to enjoy herself. After walking along the parade route for a few minutes, she stopped and stood behind a row of people sitting on a curb and watched the floats and high school bands go by.

The floats were elaborate works of art representing various groups and peoples of the city, usually with a reference
to the theme of the parade. A float representing a local children's recreational club passed by, kids in matching shirts
waving from the float platform to the crowd. Around the
children were pillars made to look like humans and stereo-
typical human-shaped robots, their hands outstretched and
meeting to form arches. The arches declared in large letters,
"47th Annual Labor Day Parade," with a subtext beneath that
read, "Celebrating the Value of People Apart from Work".

"Whoa, cool!" some of the kids sitting on the side of the
road yelled. Maria could not tell what they were excited about,
but then she remembered she did not have her virtual display.
She pointed her tablet at the float and the screen displayed the
street in front of her in augmented reality. Virtual fireworks
were shooting from the float and a massive virtual robot and
human were walking hand in hand behind it.

Maria smiled to herself at the cheesy robot depiction. Hu-
manoid robots were rare. Usually robots were shaped however was needed to accomplish a particular task, and most
specialized tasks did not require the diverse abilities that the
human form provided. Still, she supposed it made for a nicer
image than a human shaking hands with factory equipment.

She had learned back in school that Labor Day had not
always been the big celebration that it was now. It had surprised her to learn that it used to be a day that was meant to
honor labor and the only special thing about it was that a lot
of people got the day off work. That had changed in 2074,

when years of riots and unrest had culminated in the passage of new laws and official recognition of a cultural shift in views on labor. The riots had been sparked by high unemployment and depressed wages, as it became quicker to train machines for many jobs than it was to train humans. New technology had created new jobs, but many of the new jobs could be learned by machines faster than they could be by a human. Job-retraining programs had been created by the millions to help people find work, but by the time many people had completed their training, they had found that a computer had already learned their job. People who were out of work and out of options took to the streets, protesting, rioting, and looting. After years of inaction and inadequate solutions, Congress finally passed a right to live bill, taxing the massive wealth that was concentrated around those who owned the machine workforce and redistributing it to the public. Since then, work had no longer been a necessity; instead, many people simply did what they wanted after their schooling. There were still many jobs, like Maria's, but with the oversupply of human labor, the work week had been shortened and the jobs were worked by people who wanted to work them and who wanted the supplemental income instead of by people who needed the jobs to survive.

The first few years of this transition had been difficult, with rising suicide rates and depression in the population of people who no longer had jobs and who derived meaning from their work. But the education system quickly adjusted, increasing the focus on developing and pursuing personal

interests and fostering relationships. The culture had adjusted
too, and within a decade the suicide rates had decreased as
people learned to value their lives apart from labor.

Maria was too young to have noticed any problems, and
by the time her family had moved to America, the new system
had been operating smoothly for decades. She supposed that
was why Labor Day had been refreshed a few years after the
laws changed, to remind people like her that things were not
always so nice and that it took a lot of work to make it this
way. Whatever the reason, it had worked, and Labor Day was
one of the big holidays of the year.

Her reverie broke with a sudden pang of panic and she
checked the time on her tablet, fearing that she would be late.
She was relieved to find she still had an hour to go until they
were to rendezvous near the DARPA headquarters. Wanting
to be closer to her destination, she began walking along the
parade route in the general direction of the headquarters. She
had been to Arlington several times in the past, but she was
not familiar enough with the area to navigate it easily. Which
was why she had spent some time memorizing the local area
when she had checked the flights back in La Ceiba. She could
not be seen looking at the DARPA headquarters on the map
she had on her tablet, as it could make SEER monitor her more
closely.

Maria weaved her way through the crowded sidewalk,
watching the parade as it passed by, moving the opposite direction. The train of floats turned a corner ahead of her, and
she followed the sidewalk around a coffee shop on the corner,

one of the many shops making up the ground floor of the ten-story office buildings on the block.

She turned the corner and looked down the block, where the parade continued into the distance. As her eyes passed over the sidewalk, her heart dropped into her stomach.

Sandara, her co-worker and the last person she had talked to before being abducted, was walking toward her, hand in hand with her husband and only twenty feet away. Sandara was looking at her husband, but before Maria had time to react, she had turned her head toward her. Their eyes met, and recognition flickered over Sandara's face. Maria jerked her head down, ducking slightly to lose herself in the crowd.

She had to hide, but she was too exposed. The parade blocked her in to her left, and she could turn around, but she was worried about her ability to put distance between her and Sandara with the crowd. Plus, hurrying back the way she came for no reason would look suspicious to SEER. The only choice was the coffee shop. She dodged through the crowd as fast as she could without drawing too much attention. The door slid open and she entered the shop, her head darting around to find what she was looking for. Spying it, she strode between the small tables and the line at the dispenser and toward the bathroom, hoping that it was not occupied. She was in luck, and the door opened for her as she approached and locked behind her.

She took the battery out of her tablet to disable it. This was one of the few places she could have real privacy, with no cameras, and she did not intend to violate that. She stood and waited for her heart rate to slow, hoping that her behavior would not alert SEER and that it just looked like a sudden need to use the restroom. Several minutes passed as Maria tried to calm herself, hoping that Sandara was not waiting in the coffee shop to see if it was her.

A sudden knock at the door startled her, sending a cold wave over her body. She did not respond, hoping that whoever it was would just go away. They knocked again, sounding impatient.

"It's occupied," Maria said, trying to disguise her voice in case it was Sandara. There were no more knocks, and after several moments she heard a flush and the opening and relocking of the restroom adjacent to hers. Air rushed from her mouth as she let out the breath she had been holding.

She decided she had waited long enough, and she turned to the toilet to flush it when something scurried under the door and into the room. Springing back and holding in a yell of surprise, she made to jump onto the toilet to escape the mouse or roach. But the object slowed to a stop in the middle of the floor, and she could see that it was not alive.

Cautiously stepping forward and stooping down, she could tell that it was some kind of tiny robot, the size of a large roach but with wheels, like a toy car. She picked it up, and as soon as she touched it, a small light shot out from it. Her brow wrinkled in confusion, and she shone the light toward the wall. Words appeared, several lines of red text. They read:

> Change of plans, regroup at empty building at cor-
> ner of N. Quincy and N. Glebe immediately. Flush
> this bot after memorizing.

A change of plans, but why? Had something bad happened? Sweat broke out on her brow. She was already nervous
enough when everything was going according to plan, but
now the plans were changing and that meant there were problems. Her hands shook as she realized that her chances of
being killed or imprisoned had just increased substantially.

Maria took a minute to breathe deeply and think it
through. Maybe some new information had been learned
and they needed time to discuss the plan before going forward. Or maybe one of them had been delayed and they
needed to wait. But meeting up somewhere beforehand was
risky. SEER would be on high alert if nine foreigners who
were supposed to be strangers converged on one location.
Maybe they had hacked a surveillance drone like they had
when Maria had been kidnapped. But even so, SEER would
still know if a bunch of new arrivals disappeared from its
surveillance. Whatever the reason, they must only intend to
meet briefly before executing the plan. Any longer than a few
minutes and surveillance drones would be there to see what
was going on.

Another thought crossed her mind, one that chilled her.
What if they had been found out? What if the government
had sent her this message to lead her to a nice quiet place
where she could be arrested without causing a scene or risking

civilian lives if she was dangerous? It was a worrying thought, but she realized it did not matter, and was pretty unlikely. If they had been discovered, then it made little difference if she was captured here or at some other place. If it was the government trying to trick her, they already knew where she was, so even if she did not go, she would still be arrested anyway.

The only choice was to go to the address, she concluded. She felt that it was most likely from her team, since it seemed unlikely the government would go to the trouble of sending her a discreet message to get her to go somewhere else instead of just arresting her here. Besides, this was a clever way of getting a message to her. Someone from her team must be monitoring the rest of the team, probably with a drone, either a hacked SEER drone or one of their own with a way to send data without it being intercepted by SEER. And this little roach-bot could not be remotely controlled for fear of the signal being intercepted, so one of her team members had to have followed her, waiting for a chance to drop it on the ground where no one would see. It was a glorified note, one that could maybe pass for a toy or an insect if glimpsed from a drone or street camera.

She was calmer now, her resolve recovered by the knowledge that her only choice was to go to the address. Her eyes passed over the hidden message ten more times, committing it to memory. Then she tossed the bot into the toilet and waved at the flush sensor, sending it swirling down the drain.

Maria washed her hands to uphold the illusion of using the restroom and stepped through the automatic door. She tried not to move her head too much, but her eyes darted around the room to see if Sandara was waiting. She did not see her, and Maria was almost disappointed. It would be so nice to be able to talk and laugh with her again without all this danger she was mixed up in and without knowing everything she had learned.

The parade was still in full swing as she stepped back out of the coffee shop. She walked down the street for a while, feigning interest in the floats, before pulling out her tablet and opening the map application. She did a manual search for nearby food, since SEER did not have enough data on her new identity to predict what she would search for. And that was good, because she was not at all interested in nearby food. Her eyes scanned the map, making sure to only look at the little food icons so that the tablet's eye tracking data did not contradict her search. There were restaurants all over the place, and she was able to discreetly find the rendezvous address on the map. It was only a few blocks away, and it was only a couple buildings down from the DARPA headquarters.

The walk took her twenty minutes at her nonchalant pace, following the parade route and occasionally stopping to take pictures or hold up her tablet to see the virtual part of the parade. She felt out of place with her antique technology. Everyone else had the orb virtual displays that she was used to, with the occasional older person using the outdated head-mounted display. But her tablet was even more outdated than that. Still, it fit her role as a foreigner from a poor rural area quite well.

Her walk took her the long way around the block to the address, so as to avoid passing by the DARPA building. She was

free to do as she pleased, but she was worried that she would
have some kind of visible nervous reaction if she walked by the
headquarters, something that could make her look suspicious.
The parade had parted ways with her a block ago, and now she
was walking down Glebe Road under the pretext of going to
the pizza place one building over from the corner of Quincy
and Glebe.

The pizza place was one of a few stores along a strip of
retail outlets on the first floor of a five-story apartment complex. As she drew closer, a wonderful aroma of baking dough,
cheese, and cultured meat reached her nose, emanating from
the small shop. But she was not here for pizza, and how she
acted here was critical for avoiding increased scrutiny.

She paused outside, reading the menu posted on the window. Feigning disappointment, she turned and continued
walking toward the corner, looking around as if taking in the
city or looking for other food options.

After passing the apartment building, she found herself
gazing at the address that the message bot had shown her.
It was an old pod rental building, a large, three-story office
with a huge parking lot in the front, devoid of pods. It was
strange to her to see such a large parking lot. Lots like these
were rare now, except at pod rental businesses. She remembered learning in school how the advent of pods had virtually
eliminated vehicle ownership, as it was far cheaper to rent a
pod when you needed it. Parking lots were no longer needed
at most places, and all of the extra space was used for larger
buildings and denser cities. Instead there were now just a few

stalls or a pull-off at most places to allow room for people to be dropped off and picked up.

The pod rental business in front of her was a relic, the building old and abandoned. She guessed it was one of the rental businesses that tried to go it alone with their own passenger data instead of paying for access to SEER data. SEER access was cheap, but when it was in its early stages, it was seen by some as an unnecessary expense, and not particularly useful. That proved to be an incorrect assessment, as the businesses using SEER data flourished. The ability to predict customers' needs was a boon, enabling superior customer service. It had supercharged every industry, boosting production at existing businesses and creating thousands of new businesses. Firms were created to supply the data to businesses, firms that had to win government contracts and be subjected to strict government privacy rules. Data administrators bought access to SEER data and its human behavior predictions, tailored it for different uses, encapsulated it for privacy, and then rented data access to businesses. This allowed the data to be used throughout nearly every product, all while keeping people's information private and secure, or at least private as far as the eyes of other humans were concerned. And, of course, as part of the data usage agreement, SEER was able to gather more data through every product. Combine the data from consumer technology and from the drone and camera surveillance network and SEER had eyes everywhere. But they were electronic eyes, eyes that people took no offense to watching their every move.

Maria crossed the small side street to reach the building and then walked down the sidewalk, heading for the entrance. She mentally calmed herself before entering, wondering if the doors would even be unlocked. Even if they were, the moment she entered the building, SEER would likely dispatch police drones to investigate her for trespassing. She hoped that her team had it well under control. Grasping the door handle, she checked her wrist and her pocket one more time, making sure she had her portable drives.

The door was automatic, but the power to the building was off, so she pulled on it. It opened, and she stepped inside into a dim lobby, the only light coming from the sunlight streaming in through the windows. There was no one in sight, just a dusty receptionist desk and a few couches. She took timid steps toward the hallway ahead of her, which ran to her left and to her right, a sign on the wall indicating the direction of the elevator, stairs, and restrooms. Her head turned each direction, unsure of where to go, when a drone popped into the hallway near the stair sign and sped toward her. She backed away instinctively, but then she recognized it as one of the types of drones Vasu had, a medium-sized shield drone with a rotor deck a little narrower than her shoulders and a shield in the front, covering the main drone body. The spherical body mounted below the rotors had two fierce-looking barrels protruding from it under the shield, and the sphere itself was a black glass-like material which hid its cameras and sensors.

"Follow me," came a pleasant computerized voice, and the drone retreated back to the stairs. Maria followed it up the stairs and down the second floor hallway, past rows of cubicles and offices. It stopped at a door, a plaque on the wall bearing the words "conference room". The drone sped off down the hallway, and Maria was unsure for a moment whether she should stay or follow it. Then the door opened, and Maria froze.

"Who are you?" Maria said, backing away from an unknown woman with long red hair, dressed in a form-fitting black bodysuit. "Why did you bring me here?" The woman was blocking the door, and Maria could not tell how many more were in the room.

"Please, come in," the woman said in a calm voice.

Maria turned and ran back down the hallway. Whoever these people were, they were not with her team, and that meant her team would still be meeting at the DARPA headquarters. She was their way in; she had to get to them.

Another woman stepped out of a cubicle aisle into the hallway, blocking her path. This one was dressed the same, but had short, curly black hair. Maria was startled into a brief moment of hesitation, but then she leaned her shoulder forward and drove as hard as she could into the woman, sending her sprawling. The woman managed to grab a hold of Maria's leg as she fell, and Maria felt her world turn sideways and her body slam into the floor.

Maria thrashed her leg and pulled at the thin carpet, scrambling away from the dark-haired woman, but the woman was too fast. The woman gained her feet and ran up to Maria, driving a knee into her ribs as Maria tried to stand. Maria felt the air being forced out of her lungs and mouth in a great gasp. Pain churned in her stomach like her organs were being squeezed by a giant hand.

Maria doubled over, leaning against the dark-haired woman. Clutching at the woman's arms for support, Maria feigned weakness, or at least half feigned. The dark-haired woman grabbed her to help her stand upright, but then Maria drove an elbow into her exposed stomach, throwing her weight behind it and driving the woman into a cubicle wall. It collapsed with a crash, and the dark-haired woman collapsed with it.

Maria staggered to her feet and strode forward to run, but then there was a sharp pain in her shins and her feet were swept out from under her. She hit the floor hard, pain shooting through her left shoulder. Her breath came in gasps, the wind knocked out of her again. A knee pressed between her shoulder blades and red hair dangled down into her view. Maria reached weakly for it, but a hand caught her wrist.

"I don't think so," the red-head said. "Are you alright, Anita?" she called to the dark-haired woman.

"Everything's fine but my pride," a voice, evidently belonging to Anita, replied. Maria heard a creak as the collapsed cubicle shifted.

"Yeah she's scrappy. She was going for my hair just a second ago. Help me get her up."

They grabbed her by each arm and pulled her to her feet, walking her to the conference room door. Anita opened the door and they guided her in. Maria was too nervous and fatigued to count, but there were roughly ten people sitting around a large conference table, all wearing black body suits, a mix of women and men.

A woman at the head of the table stood up. Maria had only seen her once before, but she recognized her immediately. "We've been waiting for you, Maria," Reyah said. "You're going to get us into SEER."

Chapter 12

Maria stood there, Anita and the red-headed woman standing on each side. Some of the people at the table were looking at her, interested to see how she would react. The rest seemed to be busy with other tasks. Reyah stood at the other end of the table, dressed in the same black jumpsuit as the rest of them, her black hair pulled back in a ponytail.

"I won't help you," Maria said.

"You have no choice," Reyah replied amicably. "There's only one shot at this. You're with us now, so you have to take it. Either you help us and we destroy SEER or you don't help us and SEER continues to be used to control us all. Your team is out there in the city, unable to continue because you're missing. They'll be unsure and searching for you, and eventually they'll slip up and get caught by SEER. So we act, or this once in a lifetime opportunity to strike is gone forever."

Maria frowned. "You've already blown it, police drones are on their way to investigate me for trespassing."

Reyah smiled. "We have that covered. Before Vincent and I left SEER, I managed to sneak some code into SEER's database that would reroute the camera data in this region. Instead of going straight to SEER for analysis, we're able to tinker with it first. We run filters to make the data show what we want it to show and hide what we want it to hide, and then we send it on to SEER for it to analyze. That's how we were able to set up shop here, and it's why you trespassing in this abandoned building won't alert the police drones. Of course, Vincent never knew about that, he left our operation before we set up shop here, and I never fully trusted him enough to tell him I had done that."

Maria noted around half of Reyah's team were gesturing subtly and staring intently at virtual displays that Maria could not see, evidently monitoring the data and police activity. "And what if I would rather have the people continue to be manipulated instead of seeing you wreak havoc and destruction on them? You're talking about crippling the United States!"

"An unfortunate sacrifice, but when you let a country become dependent on a cancer, there will be some bad side effects when you rip that cancer out."

Maria scoffed. "You know there's another way, that's what we're trying to do! Give the people control and the country doesn't need to suffer disaster."

Reyah rolled her eyes. "To extend the analogy, you can't control cancer. It has to be wiped out or it will come back. If SEER remains in place, it's only a matter of time before someone tries to abuse it again. And if they do, all it takes is a few commands to keep the abuse from ever being discovered."

Reyah paused, her demeanor changing from nonchalant to intent. "Think about it, Maria. Right now SEER is capable of predicting your actions a short time into the future. It can only predict things with certainty at most a few minutes in advance because random chains of events can create last-minute influences that affect decisions. It still knows what you'll do before you know what you'll do, but only a few seconds to a few minutes beforehand. But it continues to improve. It's only a matter of time until SEER will know if a speck of dust will fly into your eye, or if you'll get a shock when you grab a sweater, or if a squirrel will run across the sidewalk in front of you. And then SEER will be able to predict what we all will do hours, then weeks, then months into the future. The longer SEER is allowed to exist, the more dangerous it becomes."

Maria frowned, realizing that it was unlikely she could change Reyah's mind, just like Vincent had been unable to. But trying was the only option, the two options Reyah had given her were untenable. "Even if you do succeed in destroy-ing it, it's only a matter of time before it gets remade. You think the Europeans or the Chinese aren't already working on their own version of SEER?"

"I'm sure they are. But there are some technologies that should be delayed as long as possible until humanity has the chance to mature, to understand the implications of the things they want to create. Nuclear weapons for example. Do you think humans were ready for that kind of power?"

"No, we weren't ready. But look at how that turned out. Almost 200 years and no nuclear attacks, not since the first two were dropped. Humanity is never ready for the problems

we invent, but we deal with them, we learn. People understand the dangers more than you give them credit for."

Reyah frowned, but then she broke into a smile. "You're
almost as bad as Vincent," she said with a chuckle. "At least
you don't have the Messiah complex that he does." Reyah
turned serious again. "Look, don't think I take this lightly.
The knowledge that we'll be causing suffering and death
weighs heavy on my conscience. But it's better to experience
hardship as a free woman than a life of leisure as a mindless
drone."

"Apparently it doesn't weigh heavily enough. It's just
collateral damage to you, justified by your idealism." Maria's
tone turned accusatory. "Just like the deaths you caused when
you turned our mission at Quantico into a full-on attack."

Reyah winced as if Maria had physically struck her. It
was the first time Maria had seen her appear anything but
relaxed and in control. Reyah's eyes turned to the floor, her
face losing color. "I... I never meant for anyone to be hurt. I
had Cass warn you so you could get out," she said, gesturing
to the red-headed woman. "I was just hoping that we could
use the chaos to bring you over to our side. I'm truly sorry.
Henry was a good man, even though we disagreed, and I'm
sure Clarissa was a good woman."

Maria felt a chill crawl up her spine. "Wait, you ... you
knew Henry?"

Reyah looked puzzled. "Of course I knew him, Vincent
and I recruited him. He was one of the first we picked up."
Understanding flashed across Reyah's face, and her mouth

turned into a wry grin. "He told you he left on his own, didn't he?"

Maria was silent, dumbstruck.

"He told you he disagreed with our end goal and so he left by himself and built his little team up from nothing," Reyah said, a statement now, not a question. "He probably neglected to mention how the rest of us were getting suspicious that he was more interested in controlling SEER himself than he was in giving control to the public. How he knew we saw right through his argument for keeping SEER around and returning it to the people, so he took his little group and stole off with a bunch of our equipment."

"His group?" Maria asked, her voice numb and quiet.

"I told you not to trust him, Maria," Reyah said, ignoring her question, her tone triumphant. "Don't you see? This is why it has to be destroyed! People begin to think they're the only ones who can be trusted with the power, the only ones who know the true and just way to use it."

"Who else was with him?" Maria asked, more forceful this time, dreading the answer.

This time Reyah acknowledged her. "Let's see, there was Lily, Tiron, Min, Henry like I said, Clarissa he picked up after—"

Reyah was cut off as the ceiling caved in with a boom that made Maria's ears ring. The ruins of the ceiling crashed down onto the table, sending up a cloud of dust that mixed with the smoke from the explosion.

"Grab on," came a shout from above, and a black baton with a line attached to it struck Maria in the chest. Maria

grabbed for it, shaking off the sudden shock that had frozen
her in place. Cass was still reeling, driven to one knee by a
blow from a ceiling tile. The rest at the table were stunned
and coughing, trying to regain their feet. But Anita reacted,
grabbing onto Maria's legs as the line retracted and pulled
Maria off the floor. Maria lashed out and felt her foot connect
with Anita's chest, Anita's hands releasing.

The baton dragged Maria upward through the wreckage
of the drop ceiling and the twisted steel and concrete of the
floor above. At the top, she was pulled to the side by Irina,
safely onto the solid floor. Irina detached the tool from the
ceiling with a press of a button. Antonio was there too, his
weapon in hand.

"This way!" Irina yelled, and they took off down the
hallway. The sound of Reyah's shouted orders chased after
them. Maria's mind was still reeling, too disoriented by it all
to decide what she should do about what she had just learned.
Lily and Min were with Vincent. Henry had been too. And
Reyah had sounded like she would name more. Could she
trust anyone? If she could not trust her own team, could she
really trust the public to deal with the knowledge of SEER's
true power? Questions churned through her mind, but she
shoved them aside. She had been rescued, and that meant she
would not be forced to destroy SEER. There was still a chance
to make the right call, whatever that might be. As long as they
could make it to the command console alive.

"Out the window!" Irina shouted. Maria's thoughts
jerked back to the present. What did she mean? They were
three stories up! Antonio raised his weapon and shot a short

burst at the glass wall at the end of the hall. The glass shattered and fell away, leaving a jagged hole. Irina fired a shot from her weapon at the floor in front of the window and Antonio did the same. But the rounds did not ricochet, instead they trailed wire behind them and punched through the carpet, embedding into the concrete.

"Grab on!" Irina shouted, and then they were leaping out the window at full speed. Maria clutched desperately to Irina in midair, hanging on around her shoulders. They soared out over the grass below, wire trailing out from Irina and Antonio's belts. It adjusted automatically, slowing their fall until they landed on the lawn with only a gentle bump. A quick press of a button and the wire wound itself back up on their belts, their feet already pounding across the ground, with Maria following close behind.

Up ahead was a block of commercial buildings, people milling among the restaurants and small shops. Behind the smaller buildings stood the DARPA headquarters, seven stories of glass and steel. The building itself did not look out of place among its surroundings, but knowing that it was home to cutting-edge military research and a computer program that had the ability to control the entire country made it seem extremely out of place among the nondescript commercial buildings around it. In fact, Maria imagined this whole scene looked ridiculous, three people running for their lives through the middle of a crowd of casual shoppers. She would have laughed if she had not been so terrified.

Maria looked back at the abandoned building just in time to see drones stream out from the broken window like bats from a cave. She knew they could not hurt her, not if Reyah wanted access to SEER. But they could still hurt her team. "Drones behind us!" Maria shouted between gasps as they weaved their way through businesses and confused customers. "Shouldn't we put on camo-suits?"

"There's no time!" Antonio yelled back over his shoulder. "This battle will be won with firepower!"

"Where's ours then?" she shouted back. But then she saw it. Streaming across the road on the other side of the DARPA building were hundreds of drones, most of them flying through the air at maximum speed, although there were a few large drones rolling across the ground that looked like miniature tanks. And beside them ran Vincent, Min, Vasu, Lily, Zu, and Karen.

They raced across the DARPA lawn, heading for the building, which was already going into lockdown. A closely spaced line of bollards rose from the ground to block approaching vehicles, creating an intermittent fence twenty feet away from the edge of the building. Fortunately, the mini-tanks were small enough to fit through, being only half the size of a pod. Police drones swooped down from the sky, but they were shredded immediately in a hail of explosive drone-fire. Half of Vasu's drones peeled off to intercept Reyah's, but Reyah's drones hung back, not engaging.

They sprinted through the vehicle barrier and toward the glass wall of the building. Vincent's squad was nearly to them when Antonio's voice rang out. "Down!" he shouted, and Maria obeyed, diving to the grass. A loud whir sounded, accompanied by a deep vibration that rattled her organs. She looked up to see automated sentry guns on the corners of the building just below the second floor, having folded down from the sides of the building. They were unleashing a stream of gunfire, disintegrating drones in the hail of bullets. One of the steel vehicle bollards was ripped in half as a torrent of rounds chased a drone across it. The sentries were moving at lightning speed, acquiring new targets and reducing them to scrap faster than Maria could blink. Vasu's drones were returning fire but the sentry guns were encased in a sphere of steel with only the thick metal barrel protruding. The numerous hits from the drones only managed to gouge and dent the surface. The sentries had been firing for less than a second and already nearly twenty drones had been ripped apart.

Maria's heart dropped into her stomach as the sentry on their corner of the building swiveled toward Irina, who had been raising her gun to aim at it. Maria watched in horror, expecting Irina to be turned into red dust at any moment.

Before the sentry could get a shot off, it was hit by a storm of rounds, each one punching through the steel armor and turning the sentry into a mass of twisted metal. Maria turned towards Vincent's group to see that the mini-tanks had opened fire, their gun turrets shooting piercing rounds as fast as the sentries. One of them was taken down by the second sentry, torn apart in a shower of sparks and metal shrapnel, but the other five snapped their turrets around and turned the sentry into a twin of the other.

With the sentries gone, they scrambled to their feet and ran to the building, Vasu's drones flying in formation around them. Reyah's drones still held back, floating in a menacing cloud away from the building. So far their only resistance had been a few local police drones, but it was only a matter of time until the Army showed up.

Behind them, the ground erupted upward like water that had been struck with a stone, knocking Maria off her feet and swallowing up a quarter of Vasu's drones. Her ears rung from the sound and her head spun, preventing her from getting back up. She looked up at the sky to see three helicopters soaring in above the buildings, surrounded by hundreds of drones. The Army had arrived.

The three helicopters swooped down toward them, the drones around them filling the sky like a horde of locusts. The helicopters had a rotor on each side of their body attached to a kind of wing, tilting upright as they slowed their approach. They were silver and angular, fierce-looking machines with no windows, controlled entirely by SEER. And even fiercer were the guns and missiles mounted to the belly and sides of each chopper.

The Army drones dove at the group like a cloud of falling arrows, spewing blitz rounds toward Maria and her team. Vasu's drones moved to intercept, but then Reyah's drones were there, swooping in at the Army drones and cutting through them from the side. Drones fell from the sky all around them as the battle filled the air, explosive pellets and blitz rounds creating a fireworks show of sound and light.

"Inside, now!" Vincent shouted, and one of the mini-tanks fired at the glass wall, the rounds punching through it until there was a wide opening. Maria could see from the shards that the glass had been nearly three inches thick, able to stop most bullets, but not the rounds the mini-tanks were shooting.

They rushed through the opening as the roar of helicopter rotors filled the air. Maria looked back to see the nearest helicopter open fire, a stream of bullets chewing their way through a cloud of drones and across the building toward her. The mini-tanks fired back as they rolled inside, their rounds shredding through the chopper just as it unleashed a missile. The chopper veered out of control and the missile rocketed off target. The missile smashed into the second floor toward the end of the building with a fiery blast, rattling the building and spraying glass and burning debris all over the lawn.

"Don't stop, follow me!" Antonio yelled to them. "They won't stop coming until we take control!"

They rounded a corner just as the second and third helicopters rained down on them with a volley of machine gun blasts and missiles, reducing the hallway they had just left to rubble. Two of the mini-tanks were swallowed up in the fire, but the remaining three rounded the corner at top speed, turrets spitting at the choppers and drones. All around her, Vasu's shield drones were blocking shots from the Army drones that were streaming into the building, and the shield drones were returning fire with their explosive rounds. Reyah's drones had followed them too, going on the offensive against the Army drones.

The noise was deafening, a non-stop scream of whirring rotors, explosions, and shrieking metal. Maria's ears were battered by the sound, unprotected without her suit and its noise-dampening tech. Blitz rounds and craters coated the walls all around them as the drones dodged and exchanged fire, any shot that would have hit the team intercepted by the shield drones. Dead machines littered the floor, smoking and burning in heaps on the ground.

"Why are Reyah's drones helping us?" Vasu yelled above the din as they sprinted down an interior hallway.

"I don't know!" Vincent yelled back, nothing else to be said. It was a question they could discuss if they made it through this mess alive.

Explosions rocked the building, the two remaining helicopters unloading a steady barrage of missiles against the ground floor. Walls blasted inward around the exterior and their floor quickly filled with smoke and fire.

"They're gonna take down their own building!" Maria yelled, hardly able to hear her own voice.

"They will!" Vincent shouted back at her. "They know we could take down the country if we get our hands on SEER!"

At the front of the group, Antonio opened a door to a stairway and ushered them in. "Keep going all the way down!" he yelled, letting Irina take the lead. They entered one by one, drones flying in after them like giant mosquitoes looking for their next meal.

Vasu stopped next to Antonio and waited for Maria to pass. "Your gun," he said, handing her weapon to her as she went by. She nodded, slinging the small ammo pack over her shoulder and hurrying down the stairs after the others. Antonio slammed the door shut behind Vasu and the minitanks, trying to keep the Army drones out, but it was no use.

The door splintered open with a series of blasts, and a stream of Army drones, Vasu's drones, and Reyah's drones flew in after them.

They ran down several flights of stairs before reaching the bottom. The mini-tanks rolled smoothly down behind her, their dual front and back treads each able to rotate to traverse obstacles such as stairs. At the bottom they were greeted by a small room with a single metal security door, a sign on the door stating:

NO UNAUTHORIZED ENTRY, TRESPASSERS
WILL BE SHOT WITHOUT WARNING.

"Do you need me to open—" Maria shouted down, but was cut off as Irina fired a door-buster, blowing it off its hinges. Vincent made to run through the door, but Irina shot out an arm to block him.

"Don't," she said, and then pointed as two drones locked in combat swooped through the door and turned down the hallway beyond. The thunder of guns sounded immediately, and pieces of drone flew across the door opening.

"We're running out of time back here," Antonio called from the landing above them as he shot at drones up the stairs from him. She could tell he was right. Smoking carcasses were piled up all around them, but the Army drones kept coming. They had maybe fifty shield drones left, and only a couple of Reyah's drones remained. But they still had three of Vasu's mini-tanks, which were worth more than a typical drone. Their turrets were a blur, acquiring new targets and shredding them. The Army drones were pelting the mini-tanks with round after round, the mini-tanks too slow to avoid them, but their heavy armor protected the core of the tanks from being electrified by the blitz rounds. Some of the Army drones had switched to their own explosive rounds, but these just left the mini-tanks pockmarked, smoking, and mostly unharmed. Still, Maria knew it could not last forever. It was only a matter of time until the slower, heavier weaponry arrived, or until the mini-tanks took too much damage to function.

Irina gestured and the three mini-tanks pulled up next to her. Another gesture and five shield drones darted out into the hallway, the mini-tanks close behind, their guns surging. The thunder sounded again and one of the mini-tanks was torn to ribbons. The other two were a blur, their turrets acquiring and unloading on targets before Maria's eyes could even register it. One of them was hit in the forward tread with several rounds, but before more could strike, the shooting was done. The mini-tanks turned their attention back to the Army drones swarming around Maria and the others.

Irina sent another squad of five drones out into the hallway, but the thunder did not return. "Follow me!" she yelled, moving ahead through the door.

The hallway was wide and long and made entirely of concrete. It extended a hundred feet to their right. At the end of it was a steel door built into a steel wall. Near the steel wall were six massive heaps of mangled and smoking metal, what had once been sentry guns protruding from the concrete wall of the hallway along the height of it.

The team ran for the door, followed by a cloud of exploding drones and streaking projectiles. After a handful of seconds that felt like hours, they arrived at the door and came to an abrupt stop.

"Stand back," Irina said, raising her gun and letting loose a door-buster round. The resulting explosion left a cloud of acrid smoke. But when the smoke cleared the door was unharmed, only a black scorch mark left as evidence of the blast.

"I think this is it," Vincent said. "A massive steel box too thick to break through."

Zu looked over at Maria and gave her a ragged smile. "I think that means you're up."

Maria took a deep breath. She did not think it was possible to be more terrified than she had been in the last ten minutes, but somehow she succeeded. She walked to the door and inspected it, trying to focus with shaking hands and the sounds of the battle behind her. The door was featureless, a smooth steel door without even a handle. She looked all over it for any kind of camera or access code entry and found none.

"It must use advanced biometrics from a tiny camera I can't see," she said, "which means there's no access terminal for me to plug in my program."

Vincent looked startled. "Can you not get us in?"

"I think I can, this room has to have power and a cable network connection to it, and it should be somewhere accessible for maintenance. Access is probably shut down entirely right now with the alarm, but if we can find the conduit, there should be a port with it where they could troubleshoot the door." Maria glanced all around, seeing nothing. "Help me look!" she said to the others. "I need scanning equipment. Vasu, what do you have?"

The shield drones formed up behind them, making a defensive line to keep the area near the door clear. Irina and Antonio took positions on either side of the hallway, shooting at any drones that threatened to break through the line while the rest of the team scoured the area for any sign of an access panel. Vasu scanned all of the nearby walls for any kind of electrical signal but found nothing.

"Maria," Antonio called to her, "we don't have much time here."

She looked back at the hallway and her heart sank. He was right. The shield drones still outnumbered the Army drones, but only by a few, and there were more Army drones streaming in all the time. The two remaining mini-tanks were the only thing keeping them from being overwhelmed, as they could cut down Army drones almost as rapidly as they arrived. But they were looking pretty ragged, their armor flaking off in places, and their ammo would not last forever.

"Come on, it's got to be here, it has to," she muttered to herself, feeling sick. Could she be wrong? Maybe they had some advanced technology she had never heard of that kept this thing running. But it seemed so unlikely. It would be inefficient and a security risk if it was off grid and had to be refueled, and even then it would still need a network connection, and wireless was not secure.

"Maria!" Antonio called again, an edge of panic in his voice. She glanced back to see that the Army drones had finally taken down one of the mini-tanks, an explosive round penetrating its weakened armor, smoke rising from a crater where its turret had been.

Maria crawled across the floor on hands and knees, looking for some kind of hidden panel. It had to be there! But she could not see it. A wave of nausea washed over her as she realized she had just gotten her whole team killed. She put her head in her hands, trying to stay conscious.

And then she saw it. With her face inches from the floor, she could see a slight variation in the concrete. "Everybody back, and get down!" she yelled, waving them away from the door. "Irina, door-busters!"

Irina hurried over, looking at where Maria was pointing. "False floor," Maria said, breathless, and Irina understood instantly. Maria scurried away from the door and lay with the others, where she let loose a barrage of gunfire toward the Army drones streaming into the hallway. Sparks flew from three of the drones and they crashed to the floor. Behind her there were two consecutive blasts, a pause, and then two more, rumbling the floor beneath her and sending up a cloud of dust.

"It's there," Irina shouted, "a steel panel!"

Maria scrambled back to her and helped her clear away the rubble. Irina's shots had uncovered a two-foot-wide strip of steel encased in the concrete. It had been covered with a moisture barrier to prevent the concrete from adhering to it, leaving the panel below in good shape. This maintenance panel was a necessity, Maria knew, something they would have used in case there were issues with the door. But having it be too accessible would have been a security risk. Saboteurs could come cut the lines or try to hack into a maintenance panel, so they had encased it in a half a foot of concrete and tried to blend it into the floor.

The panel lid was bolted down, but the part she was interested in had a hinged cover made from thick steel. Maria could have cried tears of joy when she opened it and found the small panel of status lights with several access ports. She tore her portable drive from her wrist and plugged it in. Next she unfolded her tablet from her pocket and plugged it into her drive. A flick of her wrist and the door program was selected and running.

"I hope that program works fast," Min said as text scrolled by on Maria's tablet. Min had no more than finished speaking when the door opened inward with a hiss.

"You were saying?" Maria grinned in relief, snatched up her portable drive and dashed for the door with the rest of them. She spared a glance back as they darted inside to see four Army drones burst around the corner and fire a stream of explosive rounds at the last mini-tank. It was too much for it, and the precision aim exploited a damaged spot in its armor, punching a hole the rest of the way inside the tank and demolishing it. The last five shield drones peeled off and swooped through the opening as Irina slammed the two-foot-thick steel door with an echoing boom. The boom was followed by smaller blasts as the door blocked a volley of explosive rounds that had been on their way toward them.

It was quiet in the room, and they stopped to catch their breath. The room was plain, with steel floors, walls, and ceiling. But lining the walls were racks and racks of servers with blinking lights. They filled the three walls opposite the door, leaving only the entry wall empty. The only other feature was a light hanging over a metal desk in the center of the room. On it were two regular monitors, one turned off and one glowing white. Maria examined it closely as she steadied her breathing. The desk was metal and simple, and the monitors were modern. Although rare, monitors were still used in certain applications, and were inexpensive. Maria guessed that one was a backup. Best to have two of everything for such a crucial piece of technology.

Conduits ran along the floor between the servers and the desk, and up the wall to the light overhead. This was it. This controlled the entire country. It did not control the drones or any other technology directly, she knew. This computer's only purpose was to issue commands to the SEER servers containing the data, telling it what goals to accomplish. Government and private business both used SEER's data, and were therefore controlled by SEER. Even though SEER could not directly control private technology, it directed it nonetheless by the data it provided. If SEER wanted a pod to slow down, it told the pod computer that the passenger wanted the pod to slow down. If SEER wanted someone to see a certain video, it told the internet browser that its user wanted to see that video. SEER told the technology what a person wanted to do, see, or buy next, and, eager to provide the best user experience, the technology complied. Controlling the data meant controlling the populace.

This control room was one of several, Maria knew, scattered around the country. The servers lining the walls were the brains of SEER. They turned the commands entered into the computer into specific actions that could be carried out by SEER's data servers, like the one at Quantico, to achieve the entered command. The other control rooms around the country would have the same setup, exact copies of this room that could be used to enter commands in the event that this one was captured or destroyed.

Maria walked to the console and sat in the cold metal chair, setting her weapon on the desk. The one lit screen was white with the words "EMERGENCY LOCKOUT, NO ACCESS" in large black text across it. Ignoring it, she inserted her portable drive into a port on the monitor. Her available programs popped up on her tablet. She took a deep breath and selected the SEER access program.

She sat and watched as text scrolled across her vision. No one spoke, words feeling wrong in the tense atmosphere. Vincent paced, Antonio and Irina stood near the door, weapons ready, and the rest stood and nervously watched Maria at the desk.

A muffled blast rattled the floor and made her jump. The light flickered overhead but stayed on. She turned to Irina and Antonio, a questioning look on her face.

"How much longer, Maria?" was all Antonio said, his voice grave.

"Shouldn't be long," she answered.

"What if they cut the power or the network line?" Karen asked. "Then you can't issue any commands."

"There's more than just the one set of lines," Vasu answered. "The ones we saw out there are accessible for maintenance in case there are problems, but the main set of lines is probably buried deep in the concrete."

Maria nodded. "He's right," she said, "and the power will have a series of backup generators in case they tried to shut it off. The network line is probably deep and they may even have hard wired it all the way to Quantico. However they set this up, they had to make it so that it could survive a bombing or a military attack. The downside for the government is there's no easy way to stop us now that we're in. Other than take back the room."

As if punctuating her sentence, another explosion shook the room. Maria drummed her fingers nervously on the desk as her program continued to churn out progress logs.

"So once we get in and make commands, what stops another command console somewhere else from just undoing our commands?" asked Lily.

"If I get in—" Maria started, but a sharp look from Vincent made her pause. "Sorry, *when* I get in, my program will automatically change the credentials, making the other consoles unable to access and input SEER commands without the security codes we—"

The screen changed and her program stopped, and so did Maria's sentence. "We're in," she called out in elation.

"Credentials are changed and we're ready to run our commands." She reached for the tablet to execute her command program.

A hand clamped down on her wrist, another grasped her firmly by the shoulder. "Well done, Maria," Vincent said. "Now please step away from the desk."

It was happening. She had been expecting this, hoping she was wrong about him but expecting it anyway. Her heart resumed the frantic beating it had been doing on their way inside. Maria looked up, surveying the room. Vincent was standing beside her, his hands tightly gripping her shoulder and wrist. Min and Lily had raised their weapons to point at Irina and Antonio. Vasu and Zu looked unsure, although maybe Zu understood what was happening because his eyes were darting around nervously and he was covered in a sheen of sweat.

Maria looked at Karen, who was unsurprised. Maria had been unable to tell her that it was more than just Vincent, but it did not matter now. They locked eyes, and Karen gave her a subtle nod. Maria hoped that meant she was ready with whatever measure she had come up with. Maria stood up.

"Vincent, what's going on?" Irina said, her voice a mixture of nerves and accusation.

"I'm afraid we won't be letting the public know about SEER just yet," he replied coolly.

The response seemed to shock Irina, and Vasu spoke up to ask the obvious question. "And why not?"

"Because the people can't handle it, Vasu," Vincent answered. "They can't handle this responsibility. They're not experts, they don't understand the implications and the dangers of all of this. Putting this technology in the hands of mob rule is dangerous. What if someday people get mad enough to vote in representatives who want to use it to control their political enemies? What if someone secretly takes control of SEER and uses it to control people again, with none the wiser? You know the risks, we've already talked about them. We need SEER, but we need people in control of it who understand the consequences and who can be trusted to use it ethically. We are those people."

"And so you would sit here, King of the United States, answering to no one?" Antonio spat back at him, his voice quaking with rage.

"We would answer to the call of duty, to ensure SEER is only used for the benefit of all people," Vincent said.

Antonio laughed, a short, mocking laugh. "What do you think the people in control of it right now think they're doing?" he asked. "All this manipulation, these killings, you think they're doing it just for fun? They believe that what they're doing is for the good of the people too!"

"We can't trust anyone but ourselves to do this right," Vincent replied forcefully. "You know why we're here, you know that we're trying to undo these evil practices."

"I thought I knew why we were here," Antonio replied, "but apparently I was wrong."

"There are more of us than there are of you," Irina said, lifting her weapon slightly. Lily kept her weapon trained on

Irina, warning her not to try it with a silent shake of her head. "What if we don't let you take it?" Irina continued.

Vincent made a lazy hand flick and the five remaining drones spread out, two flying over to guard Vasu and Zu, the other three for Maria, Antonio, and Irina. "We're not exactly outnumbered," he said.

"Would you really kill us?" Vasu asked.

"We don't want to kill anyone," Vincent answered firmly. "But if you try to fight us, we'll do what's necessary to defend ourselves."

Another blast sounded from outside, shaking the room even harder than before. They did not have much time. Maria looked pleadingly at Karen. What was she waiting for? Whatever she had planned, she hoped it would happen soon. Maria was beginning to worry that the secret of Min and Lily being on Vincent's side had ruined her scheme.

"I won't let you access it," Maria said, defiance in her voice. "I built a safeguard into my program. Only I can get in."

Vincent just looked at her calmly. "I'm sure you did," he said, "but we can still get in."

"What are you going to do, torture me?" Maria asked. "I can hold out until they break in."

"I don't want to hurt you," he replied, "and I don't think I would need to anyway. There's only one shot at this. Would you really throw away our only shot at change and have us all live out our lives in prison, just to keep me from controlling SEER? We would do better, Maria. There would be no manipulation or killing with us in control."

Maria realized he was probably right. It was the evil out-side the room or the evil within. But was an evil she knew better than an unknown evil that could potentially do good? It was not a choice she wanted to make. Maria looked at Karen again. "Karen, please," Maria implored her, "there isn't much time."

"She's right," Vincent said, "there isn't. Karen?"

Karen walked to the desk, avoiding Maria's gaze. She sat, navigated to the command entry, and then gestured a secret pattern at the monitor, the secret pattern that Maria had added to her code. Maria's heart sank, and with it, her hopes. "Karen, you're with him?" she asked, defeated, not wanting to believe.

"Vincent is right, Maria," Karen said. "People won't un-derstand all this, they need someone in control who can do it right, who can handle the responsibility. I'm sorry I lied to you but I had to play along, to make sure I found out what you knew. When you slept, I accessed your program and learned what you added. I modified it to give me access too."

"Run the SEER commands we prepared please, Karen," Vincent said.

Karen made to comply, reaching to add her own portable drive to the monitor. "Step away from the computer," Zu's voice boomed out, making Maria jump.

Everyone turned to look at him, bewilderment on their faces. He slowly reached into his pack, removing a large black box and holding it out in front of him. On top of the box was a timer. It read five minutes, the time slowly ticking away.

"Zu, what are you doing?" Karen breathed, speaking for all of them. It was so quiet Maria could have heard a pin drop, except for the sound of her heart pounding in her ears.

"This is a bomb," Zu said, "set to detonate in five minutes. This bomb will blow unless it receives a signal from Reyah. Reyah will only send that signal once she has confirmed that SEER's data has been destroyed."

"You're with Reyah?" Vincent exclaimed, half incredulous and half disgusted. "This whole time?"

Zu nodded. "You used her list to find people for your team, remember? She approached me first and told me that you intended to seize power. I agreed to make sure it gets destroyed instead, and then waited for you to come recruit me."

"Damn it," Vincent growled, "and you're the reason Reyah has known our every move. The tracker on the boat?"

"A decoy," Zu replied, "I was leaving small signal buoys behind the boat with information about our plans."

Maria felt like she could not breathe. Could anyone be trusted? She had liked these people! "Zu, what about what you said on the boat?" Maria asked. "About your country, and about how the people have to have the power to choose?"

"I meant what I said," Zu replied, looking at her with sad eyes. "The people must have the power to choose, and as long as SEER exists, that power is in jeopardy. No technology should exist that can bend people to a will that is not their own. I doubt we would be arguing about this if SEER was a machine that directly controlled people's minds. But it does control people, just indirectly, and it should not exist."

"Would you really kill us all?" Maria asked.

Zu turned his gaze to the floor. "I will do what I have to in order to save this country. And Reyah controls the bomb, so there's no going back. Now please, do as I say, I don't want any of us to die."

Karen looked at Vincent, unsure. The timer on the bomb was at three minutes and counting.

"Damn it, Reyah," Vincent muttered, "damn it, damn it, damn it!" He kicked the metal desk. "Do as he says. Send commands to wipe the data."

Maria felt helpless, and so alone. This was not the way this was supposed to go. They were supposed to be a team; they were supposed to be united in their efforts to stop the abuse of power. Instead they were nothing but allies of convenience, using each other for their own personal agendas. Her eyes welled up at the thought of what would happen when SEER went dark. Maria decided to try one last time as Karen began creating the command. "Thousands will die, Zu," she said, "maybe a lot more. Please, let's tell everyone this exists and let them figure out a way to fix it without so much damage."

Zu met her eyes, and she could see tears there. "I know the consequences, and I will have to live with them. But the risk is too—"

A blast ripped through the room, knocking Maria to the floor. Her ears rang and she tasted blood in her mouth. Over the loud ringing, she heard shouts and the sound of gunfire. Maria looked around, trying to see what was happening, but it was chaos. The steel door had blown off its hinges and was now embedded in the server rack on the far wall. It had flown just to the side and barely missed Maria and the desk. Drones were swarming in, and the five remaining shield drones had engaged them, but they were outnumbered and would not last much longer.

This was it. They were finished. The only thing that could save them now was taking control of SEER and the drones. Karen had been sitting at the desk, but now she lay on the floor, not moving. Maria's weapon was still sitting on the desk where she had left it, and next to it the monitor was still glowing.

Maria made to move for the desk, but her body would not cooperate. Her head was swimming and she squeezed her eyes shut to clear it and then tried again. Something was holding her back. She turned to see Vincent still clutching her shoulder, staring at her with lifeless eyes, chunks of metal jutting from his back. She recoiled in horror, pulling free from his grasp and scrambling toward the desk. He had been between her and the door when it went, and that had probably saved her life.

Maria crawled across the floor on all fours, trying not to make herself a target. She reached the desk, her fingers flying as she navigated to her program and found the routine that would automatically enter all of the commands they had created. Her heart hammered in her chest as she silently prayed that the command terminal would still work despite the damage the door had done to the servers.

Just as she was about to run the program, an Army drone turned toward her, firing a stream of blitz rounds. She only had one more gesture to make, but the blitz rounds were faster.

A shield drone, the last shield drone, swooped in front of her and intercepted the shots, catching them all. The last blitz round struck the drone full on the body, getting past the shield as it moved to block it. There was a crackle of electricity and the drone crashed to the ground.

Maria made her last gesture and the program submitted, cycling rapidly through the commands. But the Army drone was still targeting her. She reached for her weapon but she knew she could never bring it to bear in time.

A spray of gunfire tore into the drone before it could fire another shot. It disintegrated in a shower of sparks and smoking metal. She turned to see Antonio lying on the ground behind her, propping himself up on one arm and firing at the drones all around them. Maria raised her weapon and sprayed at a drone flying at him from behind, blasting it backward.

More shots rang out from behind her but she did not know from whom. They were out of shield drones and ten Army drones were bearing down on them. She knew they would not miss. They were not stopping; the servers must have been too badly damaged to execute her commands.

She raised her weapon at the drones and squeezed the trigger, not going down without a fight. Regret at being unable to stop SEER welled up in her, but she refused to die without hope. Maybe all this destruction would be too much to cover up, and maybe someone would discover the truth.

The drones went down one by one in her onslaught of bullets. It seemed too easy. Then she realized why. They were not moving. They had completely stopped. No more shots were fired; they were just hovering in place. Maria could not believe it. She turned back to the computer to find a single message waiting for her:

COMMANDS PROCESSED.

Relief flooded through her, and she slumped down to the floor, completely drained. But then she shot back up again. The bomb! She had almost forgotten. "Oh no," she breathed, scrambling over to where Zu lay on the ground. She saw two blitz rounds stuck to the back of his neck and she knew he was gone. Next to him on the ground was the bomb. Bright red letters displayed thirty-four seconds, and it was still counting.

She picked it up, her eyes darting wildly about the room as she tried to figure out what to do with it. If the door had still been attached, she could have tossed it in the hall and closed it up, but the door was embedded in the servers on the opposite wall. Twenty-five seconds. Frustration bubbled up inside her. She had not escaped death at the hands of the drones just to be killed by this stupid bomb.

That was it! She ran to the nearest drone. Taking off her weapon, she used the sling to strap the bomb to it. "Fly straight up, avoid people and go as high as you can," she said to the drone. It took off, obeying the order of its new ally, thanks to the commands she entered into SEER.

Maria ran back to Antonio, who was still lying on the ground, a piece of metal protruding from his thigh. She grabbed him under the arm and dragged him to the corner of the room, adjacent to the missing door. Maria looked around for anyone else, and saw Min climb to her feet and join them.

"Anyone else?" Maria asked. Min just shook her head sadly. Antonio moaned when he saw her response. Maria's eyes filled, and then it was like the end of the world.

A deafening boom engulfed them. The floor and walls shook violently. The hallway collapsed, spilling chunks of concrete and mangled rebar in through the door. Then it was over, just as quick as it had started. Maria looked at the rubble blocking the door and hoped there had not been any people left in the building when it blew.

Maria took a quick walk around the room, looking for signs of life, but there were none. Irina had been struck by the door when it blew open, blood covering her face. Lily had been hit by several blitz rounds, stopping her heart. Karen, Vasu, and Zu had all had the same. Vincent had been impaled with shrapnel from the door explosion. Maria walked back to Antonio and Min, weeping openly. They understood and did not ask, only crying along with her.

Antonio was in agony from the shard of metal sticking out of his thigh, and it was bleeding heavily. Maria knew the metal should not be taken out, but she had to slow the bleeding. Min helped her grab the desk chair, using it to elevate Antonio's leg above the rest of his body. The bleeding slowed, but did not stop. Antonio was hyperventilating and acting delirious, and Maria suspected it was more from the outcome of the battle than it was from the injury. She tore a scrap from her shirt, trying to calm Antonio while she did.

"Antonio, hey, deep breaths," she murmured. "I went to those places you mentioned. The falls were beautiful, one of the prettiest places I've ever seen. I even went to the arcade." His breathing slowed slightly.

"I saw your brother's plaque." His eyes lifted to hers at the mention of his brother. "And the woman at the desk said she remembered you two, she said you were good kids."

"Raul," Antonio moaned, "I'm so sorry." He continued to repeat his brother's name, but Maria shushed him softly.

"You can't blame yourself. It was SEER. You can't blame yourself for any of this, either." Maria took the scrap of her shirt and carefully placed it around the chunk of metal, applying pressure. Antonio groaned and writhed while Min tried to hold him still.

"It's my fault," Antonio growled through the pain. "I was in charge of our missions, I was responsible." He seemed more lucid the more he talked, and Maria hoped he would stay that way.

"No, you aren't responsible for that. We were a small group against a whole country. And this was all our faults," she said, glancing around at the lifeless bodies. "We could have prevented all of this if we had agreed on what to do, but we argued and gave them time to break in. We didn't trust each other and we couldn't see eye to eye. It was human stubbornness that caused all this, not you."

He seemed to hear her, but she knew it would be hard for him to let go of the guilt. It was for her. Even after learning that SEER had killed Ana, the guilt was still there. Maybe Ana would still be alive if Maria had gone to see her, or had been more persistent, or had been a better sister. Maria knew better than that, but it still did not stop the thoughts from coming. And now there were more lives lost that would weigh on her mind, more 'what ifs' that would torture her.

Antonio laid his head down, breathing deep as Maria continued to apply pressure to his elevated leg. He squeezed his eyes shut, tears rolling down the side of his face.

Min sat down beside Maria, neither of them saying anything. After some time, Min broke the silence. "I didn't want any of this. I didn't want to lie to you. I only wanted what I thought was best." She turned to meet Maria's gaze. "I'm sorry."

"I understand," Maria said. "None of us wanted any of this to happen. We just wanted to fix things."

Min looked down and wiped her eyes. "I just want to go home," she said, sobbing.

"Me too." Maria reached out and took Min's hand.

Epilogue

The pod carried her through the darkness, the only sound was the hum of the tires on the road. Trees whipped by on either side. She was bone tired but could not sleep. It felt wrong to sleep, too normal. How could she sleep after the insanity that had just occurred? How could she sleep after so many of the people she had come to care for had died in front of her eyes?

Her eyes were dry now. She was not sure if she would be able to cry again, not sure if there was anything left. She had spent most of the day with wet cheeks. After the bomb, it had taken ten hours for a rescue crew to reach them. She had spent that time taking turns with Min, putting pressure on Antonio's leg. He had been so pale and weak by the end of it. But he had made it. She was grateful for that. Not just for him, but for her. Another loss might have been the breaking point.

While Min was applying pressure, Maria had spent time making sure that she had accounted for every detail. She made sure that only she would have access to SEER, for now. She made sure that she, Antonio, and Min would be under constant drone protection. Even now there was a squad of twenty drones staying within range of her pod. She made sure that no harm or punishment would come to any of them, and she commanded SEER to wipe all its data if any of them died. She had even made sure that Reyah and her team would not be punished, only closely monitored for anti-SEER activity. But most importantly, she made sure that SEER published every last bit of information it had about the ways it had been controlling the public. Every news story about SEER would be priority number one.

Publishing this information was the real core of it, the real power holding it all together. By now the country was probably reeling from the information. Probably the whole world. She knew it must be, but she had not bothered to check. There would be time for that later. But it was out there, and that was what really guaranteed her safety. She and the others would be seen as heroes, she hoped. Heroes fighting a secret and corrupt part of the government. Even most of the government did not know what SEER was being used for, and they would be grateful to learn about it. It was hard to say what would happen, but considering that even the president had no idea about it, she would have bet money on her, Min, and Antonio receiving a presidential pardon.

While they were waiting to be rescued, Maria had ordered the Army drones to tell her how many innocent people had died in the chaos. The answer was four, and the number had been both a relief and a crushing blow. She was relieved to learn it was not more. It had been fortunate that the DARPA building was mostly empty in observance of Labor Day. Yet those four people weighed heavily on her conscience. That was four people who would still be alive if not for her and her team. She knew those four deaths would stick with her for the rest of her life.

When the excavation and rescue robots reached them, Maria had made sure that Antonio would be taken to a hospital and that he would survive, and then she had parted ways with Min. Each of them had their own business to take care of. As far as the world knew, they had been dead, but now they could pick up their old lives again. They could go out in public as themselves, protected by drones and without fear of SEER.

They promised to keep in touch. They were still her teammates, and there were still important decisions that would need to be made in the transition of power, and she would want their input. Not only that, but she would want their friendship. Even Min's, despite their different views on SEER. They had been through so much in a short time, so much that only they could understand. They needed to be there for each other.

Maria was apprehensive about how the country would react over the next few days. She was unsure what people would do when they learned that they were entirely predictable. She had commanded SEER to make every detail of what it was capable of public and prominent. People around the world were learning that everything they did could be known beforehand, and coming to terms with that information.

She had come to terms with it, she thought. She had decided that the concept of free will was not useful. All beings feel in control relative to their own intelligence. But to a more capable intelligence, those with a lesser intelligence did not appear to be in control, instead they seemed to be following a determined path, like water in a waterfall. So free will meant nothing; there was only perspective.

This conclusion meant both nothing and everything to her everyday life. The only way to live was under the assumption that she was controlling her own actions. The purpose of storing information in your brain was to use it to make future decisions. It was in everyone's best interest to use that stored information to the best of their ability, to come to the best possible action. Just like SEER did with all of its data. There was still a responsibility and a duty to use all the information available to her in her everyday life. That was the duty of all living things, to do the best they could based on everything they had at their disposal. It meant living just like she had always done.

Where it changed everything was in understanding the foundation of all human behavior. The knowledge of predictability meant understanding that no one could escape the consequences of their origins. It meant recognizing that her flaws and the flaws of others were a result of bad genetics or bad influences, or a combination of both. To her, that was the most beautiful part of it all. Understanding what made people the way they were made hatred obsolete, at least in theory. How can you be mad at someone for the things they had experienced or the things they had been born with? Instead, people could recognize the sources of their differences and combat those differences by sharing with each other. The key to better understanding each other was sharing the data that made a person who they are. Just like SEER needed data to understand a person well enough to predict their behavior, other people needed data to understand why others believe what they believe. Learning the background that formed someone's beliefs meant being tolerant of that person and recognizing what information they may need to be more tolerant of your own point of view. It meant a shift toward teaching instead of punishment, discussion instead of violence, uniting instead of dividing, and loving instead of hating.

But of course, others might see it differently. The thing that worried her most was that she had just spent two weeks with people who fully understood that they were predictable consequences of previous circumstances, and yet they had still disagreed so fiercely to the point that it had gotten most of them killed. Would the public make the same mistake?

The main thing preventing her ideal world of love and understanding was the inability of the human brain to store enough information to fully understand everyone. Sure, in theory she knew that she should not blame others for their beliefs, but in practice her brain could not comprehend everything that made up another person. No matter how hard she tried there would be beliefs she would be unable to understand, beliefs founded on a lifetime's worth of information stored in another person's brain that she would never be able to fully access. This fundamental difference in background would make it impossible to see eye to eye on many things.

She was a perfect example of the contradiction between recognizing that others should not be blamed for their beliefs and applying that recognition to her life. Anger still burned within her at those responsible for Ana's death. She knew her newfound understanding should imply that she should forgive these people and work to change their minds. Instead she wanted vengeance. She wanted to make SEER torture them the way Ana had been tortured. It had taken all her strength not to enter those vindictive commands as she sat with Min and Antonio, staring at the bodies of her fallen teammates. In the end, she had been strong enough, resisting the urge to exact revenge. Their names had been published, and the world now knew of their crimes. They would face an impartial judge and be held accountable.

In time, she hoped her anger would fade to acceptance. For now, she took solace in the fact that she had stopped the abuses SEER had been used for. The country would know Ana's story and the stories of countless others, and they would all get a say in what to do about it.

Her pod rolled silently onto a quiet residential street. It pulled to the side of the road to let her out in front of a small yellow house. As she got out, she wondered again if she had made the right call. People were going to disagree with each other. Many would be scared and confused. There would be those who shared Reyah's beliefs, and some might even share Vincent's. Had she plunged the world into conflict?

Perhaps, she thought, as she walked to the door. It was impossible for everyone to understand each other perfectly. But perfect understanding was not necessary. If people became even a little more perceptive and compassionate, the world would be a much better place. The vast array of different life experiences and knowledge among the population was valuable. SEER's future needed to be left up to the whole population, the combined wealth of knowledge and life experience that made human life in this country and on this planet vibrant. No single perspective was enough to decide for everyone else.

The light came on and the door opened as Maria approached the house. Her heart fluttered, but for once it was not from indecision or fear. No, she knew she had made the right choice. She knew the human race was capable of solving this problem, just like it had progressed despite every problem set before it.

"Who's there?" came a woman's voice from the house.

"Hi, Mom," Maria said, tears brimming in her eyes. Her mom shrieked and pulled her violently into an embrace, clutching her tight.

"You're alive, you're alive," her mother whispered over and over, as if she was trying to convince herself it was not a dream.

"What happened?" her father asked, rushing down the stairs in his robe in concern for his wife. "Are you okay?" He stopped short when he saw her and leaned against the wall in shock. He rushed in, wrapping them both in his arms.

Maria was at peace there, held tight in her parents' arms, tears on her cheeks and a smile on her face. A feeling of hope surged through her, hope for the future of humanity. There was no other way she could feel.

Acknowledgments

A lot of people have helped make this book what it is today and I am grateful to all of them. First and foremost, I want to thank my wife, Brianna. She was the first to read my book in its early stages and she has been a source of constant support and encouragement. She has provided valuable advice throughout this endeavor, ranging from the contents of this book to the appearance of its cover and the design of my website.

Some of the most valuable feedback I have received was from my beta readers, Julia Nolan and Larry Allen. Their comments and advice helped make this a stronger and cleaner story.

I am very grateful to my mom, Kim Beck, and my sister, Kayla Cunningham, for reading this book early on and offering advice and support. My sister also painted the cover of this book, and I'm delighted with how it turned out and am honored to have her work be the first thing people see when they pick it up.

My editor, Celestian Rince, has done a wonderful job and has greatly improved the reading experience by correcting my errors.

I also want to thank the community at critters.org for critiquing my book as well as other stories. The tips and comments from them are always helpful and it's the best place to go for feedback. I highly recommend it to other authors looking for critiques of their work.

Finally, thank you for reading. The purpose of writing is to share your creation with others, whether to provoke thought, or to entertain, or to evoke an emotion. I hope this book has achieved at least one of those things, and I'm thankful that you took the time to experience this story. If you liked it, I hope that you'll please leave a review and connect with me on social media or through email.

Please consider helping me out by leaving a review on Amazon or Goodreads. Visit my website for all the latest news about my work. Feel free to reach out via social media or email.

www.ryanbeckauthor.com

ryanbeckauthor@gmail.com

RYAN BECK is an author of science-fiction novels and short stories. He loves exciting and thought-provoking fiction of many different types. He lives in Iowa where he works as a bridge engineer. In his free time, Ryan is usually spending time with his wife and daughter, reading, or trying to learn a new skill.